Here's what people are saying about *Captured Lies*....

"...I loved the creative and strong characters and plots that continued to build and shock and surprise..." Sam Ryan (Author and Indie Book Reviewer)

"...This was a fast moving story, fast and driving. It simply hit the ground running, and was so thrilling and engaging, I couldn't put the book down..." Joy Nwosu Lo-Bamijoko

"...Maggie Thom will draw you into her story and keep you until you finish—no bookmarks required..." Jen Winters (Author)

"...She carefully plots characterizations in a way that not only pulls us in and makes us care about Baily's life, but makes us feel like we are right there going through it too..." Laura Clark (Author and Indie Book Reviewer)

"Maggie Thom writes a fast paced thriller laced with romance that keeps the reader interested and on edge!" InDtale Magazine

"...Captivating story, it was intricate and every time you had it figured out a shift would happen adding another layer to the puzzling story..." Musings from an Addicted Reader

"...Questions grow and so does the pace of this excellent story..." Reader's Favorite

"...you will be captured in a thrilling page turner..." Ruth King

Read... for the love of it.
Enjoy

CAPTURED
LIES

The Caspian Wine Series
Book 1
By
Maggie Thom

First Edition: Published 2012, Revised 2017

Published by: Quadessence Solutions
Cover Design ©2017 Laura Callender (Just Publish It)
Editing & Formatting: Patricia Terrell (P.I.S.C.E.S)

ISBN: 9780991727254

Read to Escape... Escape to Read...

Maggie Thom

Quadessence Solutions
Suspense/Thriller/Mysteries

Acknowledgements

Thank you to Gerry, Jazmine and Zackary, whose endless support and patience, for my constant need to write and your belief that this was possible... to my sisters - who've given me the feedback I need, the support to keep going and the kick to keep on track... to my friend Bev – for her reviews and suggestions, endlessly there for me, always making me laugh. To my friend, Christine – for your reviews and suggestions and support. You've all played a part in making this a success... :)

Other Books By Maggie Thom

Tainted Waters

Deadly Ties

The Caspian Wine Series

Deceitful Truths – Book 2

Split Seconds – Book 3

1

From the *Toronto Star*, Saturday, February 14, 1983

Two-day-old Cassidy Jane Lefevre was stolen from Gracefield Hospital, snatched from the nursery between 1:00 and 3:00 a.m. The hospital is cooperating with the official investigation. Cassidy's parents, Bottle-Up magnates Gina and Daniel Lefevre, are devastated at the loss of their first child. Five million dollars is offered for the return of their baby. There are no suspects but there are a few people of interest, including a missing nurse. In the past year, four newborns have been abducted from hospitals in Quebec and Ontario. Is there a black market?

Mary scanned the rest of the five-month-old article. It sounded so ugly. Some people were so desperate for a baby they didn't know where else to turn. Kids deserved parents who'd love them, not keep them as prizes. Rich people were all the same.

"Excuse me. Would you like something to eat or drink?"

Mary looked blankly at the stewardess. "Something to drink… oh… no... No. I'm fine, thank you." Mary folded the clipping and stuffed it in the brown envelope she'd propped beside her hip, shuffling the baby to her other arm.

"She sure is cute." Smiling, the stewardess tilted her head and clicked her tongue.

"Well, thank you. I think she is too. She's a beauty. My best… g-grandchild yet." Mary looked down at the baby sleeping in her arms and then back at the stewardess. She beamed at her. "Aren't you just the sweetest thing to say so? Thank you. It means a lot when others notice what I think is true."

"What's her name?"

Mary's hand shook as she patted her carefully coiffed, dull gray hair. Her scalp itched but she didn't dare scratch. The wig would no doubt shift, so she restrained herself, glad the charade was almost over. "C-candy."

"Ooohhh. Sweet."

"How about you? Do you have kids?"

"No."

"Oh, that's a shame. Why, I bet you'd be the best mom ever. It would sure be the cutest tyke too. You with your blonde hair and blue eyes."

"Thanks." She grinned at Mary before shifting her gaze to wink at the baby. "Sorry but I've got to keep moving. Excuse me."

The stewardess' eyes darted from Mary to the man beside her. Mary leaned on the armrest between them, closing the distance. His head whipped around to stare at her, his shoulder bumping her cheek. She smiled indulgently at him before shaking her head and shrugging her shoulders. The stewardess nodded in acknowledgement, rolling her eyes as if saying, "Men."

Mary took a deep calming breath, reminding herself that this was almost over.

As soon as the attendant moved off, asking others what they wanted, Mary sat upright. She looked around. Her gaze met a pair of blinking, owlish green eyes, partially hidden by streaky lenses that looked as thick as the bottom of a bottle. She pursed her lips as she frowned at her seatmate. He nervously pushed up his glasses before sticking his nose into the stack of papers in his hand. Rooting through the pages scattered over his tray and the empty seat on the other side of him, he was soon oblivious to her.

Mary had been tempted to ask him to scoot over so she'd have more space for the baby but was glad she hadn't. Better that people think they're together. She almost reached out and rubbed the smudge of makeup she'd left on the shoulder of his blue shirt. Absently, she gently patted her hand over her face, hoping the wrinkles that had taken hours to make hadn't been disturbed. Her pale face powder felt a bit creased, just like it was supposed to. She relaxed a tad.

Mary shifted the baby to the side so she could reach under the seat in front of her. The infant cried out. "Hold on." She snagged the diaper bag and stuffed the paper inside. "All right. All right. Do you have to wake up screaming all the time? Cripes, you're worse than... my... youngest ever was. And man, could she scream." She stifled a groan at her near-mistake. She'd be so glad when this pretend stuff was over. She grabbed the pacifier and plopped it into the baby's mouth, who gave a mulish look before starting to suck on the rubber stopper with the suction of a vacuum.

The plane jerked, hard. Mary clutched the baby to her chest as she whipped her head around in an attempt to see what was happening. The man beside her dropped his chest onto the tray table, arms splayed wide, securing all his paperwork. His bulging eyes met her glance.

A voice came over the speaker. "We're experiencing some turbulence. Everyone please return to your seats and fasten your seatbelts."

Mary looked out the window. Gray clouds, low-hanging and heavily laden, filled her view. Lightning streaked past, followed by a loud rumble. The plane jerked and shuddered.

Passengers screamed and shouted. The stewardesses called out instructions as they raced down the aisle, checking on everyone. "Please remain calm. We're going through some rough weather. Stay seated and ensure your seatbelts are secure. Put your tray tables in the upright position." The instructions were issued so quickly they were almost incomprehensible.

More booming and cracking shook the plane as though it was having a grand mal seizure. The aircraft dropped nose down. They were descending rapidly—too rapidly. The stewardesses swayed and scrabbled, grabbing seats, staggering as they lurched down the aisle toward the crew seats. The plane bucked as passengers screamed.

Mary slammed forward, smacking her head on the seat in front of her. The baby shrieked with terror. Mary forced herself back, eyeing the infant in her arms. "Shh, baby. Shh. We'll be all right."

Papers flew like frantic birds despite her seatmate's attempt to catch and hold them. Ignoring him, she peered out the window at the sky, a blur of ominous black lit to gun-metal gray every now and then by flashes of lightning. She wasn't sure what dropping out of the sky looked like but she figured this was it. It reminded her of a ride at the fair where the floor fell out from under her as she'd spun around in a drum. She'd taken that ride only once and only because she'd been teased into it. And the ride had been hell. She'd puked her guts out when she'd disembarked. Now the lurching of her stomach gave her the same sensation. She swallowed hard.

The grubby passenger regarded her with a solemn gaze. "We're going to die." Another passenger had started to pray. Everyone seemed to realize in unison that their chances of survival were slim.

"I'm going to go to hell. I know it." Mary hugged the baby to her chest. "But you don't have to go with me. I made a promise that I'd look after you. And I will." She grabbed the diaper bag, unzipped it and threw its contents onto the floor. She stuffed the screaming infant into it.

"Give me your blanket and pillow." Mary elbowed the man beside her.

He cocked his head.

"Give me your blanket and pillow."

He continued to stare blankly at her.

"Give me one of your books!"

He jerked upright and grabbed one of his manuals from the seat on the other side of him, clutching it like a treasure.

She ripped it out of his hands. He looked at her owlishly for a few seconds before again collapsing protectively over his papers, haphazardly spread over the lowered tray table.

She looked down as tear-filled blue eyes met hers. The baby's bottom lip was trembling. In the five months Mary had the baby she'd never before felt a tug in her heart. Amazed at what fear would do to her, she shook off the feeling. She hugged the diaper bag close against her well-padded belly, glad she was carrying some extra protection her taut stomach couldn't provide. She curled herself around the crying infant and held the hardcover book in front, providing the most protection she could. Her arms were rigid, the muscles screaming in protest as nearly tornado-strength aerodynamic forces tried to pry the baby from her.

"Mother of God, I hope you can hear me," she silently prayed. "I know it's been forever since we talked." *But what's twenty-eight years between friends? So many occasions I should have prayed but I didn't believe it would help.* Fear crawled up her throat, choking her as she continued her prayer. "I know I've taken the wrong path—many times. But please don't hurt this baby. She's innocent. Something I haven't been in a long time. Don't hold that against her. Take me; keep her safe. She might actually have a chance to be something."

Screaming, yelling, fear, anger—the dashing of hopes and dreams. Prayers filled the cabin. The lights flickered. The engines howled like banshees in the darkness. Thunder boomed and lightning cracked. The plane convulsed violently.

"Holy Mother of God. Holy Mother of God. Holy Mother of God." Mary chanted in an endless stream. She wanted to recite a prayer but couldn't remember any. The vision of a younger self flashed before her eyes, a young girl forced to spend hours locked away reciting prayers, the nuns convinced it was the only way she'd learn, yet none of it came back to her now.

Mary kept her head tucked, refusing to let in to the temptation to stare out the window at the ground rapidly rushing up to meet them. "John. I'm sorry big brother. I screwed up... again. This is my fault."

The baby screamed and Mary vainly tried to comfort her.

The cacophony of sounds stopped in an instant as a surreal blackness swallowed her like an insignificant minnow in the mouth of a whale.

2

Donna Saunders
Born January 5, 1952
Deceased April 21, 2012

Bailey read the information one more time, wondering when life would again make sense. She looked up from the pamphlet clutched in her hand. "What do you mean, it's all paid for?"

"Miss Saunders, I know this is a trying time for you." Mr. Summervold, the funeral director, patted her hand. "I am sorry for your loss."

Annoyed at his patronizing tone, Bailey leaned back in her chair, effectively removing her hand and herself from any contact with him. It was either that or lean forward and punch him. She definitely had the urge to hit something.

She eyed him critically. His narrow jaw would crumple and his sleek nose would either lie over on his cheek or flatten like squished potatoes. She dropped her head into her open palms, allowing exhaustion to drag her toward the dark hole of sleep. The sound of a chair rolling on the hardwood floor yanked her back to reality. Her head jerked up and she thrust out her hand like a traffic cop. "I'm fine. Just give me some answers."

Long and lean, Mr. Sommervold had been in the act of standing. Now he reluctantly sat back down. "The funeral and burial are paid in full. You don't have to worry about any of that. The ceremony will take place here at the gravesite tomorrow, Thursday, April 23. Everything is arranged. It's all in there." He waved a languid hand at the paper in her lap.

Bailey's hand shook as she looked at the picture of her mom. Her red hair stood out like a beacon and her ruby red lipstick was in complete contrast to the dye job. Her face was pale and her aqua eyes pinched as though full of pain. It's not the picture she would have chosen but then there weren't many to choose from. Her mom normally refused to let others take her picture. For Bailey's graduation, she'd made an exception. Her present had been a picture of her mom in the backyard. She'd been happy, one of those rare moments. That's the picture Bailey would have selected.

"Everything has been taken care of."

"Where did this photo come from?"

"You really should talk to Mr. Lund, your mother's lawyer. He made all the arrangements."

Mr. Sommervold stood, his immaculate charcoal gray suit crisp as though he'd just put it on, though she knew he'd been in it for several hours already. The lady who'd met Bailey at the door had stated Mr. Sommervold started at 6:00 a.m. and was there most days until 6:00 p.m. Funeral directors didn't get a day off. Death was always at their door.

"But how?" Bailey got to her feet, stared at her clothes and brushed her hands down her wrinkled emerald-green dress. *When did I put this on?* She rubbed her finger over the faux silk material. Her mom had bought it for her four or five years before. *I choose to wear it for the first time when you can't see it?* She rubbed her forehead, squeezing hard to push away the headache pounding her skull.

Everything that hadn't been right between them came rushing to the surface. Stopping the flow of memories took some effort. The tears that filled her eyes took her by surprise. Where had they come from? She'd cried enough over the last two days to fill a dam. She pinched the bridge of her nose. *Not now. Not now. Not now. Just let me get through this.*

"Are you all right?"

Stupid question, if I laugh, will he think I've cracked up? She felt like she was. The 2:00 a.m. phone call she'd received about forty-eight hours before hadn't been what she'd expected. If it had been her mom saying their fight had gone far enough and Bailey should grow up and let it go... yes. She was all right with that. Being told her mom was dead... no. She'd caught the first flight out of Victoria and landed in Calgary, rented a car and headed to Foothills Hospital where she'd learned her mom's heart had given out. The doctors had done everything they could but couldn't explain how that could happen to a woman at age sixty. It just sometimes did. That she'd been failing for several months hadn't helped.

Bailey wasn't sure what had hit her harder—her mom being dead, or her mom having health problems and not sharing them with her.

Straightening, she squared her shoulders. "Just tell me who paid the money for her funeral. Who organized it? It doesn't make any sense." She stopped short of telling him that her mom had no friends, just Bailey.

Mr. Sommervold pushed up his round wire-rimmed glasses from where they'd slid down his nose.

"I'm not leaving without answers."

The door opened as his assistant, a stunning auburn-haired woman, poked her head in. "Mr. Sommervold, the Greenings are here. They have a few things they'd like to discuss with you before the funeral this afternoon."

Solemn-faced, he nodded then turned to face Bailey. "I don't know who paid for it. Mr. Lund sent me a letter stating her wishes. He also provided a second letter." He opened the folder in front of him, pulled out an envelope, closed the file and dropped it into the bottom drawer of his desk. After a short hesitation, he slid the envelope across to Bailey.

She stared at him for a moment before picking it up. Her name was scrawled across it in her mother's handwriting. She pressed it between her palms.

"I'm sure this will answer some of your questions. For any others you have, you'll need to talk to Mr. Lund. Here's his business card."

Bailey stared at the envelope. Would it give her the answers she needed?

"Now if you'll excuse me. I have other clients I need to see."

She jerked up her head. Mr. Sommervold was standing in the open doorway, obviously waiting for her to leave. A bit dazed, she stood shakily and walked past him to the main foyer, where she stopped.

Everything seemed surreal. Even the rich, immaculate oak entranceway was too perfect, too daunting. Soft hymn music drifted through the building. Quiet voices drifted to her in whispered, reverent tones heard only at solemn times. They made everything feel more unnatural.

She felt like a character in dream—no; a nightmare. An unexpected shiver shook her out of her reverie.

She strode out of the building to her rented Hyundai. Once inside she stared at the paper clenched in her left hand. There were designs and pictures covering the back of the envelope. Many would dismiss them as doodles but Bailey knew better. She just wasn't prepared to decipher what her mom couldn't tell her straight out. Tracing her finger absently over the heart that had three stick figures within it made her pause, for it looked like a family.

Are you saying you'd wished Dad had been in my life? Whoever he was.

Realizing that she wasn't in any space to deal with what that could mean, she shook off those thoughts. Sliding her finger under the edge she worked her way across the top, peeling it open. She pulled out the slim, folded piece of paper inside.

Bailey, I know you have a lot of questions. That's just the way you are. You deserve the answers but I can only give you some. I planned my own funeral so it would be one less worry for you. Just go back to the life you had. Keep helping the poor families. I am very proud of you, Bailey. I'm sorry for all the misunderstandings between us. They're all my fault. Not yours. You're a good girl, one any family would be proud of. It's a miracle that you came into my life. I love you… although I don't really have the right.

Mom

Bailey crumpled the paper in one hand as her tears obscured her vision. Why had she never cleared up that lie about her career?

3

"I found her."

"Oh?"

Guy fought back a smile and wondered how one person could convey so much information in such a short word—doubt... disdain... disbelief.

"Yes Gramama, I did." He allowed himself a full grin, mostly because his not-even-related-grandmother wasn't with him to see it and give him hell. He was the only person who could get away with calling Dorothea Lindell that affectionate name. He'd never understood why she'd opened her arms to him anyway, given his dubious heritage.

"Wipe that smirk off your face. I'm not too old to still take a round out of you." Her indrawn breath sounded like a shop vacuum sucking up a pool of water.

Oooh, I'm scared, Grams. He waited her out.

"How do you know it's her?"

"Well, Gramama, I know because I'm good at looking at a picture and seeing similar details in someone else's face. That's why you hired me to find her. Of course my charm and good looks had to have played a part in that." He had shown her the facial recognition software they'd used to confirm Bailey was a match. It had confirmed Dorothea's request that he find her.

She snorted in mock disgust while Guy continued to smile. He loved his relationship with her. He was very fortunate to have it or any acknowledged connection with her. She was a lot softer than people knew but he didn't plan to share that bit of news.

"Are you sure it's her?"

He could hear the hope and the fear of what that meant and what it could mean. "I am."

There was a long silence. He couldn't imagine how difficult this was for her. Even though she'd sent him to find her, the shock after all these years had to devastating. Especially with all it implied—someone had stolen her granddaughter.

"Just a moment."

He could hear his grandmother's muffled voice along with a man's. Uncle Geoffrey—or at least that was what his step-grandmother had hoped Guy would come to know him as—was angry as usual. Guy flinched, an automatic response. They'd never gotten along. Geoffrey had hated Guy from the moment they'd met.

"What the hell do you mean to bring that brat into this family?"

"Watch your mouth, Geoffrey. He is my grandson and will be treated as such."

"He's no blood relative of mine."

"No he's not but he's important to me. If nothing else, you owe me the respect I deserve and you need to trust me. I'm asking you to accept this boy."

"You want me to accept the grandchild of a maid, whose daughter swears she was raped here, on our property? Hasn't

she brought enough embarrassment to this family? You want to raise that brat as one of us?"

"You ever talk like that to me again and you're out."

Geoffrey had backed down immediately but he'd seemed angry enough to strike her. And he'd never accepted Guy, treating him the same way he treated chewing gum clinging to the bottom of his five-hundred-dollar shoes, doing whatever he had to do to get rid of it.

Many years later, Guy realized that his grandma held the reins at Caspian Winery. She'd given them to Geoffrey when someone had leaked to the media that her husband, Joseph, was his father. Guy would have loved that. The real reason she'd given up the reins for a while was because Joseph had cancer. He'd been fighting for his life and she'd been right there beside him. Once he'd pulled through all the chemotherapy and radiation and seemed to be on the mend, she'd taken back the CEO position but Geoff remained her right-hand person and had continued to act as though he owned the place.

And nothing had changed. Guy had learned to stay out of Geoff's way.

"Guy, we've got a problem," his grandmother said.

Guy shook off that horrid memory of meeting Geoff. What else was new? Geoffrey always had something crawling up his butt. Guy just hoped his grandmother hadn't shared with him what he was really doing. "What do you mean a problem?"

"Geoffrey just told me we're having issues with our new acquisition in Southern California. They want more money. Since I've been bragging about your skills as a negotiator, he seems to think I should hire you to run our south shore winery. Well, the one that will be ours if he doesn't screw up the deal. You'd be very good at least when I got done with you, anyway." She huffed.

"Thanks but I don't—"

"Of course you don't have time right now. I need you to keep working this case."

Guy shuddered. He wished he had the nerve to tell her outright there was no way he would be going into the family business. Ever. Definitely not while Geoff was there.

After a short silence, she said, "Send me a report on all you've found out already. And no, don't email it to me. And yes, I do know how to use it. I just don't trust it. You can tell me all the firewalls and antiviruses that keep it safe but I believe if someone wants the information they'll find a way to hack in. Fax it to me. Make sure it's her, Guy. Make sure."

He tapped his index finger on his chin, a quirk he'd involuntarily picked up from his grandfather. He chuckled, remembering his grandfather always done that whenever his grandmother challenged him. "It's her, Gramama. If you could see her, you'd know it too. Don't worry, I know what I need to do. I'll keep this quiet as long as I can. You need to prepare Gina and Daniel, though. They need to hear this from you."

She huffed again. "Don't tell me how to handle my daughter. I'll let them know when I'm good and ready. And when I am as convinced as you are that she is the one. I won't have her hurt this family again. When I meet her I'll decide what's right."

He shook his head. He understood her anger but she couldn't blame it on a kidnapped baby, the only innocent party in the mess.

"Take care of yourself," she said as she rang off.

He wished she hadn't said that. She wasn't sentimental, so a strong sense of foreboding hit him like a smack in the face with a newly caught fish. Uneasy, he stared at the phone as he tapped the end button on his Smartphone and then searched for his business partner's number.

He watched the woman known as Bailey Saunders walk out of the funeral home, looking dazed and confused. He had to add to her burdens and regret struck him, along with sheer fatigue. He almost wished he'd taken that vacation he'd been putting off. And off. And off. But as soon as this was done he was going to go far away and lie on a beach.

Despite the hard work, he loved being a computer geek. Although he'd only been at it for a little more than a year with his partner, Graham Knight, Guy had excelled. Knights Associates had been tough slugging for a while to get clients. And when they had business, the hours had been long and grueling.

Their other cases tended to involve cheating spouses but the work was impersonal. The private investigators who hired them wanted any online traces of emails and pictures that would support their theories of infidelity. He and Graham didn't care for those jobs but they had paid the bills in the beginning. Some interesting cases had come along from the police department, wanting them to check fraudulent activity in a few companies. Then Guy's grandma had approached him with finding the lost baby, a task way outside their normal work. Finding someone who was stolen almost thirty years before wasn't their usual assignment and although it fascinated him, he hadn't wanted to take it. In fact, he'd begged Graham to do it. Graham had just smiled that knowing smile and had shaken his head.

The tears that had filled his grandmother's eyes when she'd asked had really been his undoing. He'd never seen her shed a tear or even come close. And she'd had plenty of reasons to over the years, especially when he'd been brought into the fold—an offspring from an ugly situation and no relation to her at all. But she hadn't turned him away and had insisted that he consider her his grandmother. She hadn't turned him away when his mother had died in a car accident, nor when the scandal of rape had hit the newspapers, for a second time. Nor when his grandfather, her husband, her friend, had died suddenly.

She'd taken it all in stride. Her one goal had been to protect him at all costs. She'd known he was innocent and would not let the media nor his maternal money-grabbing grandmother use him to smear the Lindell name and gain fortune.

He tapped his fingers on the steering wheel. He would do anything for Dorothea. She'd been the one to save him from a life of hell in foster homes; for that alone, he'd have helped her.

Hitting the number two on his favorites, he waited for it to be answered.

"Are you calling because you need advice, you miss me or your grandma is giving you a hard time?" Graham asked.

Guy smiled. "Kiss mine."

"Ah but then one would presume that I wanted to and after catching Mr. Simon doing that exact deed with Mr. Traemont, I don't know that I'll ever be able to get that vision out of my head. I think the only thing worse was telling Mr. Simon's wife, 'yes, he was cheating but no, it wasn't a younger woman but a younger man.' Not cool, especially when we are talking underage. And catching anyone in the act, is not a vision I care to carry around."

Guy burst out laughing. Graham had worked as a private investigator for a large company for a few years. He'd been hired on to do computer work for them but he'd soon found that they'd really needed an extra body to do legwork and he'd been it. Investigations had never been something he'd wanted to do but he loved to share the stories of the stakeouts he'd been on.

"How's it going? Any luck?"

"Well, after covertly entering the plane and flying all the way across country, I landed in the airport. After several hours of sleuthing—"

"Don't tell me you got some dumb luck and found her right away?"

"You won't believe it. This case might be over before it starts."

"What happened?"

"I get off the airplane at Victoria Airport, walk into the terminal and guess what? There she is in line getting on a plane. So I get in line, buy a ticket and now I'm in Calgary."

"Alberta? What in the world are you doing there? Are you sure you didn't just decide to take that vacation you keep saying you will and are actually calling me from Cancun after one too many rum punches?"

He tapped his finger on his chin as he took a deep breath. Things were good. "I seriously am doing that once this case is over. In fact, I should get Sherry to book me a trip for next week."

"You think it'll be over that fast?"

He'd thought a lot about it. His role was to find her and tell her who she really was which made him uncomfortable. How would she feel? Then he'd hand her over to his step-grandmother who would decide how to handle the rest. He'd already done half the job. "Yeah, it's looking like it."

"So what's in Calgary?"

"Her mother. And unfortunately her mother's funeral."

"Shit. Sorry to hear that. It'll make it tough telling her she's not who she thinks she is."

You have no idea. "I've got to go. Tell Sherry to check out some prices for me. Hmm... Hawaii, I think."

"Good choice, ol' boy. Ta ta for now."

Guy chuckled as he ended the conversation. Graham's snobby British accent was bad but it sure lifted Guy's spirits.

Glancing out his window, he noted that Bailey was finally on the move. He started his SUV and pulled into traffic four cars behind her. His gut clenched, twisting his insides. This case might not to have the quick finish he wanted.

4

"Mr. Lund? Miss Bailey Saunders is here to see you."

Bailey stood by the reception desk tapping her fingernails on the polished wood surface. The secretary glared, sniffed indignantly and then shifted sideways, her hand cupped around the phone mike resting against her cheek. She talked quietly into the phone receiver. A brash, no nonsense voice on the other end of that phone though, came through the earpiece, loud and clear.

"Right. Uhm, I need the file on Donna Za— No. No, forget it. I'll get it. Give me twenty minutes."

"Okay." The receptionist turned toward Bailey with an insincere smile. "Please have a seat. He'll be a while. That's why you should have an appointment."

Although Bailey wanted to slam her hands on the desk, she slid them to her sides and slowly curled her fingers into her palms until her nails pressed into the flesh. She pasted on as sincere a smile as the receptionist. "I'm sorry; I didn't get your name?"

"Isabel."

I'd have guessed miserable... Bailey squared her shoulders. "Isabel, look, I really need to see Mr. Lund. My mom just died and I..."

Isabel's demeanor changed like the flip of a coin. "I'm so sorry. That's got to be really tough."

Unsure of what to do, Bailey nodded and instinctively took a step back. Something in her actions must have gotten through to the other woman because she switched back to her professional self but with a softer edge.

"You have a seat and I'll see if I can speed up Mr. Lund. Can I get you something to drink?"

Bailey shook her head before walking across the expansive chrome and glass lobby. A picture of the CN Tower in Toronto caught her eye. As she got closer she realized it was a painting, not a print as she had first thought. It was an incredible picture. She glanced at the name of the artist. D. Zajic. *Hmmm. Never heard of him.*

She had jumped to the conclusion that the painter was male and smiled ruefully at that slip. She wanted to ask the secretary about it but was concerned the woman would continue talking to her. Wandering around the office, she looked at all the artworks displayed. Some carried the same theme of high rises in Ottawa or Toronto while a couple were nature scenes. The rest of the pictures adorning the walls were nature photographs. Someone had an eye for seeing the beauty in the mountains and in streams flowing over a rock. The scenes were amazing.

She studied one directly opposite the receptionist's desk which depicted a lake with overhanging trees in the foreground. On its left was a painting of a river and mountains. She cocked her head. The scenery looked familiar... too familiar. An icy chill crawled up her neck and wrapped around to brush at her temples. She jerked back.

"Excuse me, Miss Saunders. Mr. Lund will see you now."

Bailey glanced over her shoulder at the starched and pressed receptionist.

Shaking off her unease which she attributed to fatigue and stress, she snapped out of her trance and followed.

The receptionist led Bailey to a plush room that could have easily housed ten individual offices. Behind the desk was a well-dressed older man in a blue-gray fitted suit. His thinning white hair carefully slicked to the side and the hard lines around his mouth disclosed he was past his prime and nearing retirement. The curve of his lips might have resembled a smile, except that it never reached his hard black eyes. He strode purposefully around his massive cherry wood desk.

"Bails."

"What?" Her eyes widened as she stared hard at him, waiting for an explanation.

"Whales. I'm sorry. I was just finishing up on a case I'm working on." He extended his hand. "Miss Saunders. I'm glad to finally meet you."

She carefully schooled her face in only a slight frown but her mind was racing. Something wasn't right. Her mom was the only one who had ever called her Bails. She tilted her head, wondering if she had heard him correctly. Exhaustion and a thousand unanswered questions might have added to her wariness but she knew she needed to listen to her gut instinct. It had always served her well.

It went against every impulse she had but knowing it was the expected norm, she accepted his handshake but dropped his hand as soon as was acceptable.

"I'm really sorry for your loss. It was such a shock."

Scrutinizing him, she asked, "You weren't aware of her being sick?"

His eyes remained hard and fixed on her for a moment before he reassumed his seat behind the desk. "No. No. I was quite surprised that she had died."

Bailey pondered what she knew but nothing added up. She continued to examine his facial expression. "Yet she had her funeral organized and paid for. Who put up the money?" She sat on the plush leather chair facing him.

"Donna told me you'd be full of questions. Even if I knew, I couldn't tell you. Client Confidentiality." He sounded smug.

His attitude grated. "You don't know?"

"What I can share with you is what's in Donna's Last Will and Testament and that her funeral was paid in full, in cash."

"What's in her Will?"

"Customarily we discuss that after the funeral."

Bailey glowered at him.

He grabbed a file on top of a stack to his left. "Well…" He read aloud the formal introduction and sailed through the three pieces of paper that were the last connection she had to her mom.

She wrapped her mind around the information and asked, "Essentially I get everything except the house? What about the Dandy Candy store and inventory?" She slumped back in the soft leather chair.

"Uhm, there's a letter to do with the store." He picked up an envelope.

As she accepted it from him, she could barely restrain herself from ripping it out of his hands and leaving immediately. Turning away from him, she opened it, careful not to distort or ruin any of the doodles on it. She read the note inside then put it in her bag, careful to hide the extra page that was in the envelope. She'd save that to decipher later.

What the hell is going on? Her fists thumped against her thighs. She strode over to the large windows that overlooked the river valley. The Bow River flowed freely, winding through the concrete and noise to continue on its journey from the mountains across the prairies. She wanted to walk right into it and let the water take her where it would. Tempting, but she had to get this over with. She sighed.

Turning, a framed picture on the wall caught her attention. The name "D. Zajic" was again scribbled in the bottom right hand corner. The picture was a tree with branches that draped over a creek.

The cabin was nestled in trees, with the gurgle of a river nearby. The rutted road was rough and overgrown, hiding the entrance. She was running and laughing. A man was chasing her. She giggled and ran faster, loving the game they played.

❧⊙❧

Lund picked up his phone and dialed a number he knew well. "Follow her. Keep me informed who she talks to. Where she goes. What she does." He almost said what she finds.

"All right. Fifty thousand up front."

"That's pretty steep."

"Yeah and you wouldn't be coming to me if you weren't desperate." Lund's caller laughed. "Is she a looker?"

"Touch her and you'll answer to me." He shuddered as he thought about Payme's grimy appearance—stringy, matted brown hair, grease-stained clothes, runners that looked more like sandals now. At least that was how he had appeared the last time he'd kept his butt out of jail.

"Good one. You might be a big shot in your world. But you're nothing in mine. Remember that. The price goes up if I have to dispose of anyone." Payme, as he had been dubbed due to the graffiti he always wrote by his victims, 'pay me with your death', might have been a small, wiry man at 5'4" but also very deadly. Lund had hoped never to use Payme again; once had been more than enough. Unfortunately, fate had a different agenda and he needed someone who was loyal enough and could take her out, if the necessity came. He'd rather not get his hands dirty again, if he didn't have to.

"Hopefully we won't have to discuss that. Just keep me informed." He set down the receiver with a shaky hand, knowing he was into something that may backfire on him. He was already going to hell for what he did. What he was. What he had done.

This, though, was something he'd thought would die with Donna. Only she'd stolen a photo taken of him a long time ago and hidden it. Actually she'd led him to believe she'd destroyed it but the photocopy that had arrived today had been enough to know it still existed. He'd burned that little present in a pail with a liter of gas. It was just like Donna to reach from beyond the grave to let him know he wasn't off the hook. He'd pay for what he'd done to her.

It had been an invigorating game, letting Donna think she'd been in control. He could have taken her out at any time. He'd made so much money because of her. He chuckled as he sat straight in his chair and slowly climbed to his feet. It had been too easy. She'd been a scared rabbit, trying to act tough. He was going to miss her hard smackin' demands. She'd fed him so much information about all those men in government. Her husband included. Really he was going to miss her. She'd given him enough to blackmail at least fifty more people. Ah… the sins of the rich and powerful.

He brushed his hand back over his hair as he made his way across the room to his scotch. As he reached for a glass, he froze.

What if someone else finds it?

Feeling lightheaded, he rested his fingers on the table to steady himself. The picture should have been little more than an embarrassment, one he could have explained away or cast him as a victim. His in-laws didn't like him, though, and would do anything to get rid of him. If they knew the photo existed... well, the things he'd done to protect himself—the bribes, the blackmail, the man he'd murdered, the extortion—and the lifestyle he lived, were acceptable. People finding out about him and his real preferences in life was not. He made a lot of money from just that kind of secret. If his were known...

He shuddered. He couldn't take the chance. His game of twenty-nine years would have to end. He just had to make sure that not all parties were aware of what exactly he'd been playing at. It had been so damn invigorating and thrilling, especially knowing a degrading picture of himself existed that would have solved all their problems, had they gotten their hands on it. One of them would surely like to actually put the bullet between his eyes that he'd been threatened with on many occasions.

He had started it and now must end it.

All because of a damned picture.

5

"Oh Heavenly Father please accept Donna into your arms. Take care of her for those on earth who loved her…"

The minister's voice droned on. Bailey bowed her head, letting the tears fall freely. She couldn't understand why her mom hadn't told her she was ill. They never really talked about anything personal without it turning into a disagreement, but she didn't think that was an excuse for her mom to withhold something of this magnitude.

Bailey dug in the right pocket of her long, blue coat for a fresh tissue. All she managed to find was a mangled one that had seen better times. The left pocket was already full of used ones. She held the shredded pieces together and blew her nose as best she could. Stuffing it back in her pocket she raised her head. The few other attendees, whom she had no idea who they were, still had their heads bowed. Thankful for the reprieve from the I'm-so-sorry look everyone was giving her, she looked straight up. Clouds and blue sky mixed, letting the sun play hide-and-seek. She let herself drift with the ever-changing sky, blanking out all that was going on around her. A stiff breeze whipped around her, enveloping her in its cool biting presence. She shivered. She shifted from foot to foot. Normally two-inch heels didn't bother her but today they were pinching like crab pincers. The minister's voice carried on in a monotone that was an instant sleep inducer. She tuned him out. Sleep was something she could use. About seventy-two hours worth.

But not yet.

She'd had a conversation with her mom just the week before. It had been awkward and stilted and about the weather and politics rather than their fight several days prior. Her mom never said a word about being unwell.

But she'd known.

Bailey clenched her hands. She was tempted to look at her watch but she could hear her mom telling her it would be just plain rude. 'It's over when it's over.' She didn't want to do anything that would upset her mom on this day. Maybe she could do something just once that would make her proud.

The pressure sitting on her chest felt like a hundred-pound anvil, teetering, ready to crash. Anger, frustration, anguish, fear, sadness, rolled, twisted and churned in Bailey's stomach as all the times she and her mom used to fight ran through her mind. They came fast and furious, spinning like a top, zipping from one to another and back again. Startled by the speed with which it hit, she guiltily looked around as though exposed, as if everyone knew what she was thinking. And thinking she deserved it.

She forced her thoughts to other things. Had she called Tina before she left? She hoped her friend hadn't driven across the city to find out she wasn't there. A niggling memory of something planned with Tina and Deb this weekend popped into her mind but she couldn't remember the details. She'd have to call them.

They'd be upset. It wasn't the first time. The other times had involved her mom too. Not that her friends knew that. She'd never discussed her family or lack of it. This was another rule she'd had to live by.

It's all fixable.

Looking up, her gaze was caught by the sight of the casket. The finality of what it meant slammed into her.

This... this isn't fixable.

She buried her face in her hands and pushed hard. Not here. Not now. She wanted privacy when she let loose. Until now she'd been too numb to really take it in. But this...this was final. There was no going back. No, 'I'm sorry Mom. We disagree but that's okay; I still love you.'

Why didn't you tell me you were sick, Mom? Or did you?

A few months before, a time when she'd left her friends high and dry to zip home because of her mom's urgent and very bizarre phone call wouldn't be pushed away. She'd phoned and demanded that Bailey come home immediately.

Bailey had panicked and taken the next flight. It had been a really bizarre week. Her mom had insisted she just needed to see her daughter; they didn't spend enough time together but she wouldn't share more than that. She had sworn she was just lonely and feeling bad about the relationship they had. Everything had felt off. Bailey had felt queasy, the same feeling she'd had growing up, every time they'd fled from their latest location. At her mom's insistence, she'd finally put the bizarre behavior down to stress, being overworked, worrying too much about the store, about Bailey being in the news.

But maybe it had been something else.

Was it part of your illness, Mom?

Bailey sighed. Exhaustion rolled over her. Her hands fell to her sides, her shoulders sagged, her chin fell to her chest and her mind went blank.

"She was taken from us…"

Bailey shook her head, trying to deny what was happening. Stretching her eyes open wide, she blinked several times. Restlessly she shuffled her feet. The scent of lilac drifted up to her. The funeral home had taken care of every detail. The gravesite was covered with a carpet of lilacs. Her mother's favorite flower and fragrance from her childhood. One of the few memories she had shared with Bailey. That and the fact there were no living relatives. And the rest of her childhood was too painful to share—especially regarding why there was no other family.

"Let's bow our head in prayer. Oh Heavenly Father…"

Bailey closed her eyes while the reverend recited the words, not because she was following the ritual of prayer but because she didn't have the energy left to keep them open. She clasped her hands in front of her. A strong spring breeze whipped around her, slicing through her thin dress coat.

"Excuse me, Miss Saunders?"

It took a moment for Bailey to realize the Minister was talking to her. She blinked at him. Genuine concern was etched in his features and it pulled at Bailey with the deepest yearnings of an emotionally starved child. She barely caught herself from leaning against him. Just for a moment she wanted someone to take this away.

Stand on your own two feet, Bails. I didn't raise a weakling. Bailey snapped upright as her mom's words popped into her mind.

"The service is done. Your mother will be laid to rest in the ground later today…."

Bailey blinked several times. Too numb to talk or to really understand what he was saying, she nodded. Squeezing her hand, he said, "May God be with you."

"Thank you, Reverend," she mumbled in return. He moved toward a waiting car. The funeral was finally over. Could she finally go home and… and…

"Hello. We're Mr. and Mrs. Prichard." They grasped Bailey's limp hand. "We're so sorry for your loss."

Bailey smiled wanly at them.

"We were regulars at your mom's store. She found some of the most exotic candies I've ever tasted. That Delafee Chocolate she imported was very expensive but it was to die for." The woman's eyes opened wide as what she said registered. She turned a bright shade of red. "She'd never give away her secrets as to where she got her stuff. She was a very mysterious lady but such a pleasure. I'm really sorry she's gone."

Bailey nodded, not sure what else to do. "Thank you. Mom would be happy you're here." The middle-aged couple silently made their way toward a beautiful red convertible.

"Ooooohhhhh. My dear—"

"How tragic. This is just so wrong—"

"Your mom was in the prime of her life. I'm so sorry."

Two stooped, cane-carrying ladies popped right into her face, talking over the top of each other. Bailey looked from one to another and then gave up trying to figure out who was saying what.

"It's never the right time. But she's with God now—"

"She's walking in the hands of the Lord…"

It dawned on her these two might be professional funeral mourners. Her mom didn't have any best friends—or real friends, for that matter. Everyone was just an acquaintance. That was one of the things they'd argued about over the years. Her mom had taught her from a young age not to make friends–'they'll just hurt you or you'll hurt them'.

Her friends Tina and Deb immediately came to mind. Isn't that what she'd done to them? Again. And again. She'd tried to be in a friendship, thinking it would solve everything but it only created headaches. She sucked at it as she felt she did at most things in her life.

"Thank you. Excuse me." Bailey backed away from the two women who were openly bawling like they'd lost their very own child. Sidestepping them, Bailey made her way around the gravesite. A couple and a young girl of about twelve stepped in front of her. Bailey tried to hide her annoyance.

"Hi. We're sorry for your loss."

"Thank you." She tried to go around the threesome but the woman put her hand on her arm, detaining her. Bailey looked at them blankly.

"Your mom was so good to Taylor." The woman smiled at her daughter. "She used to watch Taylor dance. She taught her more about ballet than the instructors did. Our Taylor blossomed under your mom's guidance."

Bailey nodded. It wouldn't do any good to tell them they were at the wrong funeral. She'd begged her mom to put her in dance school but her mom had said it was an expensive waste of time. She doubted her mom even knew what a plié was. The woman gave her a quick hug before leaving.

Everyone had gone. She took a deep breath before looking at her mom's casket. The beautiful black onyx shone as though under a spotlight, draped with a white satin scarf and a large bouquet of flowers—daisies, irises, carnations, tiger lilies, pansies, roses and several others she didn't know. It exploded with colors—reds, oranges, yellows, purples—and reminded her of the hill in *The Sound of Music*, her mom's favorite movie.

I think you would have loved it, Mom. Bailey squeezed her hands together as though in prayer then pressed them against her lips for a moment. Her thoughts were rapid fire.

Were there enough flowers? Were they the right ones? Was that the right outfit for Mom? Did it really matter what she wore? The blue one was her favorite; all those frills. The red, sleek dress was the one Bailey would have chosen. It was something else from the old days her mother wouldn't talk about. Her mom had obviously arranged for the blue outfit. The funeral home already had it. But who had given it to them? How long had she known she was dying? Who had paid for the funeral? What else haven't I been told?

She took in several calming breaths. *When can I get out of here? When can I go back home?* The estate—what possessions she had—must be settled. Then she could go. *Should I have found more people to come to this?*

The letter had made it clear she had not wanted her death advertised. She had placed a small notice at the shop stating it was closed until further notice and only those who had phoned her cell to find out when it would reopen had been told she had died. Stepping backward, she took one last look before bowing her head. Pain radiated through her skull with the blunt force of a hammer. Stopping, she pressed her fingers into her temples and counted to ten.

Maybe this'll all disappear and I'll wake up.

She looked about. A bleak, dreary day greeted her along with a clear view of her mom's casket resting over the open hole that was ready to swallow her. Bailey spun around. Her eyes lit on her car and she walked briskly toward it.

6

A man stepped from the shadows of the trees to stand beside her Hyundai rental. She stopped and stared. His black suit was appropriate for a funeral but she didn't remember seeing him at the gravesite. He looked as though he'd just raised his head from prayer, his feet were still shoulder width apart and his hands were clasped loosely in front of him. Why was he looking at her so expectantly and with such a foreboding expression?

Bailey frowned as she made her way along the gravel road, her eyes never leaving his face. As she neared, she noted he wasn't as old as she'd first thought, and he was kind of cute with a young George Clooney countenance—dark and mysterious. An unexpected shudder caused her to hesitate a few feet from the car.

"Hello. I'm sorry for your loss."

She'd heard that over and over for the last few days and yet she felt that this stranger actually meant it. She watched him closely.

"Did you know my mom?"

He looked down, his whole body visibly tensing. A couple of heartbeats later he raised his head. "No. Not… No; I didn't." His sky blue eyes darkened. "I just wanted to give you my condolences." He seemed to study her for several seconds before striding away.

Bailey stared after him in confusion. Something had just happened that she couldn't quite decipher. It was as though he'd made a decision that was directly related to her. She watched him climb into a dark SUV and drive away, winding his way through the maze of roads as though he knew them well.

That hit Bailey hard. Her mom had known she was dying. Someone had paid for an elegant funeral and ceremony. Could it have been this stranger, a boyfriend she hadn't told her about? *He's kind of young, Mom, but wow.*

For a brief second that brightened her mood. It would be a relief if her mom hadn't been alone. Bailey sighed. But her mom hadn't dated and she would never have considered a younger man; she'd always said he'd be eighty and too darn weak to lift his arms.

She grabbed the car door handle. *I just want to go home.*

Her mind wouldn't stop though. Who had paid the bill? The couple with the daughter? Bailey snorted. They couldn't have known her mom, she'd never let Bailey near dance. They'd be embarrassed when they realize the mistake they'd made.

Bailey's headache pounded through her skull with jackhammer precision. She pressed her fingertips against her temples. The wind whipped up, letting its presence be known as it wound its way through the trees and gravesites. Fear came from nowhere and landed with a punch to her gut and then spidered its way throughout her body. It wasn't the noise so much as the absence of it.

Someone was watching her. She knew it. It was a feeling that had served her well in the past. Looking around, she noted the rows upon rows of granite, etched with names, dates and loving memories that surrounded her. The flowers dotting the graves and the shrubs and pine trees broke up the uniformity but it was still deserted. She couldn't help but shudder at what all that meant. For a brief second she had a vision of all the bodies rising up from the graves, with arms held forward, walking towards her.

Then the breeze which had been like a gentle caress blew with a howling force. She staggered at the impact of it. Struggling to stand upright, she looked up. Big drops of rain hit her in the face. Heavy gray clouds encased the sky. She scrambled for the door handle. Grabbing it, she yanked it open and dove in, just as the downpour started. She sat there for several minutes staring at the bleak sight. Sheets of rain obliterated her view. Fumbling around in the unfamiliar car, she managed to get it started and then found the windshield wiper switch. She flipped it to high speed. The deluge hit her window like a waterfall. The wipers were flipping as fast as possible and still weren't able to clear it for more than a second.

A chill scooted down her spine like a colony of ants. Shivering, it wasn't clear to her if it was from the cold and rain, the sense of dread that the cemetery had evoked in her, or all that she wasn't ready to acknowledge. She eased the Hyundai forward, straining in an attempt to see through the curtain of water. Puddles the size of mini lakes formed. The poorly graveled road had turned into a child's dream, a muck fest. Out of respect, she tried to drive slowly but the car kept losing traction. Fed up with absolutely everything, she sped up, ignoring the mud packs flung from the tires.

As she reached the main street, she sagged over the steering wheel as she peered out at the fast moving traffic, unfazed by the poor weather. The worst part was she shouldn't be either; this was normal weather for Victoria. Even that fleeting realization saddened her. And quick on its heels was another—had it really been home or simply a place she'd been hiding out from her mom? Shaking off those morbid thoughts, she eased onto Memorial Drive and headed east toward Deerfoot Trail.

An hour and a half later, thanks to accidents, flooding and the odd impulse to lose an imaginary tail, she pulled up to her mom's little blue house in Canyon Meadows in southwest Calgary. The rain had eased to a slow, mesmerizing drizzle. No thoughts, no sounds, no smells, nothing intruded on the glazed focus she had out her windshield.

A horn honked and she jerked upright. How long had she been sitting there? A dog shot across the street, disappearing around the corner of a house. She blinked a few times as she became aware of the fogged windshield and the chill invading the car and her thin clothes. She reached for the handle. Leaning heavily against the door, she pushed it open. Exhausted beyond anything she'd ever experienced, she lifted her left hand overhead and grabbed the support. One. Two. Three. Heave.

Awkwardly and slowly, like a person with severe arthritis, she managed to pull herself out. She wobbled a moment before she found her land legs. After opening the trunk, she pulled out her suitcase and carry-on bag.

Out of habit, she marched to the front door and lifted her hand to knock. Her mom was always in the living room. But just before her knuckles touched the wood she realized what she was doing and her fist froze in mid-air. Jerking back, she jumped down the four steps and headed around to the side. At the gate she dropped her luggage as she reached up to play with the tricky slider lock. After a few tries she got it open. Closing but not latching it, she continued to the back of the house. She hurried to the table and wooden stool set in the middle of the lawn as the chilly air wrapped around her. In the seat closest to the house a hidden clip had been installed under the seat. Once she'd retrieved the key she made her way back to the door. Her hand shook as she shoved the key in the lock. It took several attempts to unlock it.

She pushed her way in. The last time she'd left hit her like a locomotive. The fight she'd had with her mom flashed like a movie rerun. They were, as always, yelling at each other.

"Don't go, Bails. What aren't you telling me?"

"Not a damn thing, Mom. Like always, you want to control my every move. Well, not this time. And never again. You have meddled in my life for the last time. Bye, Mom."

"Bails. No!"

Bailey walked out of the house, giving the door a heavy push. The hard slam infused her with a sense of satisfaction.

"Don't come back, unless you learn some damn manners first! Someone has to look after you and I'm the one who took the job. No one else was there. I'm your mother, Bails!"

She kept walking without acknowledging her mom. Climbing into her car, she drove away.

Her visit had been the same as always.

Fighting.

Yelling.

Storming away.

Tentatively making up.

Moving on.

Bailey shook her head. If she could have the last month back she would change everything. One month. How was she supposed to know that things would change so dramatically in that time? She could have gotten her mom medical help. She could have done something.

Two years and she could change another confrontation. She'd wanted her mom to visit but she had refused, asking, "Who'd man the store? How would I get there?" Or five years ago, when they'd argued about Bailey moving east. She hadn't really decided where; it had just been a thought. But she had gone berserk, totally freaking out. She'd scared Bailey more than the hundred times they'd moved at night. Not moving east was another in her mom's one hundred and one rules that hadn't made sense.

If she could go back fourteen years to when she'd turned fifteen, she could fix it. Everything had changed that summer and nothing either one of them had done could recover the closeness they'd once felt. This time there'd be no making up. *I'm so sorry, Mom.*

Bailey felt like she went from free falling to crashing with a driving force. She dropped to the floor, tears already dripping off her face. Heavy, wracking sobs tore through her, starting in her gut and ripping outwards. Her body shook as the pain and anguish coursed through her like a hurricane barreling across the ocean to crash on land, tearing to shreds anything in its wake. She curled on her side into the smallest fetal position she could muster.

Eventually the sound of an old style ticking clock filtered through her consciousness. Opening her gritty, burning eyes, she closed them just as quickly as the last vestiges of light bounced off the brilliantly shining floor. Bailey pushed herself up, arching her neck so she could see the wall clock. 5:40. Was it morning or evening?

Beyond the window, it was still a dreary day with gray skies and muted light. She guessed evening. Shifting slightly, the hard surface dug into her tender hip. She groaned and then shivered as the cold linoleum penetrated her thin, damp clothing.

Pulling herself to her feet, she grabbed a cup from the cupboard and filled it with cold tap water. The fluoride taste turned her off but she downed it anyway, hoping it would appease her empty stomach for a while. Her stomach instantly protested by knotting up, reminding her it was more of a symbol for what she was avoiding. Somehow she found the courage to look at what she had wanted to avoid, the reason she hadn't come to the house before then.

The city newspaper lay open on a stack of newspapers, just like always. Her mom would read a bit before rushing off to work or running errands, but she'd always return to examine them from front to back. She should be returning to read more… give her opinion on what the government was doing wrong… grumble about who was still in government.

She'll be back, at any moment.

Bailey's breath hitched and she pressed her hand to her stomach. Everything else looked the same: clean, tidy, not a thing out of place.

But it wasn't the same.

She looked down at the mug in her hand – *Friends are like sunshine, there for the good times and gone for the bad.*

To avoid all of this, Bailey had chosen to stay at a hotel the last two nights. Staying now wasn't a good idea either but she didn't have a choice. She picked up the dark red luggage splayed across the floor and made her way out of the kitchen, turning right at the living room to go down the hallway. Her feet took the route that, although not done frequently, was still familiar. Her mind remained focused on the spare bedroom and thoughts of sleep. She stepped into the room and dropped her stuff in the corner.

Immediately, she heard her mom's voice, 'You have to put your stuff away. It'll get wrinkled. There's no one to pick up behind you. And don't expect it. You have to do it yourself. You're not royalty, you know.' Even living on the streets her mom had made sure that Bailey took care of the meager belongings she had. At eighteen, when Bailey had moved away, she'd been even more adamant about it.

Every chore since she could remember, had been followed by that statement.

Bailey flopped backward onto the bed, her arms flung out at her side. "Ouch." Sitting up, she pulled out the hair clip she'd carelessly put in that morning. She tossed it on the bedside stand and finger-combed her straight brown hair. She tugged on it and then winced. Something finally felt real.

So many thoughts floated through her mind. It occurred to her that she should call one of her friends, but she wasn't sure what she would say. She couldn't really tell them what was going on because she'd never really talked about her family. Her mom had sworn her to secrecy about their past—where they'd lived, what kind of work her mom had done, who her dad was— which she didn't know anyway, where she went to school, where her relatives lived, sometimes even what her real name was.

Everything was always a damn secret. Even your death.

Tired and wrung out, Bailey closed her eyes. Tears trickled out, ran down her face and into her hair. There'd be no more jokes between them—not that there had been many in a long time. Or ever really for that matter.

She yawned. She knew she should get up and shed her coat, her navy blue pantsuit, her shoes... maybe change into pajamas but she didn't have to the will that would propel her upwards. If she was lucky she'd wake up and realize this had all been a bad dream. She could call her mom and make up with her. Forgive her for being so damn obstinate. Something they definitely had in common.

Her mom's face with one of her rare smiles flashed through her mind. Just as quickly the vision of her lying in the casket followed. When did it end?

Bailey's body might have been resting but her brain wouldn't shut down. Thoughts continued to swirl for a long time, until all that was left was exhaustion, pulling her down a deep dark hole.

7

The phone rang.

Guy shifted in his seat.

It rang again.

He slouched against the car door.

It rang again.

He stared off into space, thinking he should be used to this by now but he always seemed to forget her little quirk of deciding when she'd answer.

Then came the fourth ring. "Yes."

Her tone made him feel like he'd been the one keeping her waiting. "It's her, Gramama. No mistake."

Silence. Hesitation. He knew she was torn. On one hand, wanting it to be true; on the other, she knew what this information would do to her family. "What's she like? What does she know about the kidnapping? How greedy is she?" His grandmother's voice sounded abrupt, angry.

He blew out an exasperated breath. "I haven't really had a chance to go through much with her. I don't think she knows anything."

"What does she look like? And don't tell me 'just like Mama did.' I know she's the spitting image of my mother. Those pictures you showed me told me that. What color is her hair? Is she a real brunette or is it dyed? Her eyes? Are they green-blue? How much money does she want?"

There was a loud whack sound. He jerked the phone away from his ear. She'd hit her cane against the cherry wood, Montclair credenza desk in her office; a bad habit he'd like her to stop. She needed the cane on occasion but used it more as a weapon or instrument to keep people in line than as the crutch it was supposed to be and sometimes he wished it would break in two and end her whacking habit.

The desk had once been covered in a very thick layer of varnish. His grandpa had been smart enough to get it sanded and recoated twice a year, as she was just a tad hard on it—same as she was with those in her life. His grandfather had been one of the few who'd known how to handle her and make her smile while he was doing it.

I miss you. You died too young, Gramps. Sighing, he brought himself back to the conversation as his grandmother continued, "I needed you to find her for peace of mind but you can't bring her home until you know more about her. I will not have Gina and Daniel put on an emotional roller coaster by this woman. I will not have her come into our lives and start making demands. They don't know any of this. It will be enough of a shock, if things work out. Find out what you can about her. I want to know if she's going to cost me or if she is the beautiful granddaughter she would have been, if raised by her real mother. Understand?"

Guy didn't bother telling her he'd already uncovered her background. She was twenty-nine, single, had been offered a lucrative job in Toronto with her own TV show on interior decorating. She'd moved a lot in the first eighteen years of her life then a few times after that but she'd now been in the same apartment for the last five years, the longest she'd been anywhere. He hadn't talked with any of her clients or friends because he hadn't felt the need. His task was simple: find her, tell her and get home.

The only piece to the puzzle he hadn't figured out was how she came to be with Donna Saunders. That piece was still a bit murky. Over the last six months, he'd focused his time on finding her. He still wasn't clear how his grandmother had discovered the west coast newspaper article on how Bailey had helped a needy family remodel their home. His grandmother had given him only enough facts to pique his curiosity.

"Understand?"

"Yes Gramere. I understand."

"Don't call me that. It makes me sound old. And I'm not."

He silently grinned from ear to ear and he sensed she was smiling too—not that she'd let anyone see her. That wouldn't compliment the image of the head of the Caspian Wine Company. She was a woman who, against all odds, had risen to lead an empire in a world dominated by ruthless men.

Guy admired the hell out of her.

After the distinct click from her phone, he hit the end button on his. Fighting the urge to get out of his car and stretch, he rolled his head around to loosen the tight muscles. The last time he'd slept in a car he was sure he'd been eighteen and drunk, one of the only times he'd indulged himself. If the hangover hadn't cured him, the disappointment in his grandmother's eyes had. That was the only time he'd been relieved his grandpa hadn't been alive. Guy didn't think he could have lived with his being disappointed as well.

He shifted a few more times to work out some kinks. A car wandered past and he turned his face away. Once the vehicle was gone, he looked out his window at the house two doors down the street. No movement yet. In fact, since she'd entered the day before, there hadn't been much of anything happening. He'd been tempted a time or two to check on her but his gut told him to wait. So wait he did. Fourteen hours later, he was struggling to remain patient. Get him on the computer for that long and he was fine; he could spend hours online and feel useful. When it came to long surveillance, however, he hated it and would dump it on his partner Graham whenever possible. It usually cost him tickets to a baseball game but he gladly paid it.

His stomach clenched, letting him know he was well beyond hungry. Sighing, he wished he'd thought to bring a thermos of coffee or snacks. Everything had happened so fast. He wasn't quite ready to admit that meeting Bailey had thrown him off track as well. The picture he'd seen of her in the paper—the only one he'd been able to find of her—had fully displayed her attractiveness but he hadn't been prepared for the vulnerability he'd witnessed.

He'd had his strategy planned—he'd sit down with her, gently tell her that she'd been stolen, listen to her grief, connect her with her grandmother and he'd be done. It had struck him like a sonic boom at the gravesite that he was going to rip someone's life apart, a life she'd had nothing to do with creating.

He couldn't do it at the gravesite. So now he had to figure out how to share with her what he knew. He couldn't even come up with how he'd like someone to tell him. It was one thing to say yes to his grandmother and be reassured his role would be fairly easy and another thing to actually follow through. He missed working with his computer; there were no worries about how a computer would feel. When he'd taken on this assignment, he hadn't really thought about how Bailey would take the news. At the time, it had seemed as simple as telling her and handing her over. But now that he'd seen her, he felt like he was going over Niagara Falls in a barrel, despite the fact that he hadn't even done anything yet.

Exhaustion and grit burned his eyes. He pressed his fingers gently against the lids. In the mirror, he noted red road maps that should have meant a night of debauchery—not that he'd ever really had one of those. Knowing he wasn't going to stay awake without help, he started the car and drove to the nearest service station about eight blocks away. Coffee and food were not something he was willing to give up. What made him think he needed to sleep there overnight, he didn't know, but that uneasy feeling hadn't left and in the past, it had always served him well.

Fifteen minutes later he was back in the same spot, though he realized it would have been smarter to park in a different place. Her car was still there, the telltale dew on the windshield an obvious sign it hadn't moved. And there didn't seem to be any new cars or movement in the predawn day. He'd driven down the back alley and around the block twice, just to make sure. Even though he had no reason to be that cautious, when he was on a stakeout, he liked to know who else was around and what was going on in the area.

Knowing he was going to confront her with what he knew, he nervously drank his second cup of coffee and ate his third donut. As he waited for a decent hour to knock on the door, it occurred to him there was never going to be an appropriate time to tell her what he'd come there to say.

8

Bailey rolled over for at least the tenth time, her body protesting, before flipping onto her back to stare at the ceiling. Frustrated that her eyes were wide open when she felt anything but rested, she finally gave up and swung her legs over the side of the bed. Her feet hit her shoes which she'd kicked off at some point in the night. She stood shakily and while gaining her equilibrium, she took a deep, almost defeated breath as she shrugged out of her horribly wrinkled coat and tossed it onto the chair in the corner. Her outfit wasn't in much better condition. Rubbing her hands down over the soft material of her two-piece pantsuit, she worked at smoothing out the haphazard pleats that now adorned it.

She flipped her suitcase onto the bed and opened it, removing her shampoo, toothbrush and toothpaste from the toiletry bag before heading into the bathroom across the hall. She tossed everything onto the counter and grabbed a towel from the closet just outside the door.

Ignoring her mom's voice ringing in her head, *don't waste water, Bails. It's a luxury. Don't get used to it,* she spent showered until there wasn't a drop of hot water left, despite the memories of all the times when they hadn't had enough clean water to do more than sponge bath once or twice a week.

Sorry, Mom, but I needed this. I think it's okay I used all the hot water this time.

In the bedroom, she yanked on jeans and a t-shirt and brushed her hair. Her stomach growled. *When did I eat last?* The thought was fleeting as the weight of the daunting task she had yet to do crowded her mind. *Get it done and get home* played out in the back of her mind.

After securing her hair in a ponytail, she headed to the kitchen and put two slices of bread in the toaster. She leaned against the sink and glanced outside. Clear blue skies and beautiful rays of sun greeted her. A few cars drove by. Her mom had loved that it was a quiet street off the beaten path.

The toast popped up, the metallic jangle of the toaster echoing in the empty room, barren of anything that suggested love. She had no deep connecting memories in this house. She'd barely set foot in it in the five years her mom had lived here.

One thing was clear, however; her mom was no longer here. She really was gone.

A vacuum opened up in Bailey, a hole that she didn't know how to plug. She clutched her chest as sobs rocked her body. They'd never be together again.

Dammit. Dammit. Dammit. What was going on with you, Mom?

Abandoning any pretense she would be able to stop, Bailey dropped into her mom's chair at the table, laid her head down and gave in to the gnawing pain. Tears ran down her face as she shook with the finality of it.

She'd never touch her mother again.

She'd never hear her mother's voice again.

She'd never be able to say "I'm sorry" again.

Anguish wrapped her in its claws, holding her tight, closing off her throat. It clawed at her stomach until it was on the verge of heaving. She ached in every corner of her being. Her emotional storm went on for so long, she wasn't sure it was ever going to end.

Finally, the tears subsided. Bailey remained still for a long time, feeling as damp, limp and fully wrung out as a discarded cleaning rag.

Her belly protested loudly at her failure to feed it, startling her. Pushing to her feet, she walked to the fridge, pulled out the jam and spread it on her cold toast. She nibbled on it as she made her way back and dropped down into her mom's chair. Resting her elbows on the table, she picked up her mom's cup and cradled it in her hands. *Life is a guilt trip waiting to happen.*

Her lips curled slightly. Her mom had loved that saying but Bailey had no idea why, since it was rather depressing. Turning the mug, she noted the smudge of lipstick on the back side. Ruby Red, the only color her mom would wear. She rubbed her thumb just under the spot. She could almost feel her mom's lips.

Shaking her head once more, she realized she could sit there and morosely think about all that should have been; all she regretted and all she should have done—or she could get busy with the things she had to do. Her mom's possessions needed to be sorted into those things she would take and those she'd give away. The contents of the house had been left to her while the house itself had already been taken care of. The lawyer wouldn't budge on what that had meant.

They'd never had many possessions. Her mom had never wanted to own something she couldn't leave behind or dispose of quickly, just in case she decided to move. And she had been a master mover. Twenty-seven times in the first eighteen years of her life.

She had three weeks to get everything packed and out, but she wasn't sure her new job offer would wait that long.

The envelopes her mother had left popped into her mind. She'd stashed them in the glove box in her rental. She needed to give some time to them to figure out their hidden message. *But not now* kept running through her mind. She'd have to look at it when she had more time.

She made her way to the cupboard, took out a set of keys and headed out the door. She crossed dry, brittle grass as she strode to a small shed in the back corner. She put the key in the lock and then just held it. This was yet another place she'd never been in, another secret of her mother's.

She turned the key, yanked off the lock and thrust open both doors but her forward movement was abruptly halted. A mountain of boxes filled the shed to capacity. She pried open the nearest box to reveal a stack of newspapers. Pulling frantically, she hauled newspaper after newspaper out, tossing them carelessly onto another box. Then she opened another one, only to find the same thing. Once she stopped acting like a mad woman, ripping and tearing, she realized the containers were dated.

Jan. 2004 to Dec. 2006 – Vancouver and Victoria Newspapers.

Jan. 2004 to Dec. 2006 – Edmonton Newspapers.

Jan. 2004 to Dec. 2006 – Ottawa Newspapers.

She dropped her face into her hands. What was it with her mom and the news? She'd acquired them from across the country; that was how she'd seen Bailey's picture that had led to an argument. Her mom never wanted publicity for either of them. The idea of it almost gave her a heart attack.

Or maybe it had. The article about her helping a needy family had sent her mom over the top. All Bailey had done was remodel a low-income family's home. She hadn't done it for the publicity but her boss at the time had been more than thrilled to use it to drum up business.

Reality crashed in.

"Dammit."

"Dammit."

"Dammit."

There was no way she was going to get through this, if she couldn't stop those thoughts from creeping in. Later, she could kick the crap out of herself. She shut off her mind and got to work. She finished emptying the box she'd started on and proceeded to empty five more, unsure how many she'd eventually need.

Bailey locked the door, grabbed hold of the empties and headed back to the house. She tossed them into the living room and then went back to the kitchen where she gathered garbage bags and the trash can from under the sink.

She put all of it in the hallway before returning to the kitchen wall where a list of phone numbers was posted. Scanning it, her eyes settled on *Lawn mowing — Jason.* Perhaps he would empty the shed for a few dollars. After talking with his mother for a few minutes, they arranged for a few local kids to do the job.

The phone clicked as she set it down. The simple act drained her. She rested her head on her arm for a minute and took a few deep breaths. After a brief moment, she stepped back and looked at the list of phone numbers. Not sure why, she tore it off the wall and tucked it into her pocket. Sighing, she forced herself to get to work.

Time to get things cleaned out.

9

The single closet door opened easily. Bailey grabbed blankets, sheets and towels and pushed them into a bag. Cleaners, shoe polish, bug spray and stuff she didn't want to know about, went into a box. She left the vacuum-cleaner sitting there as she knew she'd need it later on.

Next she went into the bathroom. Squatting, she opened the double doors under the sink to reveal shelves packed so tightly not even a bobby pin would have fit. Grabbing some of the soft items, she pulled on them. Several things tumbled out. Nylons, cotton balls, pads of a brand that were no longer made, hair spray, room freshener. Behind that were old cleaners, more hair spray, hair products and other junk she didn't feel like digging through. All went in the garbage. In the back were full bottles of shampoo, lotion, hair goop and other stuff she really didn't want to go through, so she dumped all of it in the bag. Her knees cracked as she stood. The toothpaste, toothbrush, soap and containers were all used and not worth keeping. Everything on top of the counter also got thrown out, as well as everything that lined the tub. Eventually, she stepped into the hallway, her immediate gaze locked on the doorway just down the hall.

"I can't go in there yet," she whispered but that didn't stop her from moving toward it, her mom's room. The door was wide open, giving her a clear view of the immaculately made bed. Bailey had been sure that she could have bounced a coin off the pristine white comforter. Her mom had reminded her that there was no one to look after her and she better remember that. It was one of the few reasons Bailey was quite glad the woman hadn't come to visit her. She'd have had to clean for two weeks just to make her place look livable. It would have taken a couple of weeks and an army of housecleaners, to reach her mother's standards.

There was no physical barrier stopping her but she couldn't step across the threshold.

Spinning on her heel, she went instead to the living room, which was dominated by a 70's-style flower-patterned love seat, a rocker-recliner and a china cabinet filled with second-hand items. She hesitated in front of the cabinet, looking through the glass at all the different salt and peppers, the cream and sugar sets. All were quite nice but had no meaning for Bailey, collected after she'd left home. A white sugar bowl covered with tiny red roses caught her attention. She opened the door and carefully picked it up. It really was beautiful and appeared to be in perfect condition. Something rattled as she brought it closer. Reaching inside, she pulled out two items.

Gasping, she stared at what she held. Both were valueless and useless. She'd been seven when she'd given her mom a tiny, plastic rose and a clamshell she'd found on the beach. It had been a Mother's Day gift. It had made her mom so happy that tears had run down her face.

Mom kept these.

The realization truly stunned her. Carefully, she tucked those two items in her pocket before putting everything back. The collection of twenty or so dishes, had been the one thing her mom had spent hours polishing and sometimes just wistfully staring at as though she'd lost her best friend. It had never made sense to Bailey and now she debated whether to keep the items. Deep down she knew she would, as it kept them connected.

Pack it up. I'll have to get some newspaper, I guess.

Bailey snorted. That was something her mom had collected a lot of and had a need to devour, every single one she'd come across. She watched every news program from sun up to sun down. Bailey had tried to teach her mom how to use a computer but that had become yet another argument; Her claim was was that it was the government's way of keeping tabs on people. She'd begged Bailey not to ever be on it, to never to allow herself a presence on it—yet another puzzle she had given up trying to figure out.

Pressure built behind her eyes and her nose got that familiar burning sensation. She closed her eyes and took a few slow deep breaths. Her fingers rubbed across her forehead until the overwhelming feeling went away.

She headed for the kitchen and the corner drawer behind the door where important papers had always been kept. She rifled through the junk but couldn't find the stack of envelopes which should have been there. Opening the deep second drawer, she grabbed the yellow pages sitting on top. It jerked loose in her hand and fell to the floor with a loud bang. Bailey jumped back, glad her pink toes were intact. A few inches more and she'd have been dancing around on one foot.

She set the book on the table and started to clean up the mess—papers, pencils (enough for a first grade classroom), paperclips and lots of menus—mostly pizza places. She threw out most of it before shoving the drawer back in.

That's weird. She was sure that her mom had kept all her important papers in those drawers—but there was nothing there.

Pushing the thought to the back of her mind, she began to unload the cupboards, fitting everything on the six-foot counter. Bailey frowned as she studied the meager belongings. Chipped plates, plastic glasses, pitted bowls, stained containers—all went in the garbage.

The horrible feeling overcame her that she was throwing out almost everything. Her mom would have been devastated.

Maybe the second-hand store would pick it up?

Bailey's eyelids dropped down, her head flopped backwards on her neck and a heavy sigh escaped her lips. There was no way she would get through this if she stopped to analyze everything she did. She needed fresh air. In her bedroom, she flipped open her suitcase and grabbed her running shoes and a gray and blue spring jacket. Once she had them on, she didn't hesitate to race out the side door.

Heading north, she noticed the neighbor's rose bushes were covered in pink and peach buds with a heady scent. She breathed in deeply. Pansies, irises and petunias filled the front of the house, although it was early in the season and frost was sure to kill off most of the plants. The next house had flowering trees and many varieties of flowers as well.

Bailey had been fifteen the last time she'd begged to plant flowers in their yard only to be met with a myriad of excuses: they moved too much or they were too much work or she was allergic despite the fact that Bailey had seen her many times stopping to admire and smell others' gardens. The final excuse had been that all those colorful blooms did was attract attention.

No flowers.

No pets.

No friends.

No pictures.

No home.

No life.

Bailey's pace increased as the memories flooded back.

She never really understood what her mom had wanted from her. She never seemed to please her or give her what she needed. There were times she wasn't even sure her mom liked her.

As a sob tore past her lips, Bailey clapped her hand over her mouth. She was running now and barely paying attention to the few vehicles traveling past. At the end of the block, she turned left for half a block and then raced into the park beyond. Majestic poplars loomed over her as she raced down the empty walking path, thankful it was midday, middle of the week. There was no one around.

Her hand clutched her chest as she sprinted on. How long she continued she didn't know but at one point she became aware of pounding feet behind her. Stopping, she whirled around. The person following behind grasped her shoulders as they collided. He spun, landing on the ground with her on top. Bailey shrieked, her elbow digging deeply into a well-muscled belly as she scrambled upward.

"Ooommph." He jerked upright and then flopped backward, his arms cradling his gut.

She backed up as the person curled on his side, gasping for breath.

"Sorry," he finally managed to croak out.

"You're the guy from yesterday." Bailey moved back a few more steps, balancing on the balls of her feet.

"Yes. Give me a minute."

"You're stalking me."

"No." He shook his head emphatically as he sat up and draped his arms over his bent knees. "Uuugggghhhh."

"Why are you following me? Was there a problem with my mother's funeral?"

The guy frowned.

"You're from the funeral home, right?"

Wary ocean blue eyes stared back at her. Secrets were hidden in those depths. That, she would bet on. She was sick and tired of the games people played. Her mother had been a master player. Bailey moved a few more steps back and spun on her heel.

"Wait. Please don't go." He sucked in some air and rolled onto his back. "I promise I won't hurt you... at least not physically."

She paused, the toe of her right foot barely touching the ground. She glanced around before slowly turning. There still wasn't anyone around. It was a rather secluded area of the park which wound down toward the river that ran through the city. Her mom had described it as overly popular, a crowded area in which she'd been unable to go for a walk without running into someone. She'd been thinking of moving again.

Great. So where in the hell are all those people today?

Bailey swung her gaze back to the guy, realizing that she probably shouldn't be taking her eyes off him. If he made a move, she wanted at least a little bit of warning.

"Look. I need to talk to you."

"So you tackled me?" Bailey glared at his bent head. "Are you freakin' nuts?"

"Right now, I'm thinking so." He continued to breathe as though he'd had the wind knocked out of him. He lifted his head. "Look, you were upset and I guess I'm a sucker for a damsel in distress."

Cute. He's cute. Why are all the nut jobs cute?

He placed his hand behind him and made a move to rise.

"Don't get up." Bailey's hand flew up like a cop directing traffic. "If you want to talk stay there or I'm out of here."

"My butt's getting wet." He raked his hand through his thick hair but it fell back into place as though he hadn't touched it. "I don't know how to say this."

"Good. Then I'm gone." Bailey spun around and started walking quickly.

"You're not you," he called out after her.

10

He quietly lifted the cane from its resting place across the desk. The walking stick was old but there was nothing spectacular about it, other than one side of it was well-worn and didn't match the maple brown of the other side. The ferrule was a bit larger than most but not so large as to draw attention to it. That's why it had taken him so long to figure out where she'd kept the key hidden all these years. Setting down his flashlight so it faced him, he pinched the rubber ferrule and gently pulled. His large garnet ring flashed in the light, prompting a smile at the gift his first lover had unknowingly given him. He never knew how she'd managed to explain to her husband that his piece of jewelry was missing.

The stopper slid off the wood with a gentle pop. The devil's smile crossed his face as two keys dropped into his hand. He walked around the desk.

There was a creaking sound from just outside the door. He froze with one foot still firmly on the ground while the other half was raised to step forward. He knew it couldn't be the old bat—that's how he'd always seen his sister, even though she was only a few years older than him—she slept like a drunken sailor. The snort that automatically rumbled up from the back of his throat was barely muffled by his hand. A long moment crept by before he dared to move. Since he heard no more noises, he imagined the odd sound as that of an old house settling its bones. The mansion had been built in the 1800's and although it was as solid as any mountain, it still had its moments. When he'd been younger, he remembered believing that the ghosts of the house were awakening to take vengeance for all the wrongs that had been done.

He knew of many of them. Actually, he was responsible for a lot of them and had been a party to many more. There was no question in his mind that he was going to hell. That just meant his time on earth was going to be anything but that. He sat in her chair, sinking into the luxury of the soft leather. His mind wandered to what he would have done had he been given this role that was rightfully his. It didn't matter in theory he was in charge of everything. He'd never been given the title or acknowledged as 'the one'.

She'd always gotten the credit.

He ignored the voice from the past reminding him he had no real right to even be there, let alone be given an opportunity to run the family business.

He pushed away his thoughts before sliding the key into the lower left-hand drawer, pulling it open. Knowing what he would find, he quickly flipped through the files—*My Will* which he'd read many times; account ledger—something he'd reviewed and was thankful she had no idea it wasn't totally accurate; *Baby Cassidy*— He jerked back as though a snake had struck at him. He pressed his hand to his chest, trying to still the frantic racing of his heart as he stared at the open drawer.

Baby Cassidy. That hadn't been there before. Slowly leaning forward, he pinched the document between his thumb and two fingers and lifted it out with a straight arm. He carefully laid it on the desk before reaching into his inside breast pocket. Pulling out a handkerchief, he wiped his forehead, damp with perspiration despite the cool temperature of the air-conditioned room.

Grabbing the top side of the file, he gently flipped it open. Guy's name jumped out at him.

That bastard is out to ruin me!

He knew his sister had been hiding something from him. His hands clenched, his body rigid, his breathing shallow and rapid as he stared at the words he had feared for almost thirty years.

Somehow, the old bat had found her.

He'd hoped he was home free, since nothing had surfaced in such a long time. After all, no one knew his secret and it was much older than that. Sitting back, he took a few deep breaths before reaching into his jacket for his cell phone. It had been a call he'd repeatedly rehearsed the first couple of years. When nothing had happened, he'd accepted that he'd gotten away with what he'd done.

Unfortunately, he'd become complacent.

Dialing the number he knew would go to the grave emblazoned on his brain, he waited for the clicks that revealed it was being rerouted. He never understood all the technology but he'd been smarter than the old hag and he'd at least kept up with how to use it. The call would be hard to trace, even for the FBI with all their fancy equipment.

He'd been leaving the man regular messages for thirty years now, but he never thought there'd be a need to change their relationship. John had come into his life at a time in which he'd needed him. John had taken care of his biggest problem—or so he'd thought.

After he thought Mary and baby Cassidy had perished, he and John had struck a new bargain. He still wasn't sure how they'd reached that point but John had brought him the best, cleanest and most creative whores there were. Discreetly, of course. It had solved his second biggest problem.

His hand shook as he dialed. They hadn't talked face to face in twenty-nine years. Their weekly arrangement was done through untraceable voicemail messages, a system that deleted all information once listened to. No one would have understood the inscrutable messages anyway; their enigmatic code had served him well for a very long time. This call would change all that. This time he called the number intended for emergencies only, a number he'd never had to call before.

"John, it's me."

There was silence and then, "I take it there's a problem."

"Yes. Babies are cute, aren't they? After twenty-nine years, having one come back from the grave is rather disconcerting." He filled John in with all he knew. His anger was palpable over the phone.

"She took Mary's life. She won't be an issue for long. But this will cost you."

"Really? You're the one who screwed up."

"If you want me to take care of it, it will not be cheap. Take it or leave it."

With reluctance he'd agreed to John's exorbitant fee, knowing after this they'd be severing ties. That meant he'd have to find someone else to feed his particular, or was that peculiar, habits.

The line went dead.

His hand shook so badly, he had a hard time hitting the end button. He mopped his forehead, again cursing his mother and father. It was their fault he was in this bind. If his father had kept his pants zipped, he wouldn't have become the Caspian's dirty little secret—and he wouldn't have been treated like the bastard he was. Anger infused his body, clenching his fists and tightening his muscles.

It took several moments of refocusing, using mind control techniques he'd practiced over the years. He'd hated the moments when the anger controlled him; it had nearly destroyed him a time or two. He had big plans, necessitating bringing himself down from the brink. Taking a final calming, deep breath, he let the tension ease from his body.

He put the folders back in the drawer, closed and locked it. The keys slid easily back into their hiding spot in the tip of the cane.

A steady humming sound startled him and he flinched, shooting the rubber ferrule out of his hand. Listening closely, he realized the staff was vacuuming the front foyer. To be the least intrusive, they often worked in unoccupied areas after everyone had gone to bed. Swearing silently, he peered around the dark room. He shined the flashlight slowly across the floor but it was too difficult to see much of anything with the thin beam of light. He might have been tempted to open the draperies but knew that would undoubtedly draw attention in the middle of the night, particularly by the night guard. Not knowing what else to do, he made his way to the door and flipped on the overhead light. If someone discovered him, he'd just have to make up some story—and then make sure the servants were so frightened of him, they wouldn't dream of mentioning it to Dorothea.

Wherever the damned piece of rubber, it wasn't in the open. Cursing, he went to the far corner and slowly walked forward, rhythmically searching from side to side.

A snapping sound from outside the window caught his attention. He stepped to the window and peered through the small gap between the curtains. The light from several lampposts lit the groomed, expansive gardens. Nothing appeared to be out of the ordinary. He waited a long moment but nothing stirred He came to the conclusion that it been one of their twenty or so outdoor cats.

He was ready to get down on his hands and knees—something he'd never done in his life—to look for the rubber tip. Being 6'2" and twenty pounds overweight meant kneeling and rising wasn't something he was looking forward to but it had to be under something. As he stepped back from the window, something bumped his shoulder. He jerked around, almost falling over. The large potted tree he'd backed into annoyed him to no end. He was about to turn away when he glanced down and there, sitting in the pot, was the rubber tip.

"I guess I shouldn't hate you after all, you grotesque, disfigured excuse for a tree. You just saved my ass."

He quickly replaced the tip and then gently set the cane across the desk. Making sure everything was in place, he walked to the door, shut off the light and stepped out of the room.

He never looked back. He'd never needed to. Being sneaky was something he prided himself on; after all, that was how he'd found out the truth about himself. And now he knew he had to get rid of Baby Cassidy. Again.

11

Bailey stopped so suddenly she wobbled. Who was this nut case? What could he mean that she wasn't who she thought she was? That didn't even make sense. Was that how he picked up women?

Slowly, she turned around. He hadn't moved from his position on the ground but he was leaning forward as though he was planning on chasing her if she took off again. She stiffened. Her gaze raked over him; dark hair, blue eyes, pursed lips and a crooked nose—maybe broken once or twice. She couldn't really tell anything from that. Broad shoulders were covered with a black leather jacket and jeans encased long and what she guessed were athletic legs. Normal. Her eyes wandered back to his face to discover hard lines there. His jaw clenched. The cords in his neck were taut as a newly cocked bow. He believed what he was telling her.

He has the wrong person. "Look. I don't know who you think I am. But I do."

He raised his eyebrows.

"Know, that is, who I am. I don't know who you're looking for but it's not me." As she talked she stepped back slowly. She wanted to tear her gaze away but there was something compelling in the depths of his eyes; something that begged for her trust yet simultaneously urged her to run like hell.

"So good luck." She balanced on the balls of her feet.

He jerked upward. "Wait!"

Every nerve in her body fired at his barked command but something about the desperation in his voice kept her in place. He hung his head and swore but didn't make any move forward.

"I have something I want to show you." His fingers slid into the pocket of his beige golf shirt. Bailey kept her eyes glued to his hand and took another step back.

"Stop." He pulled out his hands and held them in the air as if under arrest. The gentle wind tugged at a paper he held in his hand. "You need to see this."

"Uh…" She shifted her gaze around from the right to the left.

"Look. It's not a trick. I'd set it down but the wind will take it away. I promise I won't touch you."

She looked at his hands. Soft calluses ringed the palms, the hallmark of a weekend handyman. Long masculine fingers gently held the item out to her.

"Who are you?"

He swore again.

She found herself almost smiling. "All I know so far is you have the kind of language that should have gotten your mouth washed out."

"Actually it did." His lip curled upward. "My name is Guy Turner. Please look at this." His eyes were asking her to believe him and to trust him.

She could hear her mom screaming at her, ordering her never to trust anyone. Shaking that off, she looked around. Three young guys raced onto a grassy field, chucking a football back and forth.

Relieved, she said, "Don't lower your arms or I'll scream like there's no tomorrow."

He grimaced but didn't move. At about four feet from him she sprinted forward, grabbed what looked like a picture and sprinted about twenty feet away. When she looked over her shoulder he was standing in the same ridiculous pose. She couldn't believe he'd listened.

She watched him for a second before looking at the paper, an old black and white picture printed on new photo paper, thanks to modern technology. It was grainy and the woman's face was faded. Her head was tilted back slightly as she looked off to her right. The dimple high on her right cheek deemphasized the regal look she was attempting. Bailey smiled in sympathy, tempted to reach up and touch her own cheek where she'd been afflicted with the same characteristic. The woman's hair was neatly pulled into a high bun without so much as a single fly-away-strand. A gem-studded angled hair clip adorned the front.

"She looks affluent. After all not everyone could afford pictures back then." She studied Guy, who still had his arms extended as though waiting for a basketball pass. She shook her head. "Drop your hands but no sudden moves." She almost laughed when she realized how stupid that sounded. *Wild west here we come.* "Okay. So what's the deal?"

He stared at her for a moment before looking off to his right. Bailey followed his gaze. The three guys were hooting and hollering as two of them tackled the third. Testosterone at its finest.

"Look. I can assure you I do not have her crown jewels." Bailey looked at the single row of gems. "Such as they are. I doubt they're even real."

His head swung back, his gaze intent. "Oh they're real, all right. Those jewels are worth about five million dollars. Give or take a million."

Her eyes widened to their fullest extent as she took another look at the classic cut of the diamonds.

"Since I don't have any jewel thieves in my family, you've got the wrong person." Bailey moved toward him to return the picture but stopped when he swore again. She arched her brow.

"Got it." He shoved his hand through his hair. "I'm not here because those jewels are missing. I'm here because they're rightfully yours."

How the hell did I win this lottery? I didn't even buy a ticket. "Okay. Game's over. It's been fun but this is too weird—even for me." She thought she'd heard and seen it all, but this even surpassed her unorthodox childhood.

"She's your grandmother. Actually, your great-grandmother." He shifted his weight. "I'm a– I've been hired to find you."

She felt a little light-headed. She reached out her arm for something to steady her. Guy's smooth leather jacket wasn't what she'd had in mind but she was unsteady enough to clutch it.

She had family. Could this really be her relative? She'd begged her mom on many occasions to tell her about them but she had staunchly refused, never sharing anything—no names, no stories and no pictures. She glanced again at the one in her hand. "Is this where I got my dimple?" For the first time in her life, the slight imperfection didn't seem so bad.

Guy snorted with laughter. "Could be." He shifted his stance. "Look. Is there somewhere we could go to talk about this?"

She glanced up barely taking note of him. "Can I keep this?"

He nodded.

She turned away and started walking. *Could this really be my great-grandma? Wow.* Her fingers traced the face. How old was she in the picture? How many kids did she have? What kind of man did she marry? What kind of person had she been? Had she ever smiled? Not that they did that often in pictures back then. Whoever decided it was bad to look lifelike in a picture? They were always so stern.

She studied the woman's dimple in the picture and then touched her own. She'd always thought it was unique. Had anyone teased her about it way back when? Many times she'd wished it hadn't existed; it had been too damn cute. Now it connected her with someone. It meant she had family. Who was she? What was her name? Were there more pictures of her? Where was the rest of her family?

Bailey jerked to a stop. She hadn't asked any of that. What an idiot. She glanced behind her. There was no one there because she was already at the next door neighbor's blue house. She wasn't sure whether to return to the guy who had given her this gift or wait until he found her again; but something told her he'd be back.

12

Bailey hugged her arms around her waist. The warm, fuzzy feeling was so new to her that she almost staggered under the weight of the sensation. This had been her Christmas wish for twenty-nine years. Perhaps she was overreacting and there was a lot more to this story, but she wasn't ready to hear it yet. She wanted time to absorb the good feelings coursing through her. Hanging onto this new sensation, she walked the last twenty steps home.

Head bowed, she unlocked the side door and stepped through to find it all come crashing back—her mom was gone, there was packing to do, stuff to get rid of and she had a job she wanted but felt guilty about. Her mother's voice flooded her mind, telling her to stop wanting more—she didn't need relatives, she had her. Why couldn't that be enough?

"Don't do this Bailey, don't do that; someone will notice you. Don't make noise; someone will hear you. Grab your

Miss Piggy, we've got to leave, Bailey. Stop crying; there are more important things than that ratty old stuffed animal. I'll get you a new one as soon as we find a place. I'll get you new shoes too. Things will change soon, Bailey. Smile for Mom."

She wanted to scream, 'They never changed, Momma'.

Her mind was consumed with the torn, isolated feeling of being alone—only she didn't need to be lonely anymore. How could her mother have excluded the rest of their family? What could they have possibly done to be cut out of her life?

She tucked the picture of her great-grandmother in her bag before heading across the hall into the bathroom. She drenched her face with cold water; it felt jarring but also somewhat reviving. As she grabbed the peach towel hanging off to her right, the nicely folded lace facecloth fluttered to the counter. She looked at it and then at the spot where it had been hanging. Another matching towel and facecloth hung on a second peg. The water ran down her face and dripped off her chin as she stared at that spot. Everything had always been just so. Nothing had ever been out of place. Certain things were put in certain spots. She was sick and tired of it.

She mopped her face, tossed the towel on the counter and stepped out of the bathroom. She stopped in the hallway, dimly lit from the late afternoon sun filtering in through the front window. It looked dark and dingy, so much a reminder of what her life had been.

"It's dark, Momma."

"Shh. Be quiet, Bailey. We're playing hide and seek. Remember you have to be very quiet."

"No, Momma. I don't wanna play that again. No, Momma. I can't breathe. I can't breathe. Momma!"

Bailey shivered at one of many memories she'd rather forget. One of the many, when they'd snuck out in the middle of the night. Snuck away like really bad people, always in the dark. That thought stopped her for a moment. She ran into the living room, grabbed the middle of the drapes and yanked them wide open. A peeping tom would never have gotten a glimpse into this house. She yanked open the front door and quickly shoved the window up on the storm door, leaving only the screen. In the kitchen and both bedrooms she pulled up the blinds and parted the curtains to slide open the windows. Shooting out of her mom's bedroom she nearly tripped over the bag of toiletries from the bathroom. Grabbing it, she dropped it at the end of the hallway.

She stepped into the living room and pulled open drawers, flipping through the meager things she found there. She pulled open the bottom cupboards on the china cabinet to find newspapers, stacks of them, always the precious news. This stuff had to go. She grabbed several garbage bags from the kitchen and proceeded to fill them. She grabbed and stuffed, grabbed and stuffed.

Every now and then a date would catch her eye and she'd remember what was happening in her life on that day.

July 15th, 1990. The year they had moved twice—once from a cute little house in a dinky little town in northern B.C. to a dinky little town in Southern Saskatchewan to...

Bailey couldn't remember where to after that. She shoved some more paper in the bag.

December 23, 1993, the year they skipped Christmas because they were on the move to Lethbridge, Alberta.

September 5, 1995, yanked out of school the second month to move again and leave behind the one friend she'd finally made—someone who'd moved almost as much as she had.

Bailey started shredding the pages as she went. Pieces were flying as she worked like a mad woman, ripping and filling.

July 14th, 2000. Bailey stopped. She had no idea where she had been on that date—living in Vancouver, maybe? But what had she been doing? She frowned. It wouldn't come to her. After a few moments she realized how good it actually felt not to know where she was on a certain date. Due to their fluctuating lifestyle, Bailey had kept a diary. Every day had meticulously been marked down, the events recorded, because there had always been something to note. She'd always felt the need to record how she felt about each ugly move. Never allowed to whisper a word of it, she'd written it down; writing had been her solace, her friend.

She paused for a moment wondering where she'd put her diaries. Some had gotten lost over the years. She hadn't always had time or the opportunity to grab them when they'd moved. Her mom had shown up at school on three occasions to whisk her away to the next place.

February 14, 1989. Valentine's Day.

Hmmm. We lived in a trailer park. What was the name of the town?

Shrugging, she tossed it away.

June 23, 1985.

At some point she realized there were only certain newspaper dates in there. She wondered how many years' worth were in the shed.

May 1, June 1, July 1, 5, 6, 7, 10... August 1, 3, 6, 7, 8... September 1, 5, 6, 10... October 1 and many more in1983.

How come so many that year... the same year I was born?

Tired of the game and the vagabond feelings it brought back, Bailey shoved all the papers into the garbage bags. Most of them, she absently noted, were the national conglomerate papers.

She stood and looked around. Her mom had been so excited when she moved into that house. It was one of the few times that Bailey had seen her almost giddy. They'd had fun filling the house with finds from garage sales, second-hand stores and even newspaper ads. Then one day a truckload of boxes had arrived filled with things her mom had said she'd put in storage a long time ago. Bailey had become so angry that she'd left. There had been too many times there hadn't been enough money for food and yet she'd found enough to pay for storing belongings that Bailey had known nothing about.

Looking at the mess she'd made, the bits of newsprint scattered about and the large garbage bags flopped over like sumo wrestlers, she bet it had been the damn newspapers. Stepping over the bags, she grabbed some empty ones and headed for her mom's bedroom.

Bailey grabbed the bedding off the bed and stuffed it all in one bag, pillows and all. Looking from the bedside stand to the dresser she realized she couldn't do either one yet. Too private.

The closet was next. She pulled open the tinny metal doors and grabbed clothes. Meant for a figure of 5'3" and slightly rounded, Bailey knew they wouldn't come close to fitting her 5'8" athletic build. Besides, they were old-fashioned, dowdy cotton dresses like Lucy used to wear on *I Love Lucy*, her mom's favorite show.

She yanked clothes off the hangers when most of the hangers were swinging empty, she reached up for the last few dresses. Other than the first one being ugly, she paused as she caught sight of a red silk dress her mom had worn only once. Beside it were two other very stylish, expensive-looking outfits. Where had they come from? She'd never seen her wear them. *What were you hiding, Mom?*

She shoved them, along with several pairs of shoes into another bag. From the top shelf she pulled blankets, a few sweaters and a down filled winter coat.

None of it had any meaning for her. She kept up a steady pace, not looking at anything she threw out. Nor did she allow herself time to think. Next she walked into the tiny bathroom off the bedroom. The medicine cabinet was full of prescription and OTC meds. Paranoia had been her mom's best friend. Maybe she should have pushed for her to get some professional mental health intervention.

There was too much stuff.

Bailey kept tossing everything into garbage bags that were now overflowing. Everything was getting thrown out.

The phone rang. Jumping over bags and scattered garbage, she raced into the living room to grab the phone on the fourth ring.

"Hello."

"Hello."

Bailey's hand tightened on the receiver. "Who is this?"

"It's me, Guy. We talked—"

"What do you want?"

"I hope you've had enough time to go over what I told you this morning. We need to meet and discuss the rest."

Bailey clutched her hand to her churning stomach. She couldn't meet with this man; there was no way. How hard would it be for a stranger to find an old picture that looked like you? "Look, there's no money and nothing of value. And how'd you get this number?"

"Give me the chance to show you what I have. Meet me at six at Stella's Bar and Grill in Shaughnessy. Do you know where it is?"

"Yes. But what's the hurry?"

A surprised guffaw was her answer.

The silence stretched. Bailey bit her lip, working her teeth from the right side to left and back again.

"All right. I'll meet you there at six-thirty."

After a brief pause, he said, "I'm really sorry about this, Cassidy."

The distinct *click* let her know there was no use in responding.

Cassidy? Who the hell is Cassidy? Just like I thought, he has the wrong person.

13

"Hello?" He reached for the remote and flipped off the sound to the six o'clock news.

"She met with a guy in the park today. He gave her a picture or something, from the way she looked at it." Payme drew in a deep breath before spitting on the ground.

"You have to get that photo from her." Fear clawed its way up his throat and clung there, fluttering like a cave full of bats. Someone else seeing it after all this time made him sick to his stomach. He'd gotten greedy, too high on himself. Thought he was really above it all. After all, he was the son-in-law of the filthy rich, the Filmores. It occurred to him that embarrassing his rich in-laws might have been a stronger motivator than he'd previously considered. Perhaps there had been a part of him that had wanted them to be humiliated. But now he knew he'd be the one to lose everything. They'd see to that. The only saving grace for hiring Payme had been that he could have him imprisoned and the guy knew that. And since he had a few enemies in prison, the odds of him surviving were highly unlikely.

"Do it now. I want it today."

This has to end. Twenty-nine years. I make the rules. No one is going to change that due to one miscalculation.

He'd relished being in charge. Now, however, someone had changed the rules. "Do not harm her." He had plans for her. There was so much she didn't know about her mother but she might know enough to help him make money in the future. "I don't think she knows anything about what her mother was doing, or to be able to recognize who's in the photo. Get it."

After hanging up the phone, he collapsed onto his leather sofa. He knew if anyone saw that picture he was finished. He'd no longer be the middle-class kid who'd made it into the filthy rich club. He'd be finished. Worse, he'd be a joke—all the way to the jail.

The thought of being sent to prison, where he had helped send many he was supposed to have defended, was not something he could stomach. He wouldn't last a day behind bars. Bile rose in his throat. He jerked forward and ran out of the room, barely making it to the bathroom sink across the hall.

He splashed cold water on his face and rinsed his mouth, ignoring the mess he'd made. It would be good if his wife Betty thought he was ill, then maybe she'd take care of him like she had in their early years together. Knowing that was highly unlikely, he braced his arms on the edge of the sink. It had never really occurred to him what people would think if they knew about him. He'd never planned on it coming to light. The worst part would be what his dear father-in-law would do; he still held all the purse strings.

There was no way he was going to lose it all. He lifted his head and stared at the wall three feet away. He'd worked too hard for the prestige he now enjoyed. The game had taken a twist he'd never believed would come, a twist that almost had him wishing he'd never helped Donna escape her husband. He should have cut his losses a long time ago. *But it provided me with so many people to screw over.*

The thrill the game had given him had been so exhilarating. He'd played Donna and her ex like pawns in a chess match. Shuddering, he realized he was being called into check. *This is my game. I'll be the one calling checkmate.*

He hated this feeling of fear, of no longer being in control. It was so foreign to him now. But there was one thing he knew would make him feel better—something that had been caught in a photograph, the one thing that would bring him down.

Clearing his throat, he lowered his voice making it sound like a heavy smoker's as he picked up the phone and dialed a number he knew well. *I will not be beaten at the game I invented!*

❧☙

Bailey snatched the ringing phone off the hook just before heading out the door.

"All right dammit. I said I'd meet you."

A raspy, breathless sound greeted her.

"Listen dammit—"

"No, you listen."

Chills shook her body.

"Your mother got cocky and demanded too much. You're going to give me what I want—her little cash daddy."

"I don't know what you're talking about. You have the wrong number."

"No, Bails. You are the one!" His raspy, echoing laugh slithered over her like slime.

Bailey slammed the phone down and rested her head on her arm, waiting for the shakes to subside. The only person who ever called her Bails was her mom.

Pushing away from the wall, she squared her shoulders and headed out the door. She was going to find out what the hell was going on.

14

Bailey whipped into the parking lot of Stella's Bar and Grill and pulled into the first stall she could find.

With a quick glance at her watch she noted she was right on time, not her usual ten minutes to half an hour early, but then she usually was going to a meeting that she knew what it was about. This one she wasn't sure but she had a sense it was going to give her some answers but a whole lot more questions.

She jumped out of the car. Her next rental would have GPS. With the new job she was starting, she'd be able to afford it. As she approached the front of the restaurant, she hesitated. To her right was the entrance to the palm and vine sheltered patio, the foliage blocking her view of all but a few patrons. To her left was a formal front entrance large enough for Paul Bunyan to enter. The massive, intricately-carved mahogany double doors made a bold statement against the gray stone wall.

The patio appeared less intimidating so she strolled through the black wrought iron gates and up two steps.

She slowly wound her way around the high tables. There weren't a lot of people—four people occupied a table off to her right, two sat in the middle of the restaurant and two were at the bar. None, though, were her guy.

She shivered, pulling her spring jacket tighter around her as a cool breeze seemed to have followed her. Ahead was an additional area enclosed with a waist-high lattice fence and pergola with vines interwoven throughout.

She climbed another two steps. The back of her neck started to tingle. She peeked over her shoulder to discover, lounging back in a cushioned chair, her guy. He tipped his beer toward her. Her gaze met his. She'd never worked in a grocery store but she felt scanned, weighed and priced. He came to his feet as she approached the table. She raised her hand in protest before he decided to do any more gentlemanly deeds, like pull out her chair.

"I'm not Cassidy. I'm really sorry you've gone to so much trouble only to find the wrong person." She dropped her arm to her side. "I just want you to know I'm done playing your game. Too many nuts are coming out of the woodwork."

"What do you mean?"

"I mean you," she stared pointedly at him, "and the nut case who called me. I don't know how many others and frankly, I don't care. I'm done. I'm going home. So leave me alone."

His eyes never wavered from her face but he stayed silent.

Her whole life she'd been told what to do—do this, don't do that. He wasn't telling her anything; he was leaving the decision up to her. But his eyes were also letting her know he wouldn't leave her alone. Not until they'd talked.

She had no idea how long they stood staring at each other while her instincts warred inside her, but at some point she gave in and sat down. He ordered her a drink.

"Do you always get what you want?"

He shrugged and then downed half his beer. "I need you to just listen. I want to show you some things." He put up his hand like a traffic cop.

Bailey snapped her mouth closed.

"Would you like to order now?" The young waitress set down Bailey's drink.

"No thanks." Bailey tried to smile but wasn't sure it came across as anything more than a grimace.

"Not now." Guy, however, was able to give the server his full wattage grin.

"All right. Just wave when you're ready." The waitress moved off to another table.

"Have you eaten?"

"No." Bailey gulped down a healthy swig of beer.

"Dinner's on me."

"Well in that case..." She waved at the waitress who was only a few tables away. When the server came, Bailey said, "I'll have anything that has lobster in it." The truth was, she didn't particularly care for lobster and she knew she was being a bitch but she wasn't inclined to stop herself. Everyone seemed to want something from her. The waitress rattled off three dishes and Bailey chose the most expensive-sounding one. Guy ordered a steak sandwich.

She settled back and sipped her beer. For some reason she couldn't take her eyes off the cleft in his chin. It was kind of cute and somehow added to his machismo persona.

"Here's what I know—"

"What?"

"That picture I gave you is your real great grandma on your mom's side. Her name was Catherine Caspian. Here's a better picture of her."

Bailey stared, her eyes opening wide. Except for the wavy hair, it was her face. The flat forehead, high defined cheekbones, rounded chin, bumpy nose. Bailey traced her finger over the features. This was her. Why hadn't she seen this before? What the hell had her mother been hiding from her—and why? Who all these people were that were showing up in her life wanting to know things that just couldn't be true?

Her hands shook. "What color were her eyes?" It was impossible to know from the black and white picture.

"Glacial green. The same as the glacially fed lakes in the mountains. They have a distinct green-blue hue to them."

Bailey's head snapped up.

"Like yours."

He held her gaze. She stared at him for a long moment.

"I don't understand."

"I know."

She looked at the picture again. The eyes were full of mischief as if she'd been a young girl bent on defying the rules. *I would have liked to have met you.* "Okay. I want some answers. No more tap dancing. I believe I'm related to her. So where are the rest of my relatives? Why now? They wanted nothing to do with my mother for thirty years so why now?"

"How much do you know about your mother's family? Or your father's?"

"None of your business. I want to know what you know. You're the one who came looking for me. Now talk."

He guzzled the rest of his beer and then set down the bottle with a plunk. He signaled the waitress for two more.

Bailey downed her drink. She toyed with the label, carefully peeling it off the bottle. The new drinks were set in front of them. They reached for them at the same time.

"Your great-grandmother is dead."

She cocked her head and lifted her eyes skyward, blowing out an exasperated breath.

"All right. Rather obvious." He rested his elbows on the table. "Your grandmother is still alive though."

"Really?" She leaned forward with interest, her stomach pressing into the table.

"Yeah." He studied the beer label. Sighing, he stared past her for a moment as if searching for answers before meeting her gaze. "There's just your mom on her side but you have two uncles and two aunts on your dad's side. Then there are the in-law aunts and uncles."

Stunned, she flopped back into her chair. *I have family. Lots of them.* "Cousins? Are there cousins?"

"Ten first and some second and third."

Oh my God. This was too much like the dreams of her childhood, in which her family would find her and make up with her mom. They'd bring tons of gifts and everyone would hug and kiss and they'd stop moving. She'd get to have sleepovers at her grandma's, at her aunts and uncles. She'd have enough cousins to make two softball teams— real friends to play with. She'd have birthday parties— every year, and not only when her mom happened to remember—which had never been on the same date. If she hadn't had a birth certificate she'd have been thoroughly confused; it was yet another rule—never get hung up on dates.

She shook her head. "Where do they live? What are they like? Do they know about me?"

"Hi. I've got the lobster." The waitress set the plate in front of Bailey. Startled, she jerked back but the waitress was already smiling at Guy. "The steak sandwich must be yours." She set the plate in front of him, carefully arranging it.

He smiled at her, flashing almost perfect white teeth. Bailey rolled her eyes. When the girl finally moved off, she asked, "Like robbing the cradle, do you?"

He gave her an indulgent shrug before digging into his food.

She felt a twinge of guilt at her catty remark but shrugged it off. The luxurious aroma of her food soon drew her attention. The lobster was piled carefully into a coiffed mound with steamed carrots and whipped potatoes. Had it been any other time, she would have dug in and enjoyed an expensive meal that she never could have bought for herself. Only she wasn't hungry anymore; no way was she going to get anything into her knotted stomach.

She looked up and met a pair of sky blue eyes. They studied her. She tried not to squirm or to open her mouth and be flippant and for some reason, she didn't.

"Something wrong with the food?" He raised one eyebrow.

"No." Sighing, she pushed away her plate. "Enough BS, I want some answers now. How did you find me? How long have you been looking? Who hired you?" She looked out over the rapidly filling patio. "Where is my family?" She turned back and stared at the man who had the answers to her future.

And her past.

He carefully cut another piece of his steak sandwich and put it in his mouth. if there had been any other way for her to get information, she might have stormed out. But since he had answers, she picked up her beer and leaned back in her seat to wait him out. She got the feeling he was struggling with how to tell her something, she just wanted him to spit it out. She'd learned to play poker at eight but never how to really play 'the game'.

"How much do you know about your family?"

"Wrong question. You already asked that. I want to know what you know." She tipped her bottle to him. "So spill."

He held her gaze for the longest time. The overhead lantern provided a gentle, romantic glow that was faint enough that it hid his face in the shadows.

"Just bear with me. I need to know what you know, so I know where to start."

"Been practicing that line for a while?" She glanced down, her gaze caught by the knight's helmet and initial insignia on his navy blue silk shirt: K A. She wondered what the letters stood for.

"All right. Fair enough. Okay. This is going to be hard for you to hear. So…" He shoved his hand through his neatly combed hair.

"Your real name is Cassidy Lefevre. You're twenty-nine. You were born on February 12th, 1983, in Quebec."

The sounds of the other customers, the traffic passing by and the noise seemed amplified all at once. She jumped up. "Frick, I knew you had the wrong person." She mumbled some things as she sat back down just as fast. All her life had been about running; she was trying hard to change that. He had answers. She hoped.

"I know it's hard to believe but I do have the right person. You saw the picture for yourself. It's real. Your resemblance to the woman is real."

Heat crawled up her face. She was glad the place was gloomy and he wouldn't be able to see her fire engine red face. "It can't be possible." Shaking to the core of her being, she placed her hands over her mouth. "My mother…" She glanced away, not sure what she had been about to say. A few people were openly staring at them and obviously eavesdropping.

"I have a lot I need to tell you. Do you mind if we go some place quieter so I can share what I know?"

"Umm… Maybe…"

"I passed a lounge a couple of blocks from here that looked pretty empty. Want to take a chance?" After she nodded, he tossed down some bills.

He motioned for her to go first. His warm hand against her lower back was the impetus she needed to shake out of her confusion. Her strides grew faster but he matched her pace, his fingers a steady presence. It was very tempting to lean back into that warm, comforting hold, something she'd never had in her life.

"Follow me. Okay?"

"Sure," she said as she slid behind the steering wheel. She watched as he climbed into a new SUV rental.

He's from out of town too. That's how she had always defined herself; no matter where she and her mom had lived, she was never from there—she was never from anywhere. *Is that why no one could find us, Mom?*

A horn honked. She looked up to discover he was waiting for her, so she started her car and pulled out behind him. She did as he asked, all the way to the lounge. She watched him park, get out of the vehicle and walk toward where she was sitting in her car, at the entrance to the parking lot. The Guess Who's song, *Laughing*, came on the radio. It had been her mom's favorite song.

What the hell?

15

Bailey's heart felt like it was being held by a vise as it slowly squeezing the life out of it. On some level she knew he was going to tell her something that would rock her world in a way it had never been rocked before. It could have been the threat to her peace of mind or an inability to trust, but whatever it was, it was enough to compel her to hit reverse, stomp on the gas pedal and zip into the street. She'd always been in this alone. She'd find her own answers.

His eyes opened wide in shock before settling into a disappointed, knowing look. It was one she'd perfected when she'd learned, yet again, they were moving. The expression on Guy's face reminded her of too much. She burned out of there, going well over the speed limit. She whipped in and out of lanes, turned down side roads, drove around, at times a bit lost, until finally she pulled up in the back alley of her mother's place. It was just something she did on instinct; she didn't question why she'd chosen to hide her car, but her sixth sense had saved her on many occasions. Living on the streets has taught her a lot. It had only been because she'd listened to her gut that she'd saved herself.

Blowing out her breath, she let go of old memories, grabbed her bag and keys, quietly creeping across the lawn to the side door to let herself in. She unlocked and opened the door, gently closing it behind her just as she was grabbed from behind, one hand clamped over her mouth while an arm wrapped around her middle like a band of steel. She was almost overwhelmed by the stench of stale tobacco and rancid alcohol.

Not again.

"Where's the picture, bitch?"

Long ingrained instincts kicked in; she lifted her right leg forward and then drove her sneakered foot back into his knee while smashing her elbow into his ribs. He yelped and swore but didn't break his hold on her. They stumbled backward, crashing into the table. She took advantage of his loosened grip, ripping it from around her. She made it to the door and got it open a few inches before his body slammed into her, pinning her there. His hands encased her wrists. "Try that again and I'll kill you. I don't care what I've been told. Got that?"

She held herself perfectly rigid but didn't respond.

"Good. Now where is that picture?"

"At the photo store?"

"What?" He grabbed her arms with one hand and yanked a handful of hair, pulling her head back at an awkward angle. "Listen, lady, I'm not here to play games. The picture I'm looking for is old. Where is it?"

Bailey snorted in disbelief. "Pictures. You want pictures. Well, let me tell you something you big over-stuffed—"

He smacked her wrists against the door.

"Uuuuuuhhh… listen—"

He jammed his knee into the back of hers. Pain ripped through her. She sagged forward, trying to will away the agony. "There have been no photos in my life. My mom didn't believe in them. I... DON'T... HAVE... ANY."

Grabbing her left arm, he twisted it behind her back, turning her around. He marched her into the living room. In the dim light, she could barely see her way and stumbled over the mess on the floor.

"What's in those bags?"

"Newspapers."

"Where's your mom's room?"

"Kiss mine."

He jerked back and up.

She tried not to respond but she was sure her shoulders were but one thread away from being dislocated. Tentatively walking down the hallway, she tried to avoid the overturned bags of stuff that now littered the floor. When she tripped and almost took him down with her, he jerked her arm halfway up her back. She stood on tiptoe to ease the pain and the blackness that was threatening to engulf her.

"Do that again and I'll rip both arms out of their sockets."

Biting her lip so she wouldn't scream, she said, "Then turn on some damn lights. I can't see a thing and since you saw the need to redecorate, it's your fault."

"All right, turn on the bathroom light. Don't do anything funny."

She almost snorted at that because when he let go of her wrist, her injured arm flopped to her side. It took a moment for her to lift it and the muscles protested loudly when she raised her hand so she could flip the switch. He shoved her into the bedroom and although flopping on the bed was preferable to having his hands on her, she wasn't staying there in case he got ideas. A quick move and she was back on her feet but he immediately backhanded her. She fell backward onto the bed, the metallic taste of blood filling her mouth. She swiped at her lip as she propped herself onto her elbows. With a torrent of banging, crashing and smashing, he yanked open dresser drawers and dumped them. The veracity with which he moved made her cringe.

The man's right hand shook like he was thirty hours into detox. He sure didn't smell like that though. A week of soaking in a bathtub might have been able to loosen the caked dirt and grime, food, grease, sweat and other things, she didn't even want to guess at what they might be, coating his body and his clothes, but she wasn't so sure. "Where'd your mom hide pictures?"

We don't have any pictures, not even of me growing up. So I don't know what...

Bailey's eyes opened wide. The only photo she'd seen in thirty years was the one in her bag—which was somewhere on the kitchen floor. What would he want those pictures for? They were old. There was nothing... The jewels. Had someone stolen it? Was someone going to steal it?

She sat upright. He was bent over the debris now littering the floor, his butt pointing in her direction. He wasn't paying any attention to her. She lifted her feet and rammed them as hard as she could into his butt, toppling him. Then she ran, heading out through the kitchen, yanking open the door and hitting the lock on her way out. It wouldn't stop him but it might slow him down. Scooping her bag off the floor, she raced out, slamming the door behind her and sprinting across the back lawn. She spit out a mouthful of stale blood as she went. Once in her car, she hit the gas and drove away, the back tires spewing dirt and grass. Winding her way through the streets, she looked for a main road that would take her west.

Flipping open the glove box, she pulled out the two envelopes. Someone had answers. She feared it might just be her.

16

Guy sprinted across the street when he saw Bailey race through the living room, past the open front door. "Wait!"

She didn't slow down nor act like she'd heard him.

Leaping up the stairs he crashed into a small, wiry man who was barreling out. The two men stumbled then caught their balance. The smaller man moved quicker, lashing out with his left foot, catching Guy just below the knee, sending him stumbling backward into the railing. The man was already running down the block.

Fear hit Guy like a punch to the gut. *Where was Bailey? Who was that guy?*

He raced through the house following the direction he'd seen Bailey run. Zipping out the side, he glanced at the street and then sprinted toward the back fence as he looked up and down the back alley. There was no sign of her car. She was gone. Turning around, he made his way back inside. Picking his way over the littered floor, he looked for clues that might tell him what the hell had just happened.

Boxes were flipped over, bags ripped open, drawers piled on the floor, blood spots on the bed. Since there were only a few drops he assumed the person wasn't seriously hurt. The question was, was it Bailey's?

He pulled out his cell phone and made a quick call. "Graham. I need you to do some more digging into Bailey's background. Go back more than ten years. Retrace her steps. I need to fill in the blanks. I skimmed over some of the history surrounding her mom but I think there must be something I missed."

"Hello to you too. And I'm on it. What's going on?"

"Not sure. But someone broke into her mother's house and she's on the run. I need to know if this was a random burglary or connected somehow to her. I'm thinking the latter." He knew his business partner, Graham, wouldn't question his gut instinct. It had served them enough times when there was no evidence to go on. Like the time he'd caught the accountant with the impeccable record, who was walking out each day, with thousands of dollars in his lunch bag.

"On it."

Guy filled him in on what had occurred that evening. "I'm not sure where to look for her. I'm going to dig around here and see what I find. I'll get back to you."

Following her a few days before had at least given him something to work with. The only person she'd met with had been a lawyer. *Would she go to him if she was in trouble?* Clicking off his phone, he headed back down the hall. The unmade bed and clothes scattered in the spare bedroom caught his attention.

Lifting the suitcase onto the bed, Guy carefully looked through the items. *Nice underwear.* Shoving the black lace bra and panties aside, he continued to sift through her clothes. He unzipped the inside pocket. Airline ticket—old one. Double Bubble supply—which made him smile. A business card—Creative Interiors. Another one—Mr. Robert Lund, Attorney at Law—jackpot. Lund, the lawyer's office Bailey had gone to a few days before.

Holding both cards in one hand, Guy walked back to the living room. He made his way to the window by stepping past the overturned items. He didn't see anything outside that was cause for concern. It looked like the uninvited guest was long gone. He went with his gut instinct and pulled out his cell, hitting the redial button. "Graham, I need you to do a bit of digging on a Mr. Robert Lund. Lawyer. Also see if you can find a home address. I'll do some searching on my end but it might not be that easy to find. At least not if he's smart." He rattled off the information on the business card. "Also do a bit of digging, what do we know about him and his business?"

"Right. Give me ten."

His hand clenched into a fist as a tightly coiled unsettled feeling sat heavy in his gut. He absently rubbed his stomach. *How come I didn't see this one coming? Nice and easy my ass, Gramma.*

He placed his hands over his face and rubbed hard as though it could clear his mind. This was not going to be simple. Blowing out an exasperated breath, he spun around abruptly with the intention of leaving but tripped. With nothing to grab onto, he found himself sprawled across the floor. Since that was a dangerous place to be, he quickly twisted around and jumped to his feet. He booted one of the offending large bags aside.

"Ouch." He reached down and pulled back the plastic. Newspaper spilled out. Grabbing the top one, he glanced at the topics and then the date.

1985. Who the hell keeps the news that long?

1995. 1999. Who gets that many?

There were only some from each year but they were papers from across the country, certainly not something one could pick up casually at the local store. He flipped through the stacks of them, getting caught up in the stories.

Da-da-dum. Da-da-dum. Da-da-dum. Charge.

He jerked violently, ripping a paper in half. Sighing in disbelief when he realized it was his phone, he pulled it out. Why he'd let Graham's sister program that ring, he'd never know. It caught him off guard every time.

"Yeah?"

"I got his address, I'll text you."

After reading Lund's address he straightened. "What else?"

"You do realize it's after midnight?

"Yes and I also know you'll be up till the wee hours, getting all you can about the players we know exist so far. So give."

Graham's fingers clicked over the keys. "Man, you annoy the hell out of me. Mr. Charles Emerson Lund. Upstanding citizen. Lawyer since 1970. Clean as a whistle."

"So far."

"Yeah. So far. He's too clean. I get the feeling there are some deep dark secrets hidden in this guy's history. I have a few feelers out with my buddies on the police force. There's some speculation that he may be flying on the light side."

A gay lawyer?

"We'll see what comes back. He's married to Betty Filmore; the Filmores are a hair's width from billionaire status. That has to be the crown for a guy who came from a family that marginally made the millionaire mark. The Filmores have their hands in many pies. Besides buying up declining companies, turning them around and reselling them, they own sports teams, have their hand in the shipping business and are partners in a number of multinational conglomerates. Meeting and marrying Betty Filmore, did wonders for Lund's career. He's had some high profile cases. Don't know why he didn't join a major law firm and make partner. If he's got closeted sexual preferences it's not something he's really going to want the in-laws to know about. My thought is that if he's got that slant, then someone at some time has probably might have used it against him. It's too classic. Who wouldn't take advantage of it?"

After securing the house, Guy walked across the street to his SUV. "Do you ever miss it?" They'd met when the two of them were fresh out of university and both had decided to join the police force. Two years was all Guy had lasted. Fourteen months for Graham.

"Police work?" There was a pause. "No. I miss the guys though. If that druggie hadn't shot me, I'd still be there, but I'm better at behind the scenes snooping. How about you?"

"Nope. I was the worst rookie ever."

"That's only 'cause you didn't like all the rules."

Guy laughed along with Graham, recalling how he had trouble with shift work and couldn't handle the daily stress. Getting enough sleep had become an issue, and he'd started nodding off at any given time, which hadn't gone over well with the others.

"Thanks for the info. Keep me informed."

"Don't park your ass out there."

Guy took in a deep breath. He didn't plan on getting shot and although he never would have guessed it from the start, he was now questioning what really lay in store for him. The situation was not at all what it seemed.

John was about to stand when someone exited the side door. His knees were starting to cramp, his tall, muscled frame not lending itself to be folded into a pretzel for long periods. Though he remained fit, age showed itself in the graying of his hair, the etched lines in his face and the aches and pains his body invented. He stayed crouched until he was alone. The woman had almost run him down in the alley when she'd driven out of there like a maniac. A quick dive over the fence had kept her from seeing him, barely saving his hide. He hadn't been expecting her to run out. He could have killed her then but it would have been messy and he didn't want any witnesses. He would decide when and where. It would be done right. No more mistakes. This time he'd make sure she was gone.

What a freaking zoo. No one had said anything about having to deal with two men fighting over the broad. John had been scouting the house when one guy had barreled out the front door and the other had tried to stop him. The shoving match hadn't been much. The little guy had won hands down yet still got the hell out of there in a hurry.

He had been ordered to get rid of the girl. His intel inferred she was pretty much a loner with no real friends, but that seemed to have changed. He'd have to be more cautious, but he was confident he would succeed. He wasn't in any hurry to follow her. The tracking device he'd attached to her car would disclose her location at all times. Besides, he was curious about the identity of her 'friends' and whether they'd be a problem.

He'd get to her soon enough. She was the last person who had the answers some were undoubtedly seeking;

only she didn't know that and she may never know. He smiled, loving the quirkiness of it; she'd die and never know why. The thought of sharing her history with her was tempting, just to see the anguish, the tears, the fear. He let that image wash through him and shuddered as goosebumps covered his body. Killing wasn't his first love and not one he'd done often but when someone crossed him, they paid. And she had done him wrong by taking away his only family: the sister he'd tried to protect from his alcoholic father and overzealous, hypocritical, pious mother.

He had to do this quickly, get his money and get out of the country before the police finally tracked him down. They had a warrant out for his arrest. His latest roofing scam had given him hundreds of thousands of dollars and a line on the need-to-question list of the local RCMP. He chuckled wryly as he considered all he was involved in that the police had no clue about. He'd been caught once but never convicted. He wouldn't go there again. Once he was done with the girl, he would leave the country for good. He'd find fresh victims to bilk.

He waited another ten minutes before he stood. Hugging the darkness of the fence, he walked to the side of the house. His hand shook slightly as he took out his pick. Thirty seconds and he was in. He was a bit disgusted that at one time he'd have been in within five seconds, but he shook that off. He moved stealthily through the house, not making even a whisper of a sound. Though he hadn't been gainfully employed in this way in a long time, he prided himself on the fact he still had what it took despite his age.

The place was a mess and had obviously been well searched. Regardless, he still did a careful check of all vents and ceiling tiles that might have been moved, but found nothing. He needed to make sure there was no link from the past to Donna or her child, certainly nothing the cops could use to extradite him. Even countries without extradition agreements could be bribed. As his flashlight flipped over newspapers covering over half the living room floor, he noted two crumpled cards. Bending, he picked them up—one was the girl's business card and the other was a lawyer's. Acid burned in his gut as he thought about the lawyer he'd disposed of. The man had slipped evidence to the prosecution; he'd wanted John to go down for defrauding an old woman of her life savings. He smiled as he remembered how easy it had been to eliminate him.

John pulled out his cell phone and called an old acquaintance, though he knew he'd be charged heavily for the information. Five minutes later he had the home address he needed. He left the house, moving stealthily along the alley for two more blocks to where he'd parked his black car. The fine tremor in his hand was almost unnoticeable but was enough that the key didn't slide in smoothly the way it should have.

A drink would have been a nice but he'd never allowed himself to indulge—at least not while he was in the middle of something big. And this was big. He was facing the end to a thirty-five-year career, which, he conceded, had really ended when his sister Mary had been killed. Thinking of her still saddened him, but it also made him mad. He still blamed that infant for his sister's death and for preventing him from collecting thousands of dollars from the people who were to be her new parents. Mary had looked after that baby for months and finding out that toddler had survived into adulthood was too much. Truth be told, he would have killed the girl for nothing but he was a businessman. He planned to get paid and get paid well. That kid had robbed him of a lucrative career—snatching infants from wealthy parents who had an enemy they often didn't even realize. He'd been hired by family members, relatives, business partners. It hadn't been easy to kidnap silver-spooned babies but that's why those hiring him had to have very deep pockets and ingenious resources. He'd had to abandon that prolific career when Mary died.

He wasn't going to spend his retirement behind bars, and he had no plans nor desire to go to jail; certainly not because of one dumb bitch who could ruin it all.

He'd do what needed to be done. Then he'd leave for a long vacation, perhaps somewhere south where extradition was unlikely.

The two men who'd stumbled out of the house came to mind. He might have to charge more money for complications. Killing three was really no different than killing one.

17

There was a loud pounding sound.

The phone rang.

The banging happened again.

The phone rang.

Fumbling in the dark, he reached out to slap at his touch-sensitive lamp. It flickered on. Squinting, he glanced at the clock—12:45.

The phone rang.

The incessant thumping continued.

He swung his legs out of bed, ignored the phone, pressed his hand to his face and stood.

"Mr. Lund, open this door. It's me, Bailey Saunders. I need to talk to you. I think she knew stuff. Stuff that could get one killed." Her voice drifted in through his open, second story window.

He jerked upright, frozen for a moment, before sinking weakly to the bed. Realizing his wife wasn't complaining about the noise, he rose once more and walked across the hall to her bedroom. He briefly knocked before opening her door. In that moment, it dawned on him that she was at her sister's for the weekend. Overcome with relief, he returned to his room and slumped against the door frame.

"Open up. Please! This is important."

He went into his bathroom, donned his robe and tied the sash around his ample middle. Annoyed at not having the opportunity to at least get dressed, he took his time going down the stairs. He schooled his face into one of concern before pulling open the door.

"Miss Saunders, call my office in the morning for an appointment, and I'll be happy to discuss whatever is causing you so much distress." His white knuckles clung to the back of the door while he smiled at her reassuringly.

She tilted her head and stared at him before addressing him. "You've known my mom a long time."

His mind quickly reviewed the odds of answering that backfiring on him. "Y-yes."

She moved a little closer. "A very long time."

The way she said it sent shivers up his spine, nearly causing his bowels to empty. He stepped back and started to close the door. "Really. Call me in the morning. We can go down memory—"

She shoved him inside and slammed the door behind her. Leaning against it, she glared at him. "Let me tell you something about myself, Mr. Lund. I'm a very good judge of character. I know that when a man is sugary sweet to you, he wants something, usually to steal you blind. I know that when a man puts his hand on the thigh of an eight-year-old…" She stared pointedly at him.

He gulped. *How could she know?* She had the picture. He should have told Payme to remove the problem, not follow it.

"He's not looking for a Boy Scout badge. No, he wants to be the one to initiate that young virgin into the real world. And I know when someone is being honest with me."

Walking past him, she turned into the first room on the left. Not sure what to do, he followed her. She was already helping herself to his Port. The way she was gulping his $49,000, 1943 bottle instantly enraged him. His blood pounded through his arteries and exploded into his face with a radiant heat. He reminded himself that she was just a street hustler but none were better than he was. *You may drink my special brew but you will never be my equal.*

Swallowing his anger, he used it to straighten his spine and with several deep breaths, he was able to bring his blood pressure back under control. He walked to where she was standing by his dark maple liquor cabinet and poured himself two fingers of his best Scotch. Her eyes never left his face as he swirled the drink before taking a lengthy sip. Instantly, he felt himself relax. He was back in control.

Maybe she'll learn a few refined skills.

He moved to his fireplace and with the flip of a switch, it burst into flames. Warmth permeated the room. He settled into his high-back leather chair, facing the fire.

"Come join me, my dear. I've learned that life is too short to get stressed over the little stuff." He smiled winningly at her.

She moved to a chair placed opposite to his. Slowly he sank back into the comfort of it. He looked at her. She was staring at the flames, lost in thought.

"So what can I do for you, dear? I know this is a tough time for you. If you want, I can have someone come and pack the house for you. During these situations I know how difficult it can be."

"No."

She didn't even turn her head to address him. With a hand trembling with anger at her social faux pas, he took another sip of his drink. The rich, smooth taste slid down his throat, first with a tingle and then exploding into an array of flavor. He closed his eyes as he let himself get lost in the sensation, allowing only a tiny shudder.

He set his glass on his custom designed maple table, the engraved vines climbing up the pedestal to end at an orchid shaped glass top. He rubbed his fingers back and forth over the smooth surface. Of all his collections, this was his prize. It was gaudy, it was impractical, and it spoke of having an excess of money. The Filmores, his in-laws, were filthy rich, partly because of him. The fact that they'd started with millions and had thrived without him was of no importance. He'd been the reason they were so successful at taking over small companies, revamping them and selling them for an ungodly amount of money.

As a token they'd given him a commission, not part of the business that he felt was his due. So he'd had to find his own wealth, his own sideline. He tapped the antique beside him. His thoughts returned to it. The rare piece would be worth millions one day and might be already. It was an insurance policy in the event he had to leave in a hurry and needed money quickly. He'd had four guys bidding for it for years; one day soon, one might be the winner.

"You said the cops would be interested in my past. I think you have…"

She waved her hand at him. "I just needed to get your attention so you'd let me in."

Allowing a tiny inner sigh of relief, he smoothed his hand over his silk robe, not unlike one worn by Hugh Heffner, a man he felt he emulated in many ways—quiet, suave, sophisticated. The part he hadn't quite mastered was Heffner's disregard for public opinion. Slowly Lund sat forward and faced his now quiet, uninvited guest. He wasn't quite ready to believe she knew nothing about the relationship he'd had with her mother. She turned to look at him. The side of her face was swollen and red. Blood was caked around the edge of her nostril.

He frowned, wondering if his guy had gotten into a tussle with her. "My dear, what happened? Let me get some ice for that."

She waved him off and stood. "I'm fine. Here's what I need to know." She smiled in a way that made his stomach flop as though plummeting down a twenty-story amusement park drop tower.

"You're the man who used to meet us each summer. I was about five the last time I saw you. It was at a cabin. I need to know what was going on with my mother at that time. What relationship did you have with her?"

He gazed into the flames. "We were old acquaintances. I've known her a long time. Yes, you and she used to come to a cabin I owned in northern Alberta." He looked at her and smiled. "Those were great times. You were such a daredevil child. Always on the go. You used to love lazy days on my fishing boat. You'd scream with joy."

Her eyes now held the gleam of restored memories but her shoulders slumped. "That's it? You were friends?"

He leaned forward. "Yes, dear. What were you looking for, something a little more clandestine?"

A sad smile curved her lips.

He wasn't sure what to make of it. "Your mom was a good person. We kept in touch for a while but she moved so much I only saw her a few times. Well, up until the last six months." He looked at her with understanding. "I'm sorry I couldn't be of more help."

Feeling better than he had in a long time, he looked compassionately at her. "Your mom really wasn't one to keep much, was she? Will the cleaning up take you very long?"

She shook her head as she stared at the liquid swishing

around the glass in her hand. "No. I'm pretty much done. I just need to have the second-hand store pick up most of the stuff. The rest is garbage."

"You know, there used to be pictures of when you used to join me at the cabin. I've since sold that place but would love those pictures."

Her blue eyes glaciated. "Pictures? You've got to be kidding. There are no photos, paintings, drawings. Nothing. Never has been. If there ever were any, she got rid of them a long time ago.." She jumped to her feet, eyes wide, chest heaving. Then she stopped and stared off into space. "That's not true. There was one. Mom kept it under wraps. She'd take it out every now and then and look at it. Then one day she just ripped it to shreds. She said something like, 'enough of the lies, you'll never hurt me again'." Bailey paused. "She set the pieces on a plate, took out her lighter, lit it and watched it burn. Tears were streaming down her face. It was odd. I never understood it. And she never talked about it."

Lund was leaning so far forward he was on the verge of falling out of his chair. "Di…" He cleared his throat. "D-did you ever, umm, see the picture?"

"I peeked over her shoulder once when she wasn't paying close attention."

"And?"

When her head whipped around and she frowned at him, he realized his mistake. "I'm sorry; I didn't mean to sound so harsh. I just got caught up in the story. Please continue."

She focused on him. He tried not to fidget as he practiced his polished look, one he hoped people interpreted as genuine sincerity and understanding when his thoughts were anything but.

"It was a grainy, old picture, so worn and crumpled that I could barely make out the images of the people in it. She noticed me right away and concealed it."

Lund blew out his held breath. "I'm sorry to hear that. No other pictures, eh? I guess with moving so much it was hard to keep anything."

"There are none of me." Sighing, she studied him before turning, only to stop and face him again. "Where's her money?"

"What?" He worked very hard to keep his eyebrows from shooting into his hairline. He jammed his fists into the pockets of his silk robe.

"Where's the money she was making from the store?"

He cocked his head slightly and assumed his genuine, caring expression. "My dear, I'm not sure what your mother told you but she really wasn't all that good with finances. It slipped through her fingers like oil. She loved extravagant purchases; why, her favorite chocolate cost a small fortune." *However, I do have a nice bit of cash put away thanks to her.* "You see, I gave her the loan for the store and I just couldn't curb her spending. I know she'd had it tough for years, so I felt I should indulge her some. Not a good way to run a business. But I'm glad I did it. Who knew she'd have such a short time on earth?" He rose, reaching out to pat her on the shoulder but she side-stepped him. Clenching his teeth, he forced himself to smile. "I'm really sorry, dear."

She hesitated at the door but didn't even have the decency to turn and face him before asking, "Uhm, do you have a bathroom I could use?"

Confident he'd successfully diverted her questions, he nodded toward the corridor as he answered her request.

"Just down the hall, second door on your left."

"Thanks." She started to turn but hesitated. "I don't know how to say this but, well… I have…"

"What, dear?"

"Well I have, you know, cramps. It's my time of the month. I don't think I have anything to use."

He had a hard time containing his disgust.

"I feel like I'm kind of leaking. It's so gross. But I just don't know what to do. Would your wife or kids have any tam—"

Horrified, he waved her away. There was nothing he hated more than hearing about women's issues. "Upstairs. My wife's bathroom is the third door on the right. She keeps supplies for when the girls come. Look in the big cupboard."

He shuddered as she walked up the ornately curved oak stairs before returning to his chair by the fire. He took the first calm breath he'd had in more than six months, ever since Donna had shown up at his office demanding answers. Picking up his glass and swishing the contents, he allowed himself to indulge in his luxuries.

The picture is gone.

Instantly he felt annoyed at being duped by Donna again after all these years. She'd brought him a photocopy. She'd sworn to destroy the picture so there was only that one copy. No one would have been able to decipher much in the grainy reprint, but it had been enough to get his back up. If she hadn't been dying…

He could barely contain his mirth as he thought about the measly ten thousand dollars he'd given her three months before to get her off his back. She'd been satisfied with that. He was just glad she'd been so gullible. It had been easy to lie to her all those years; even at the end when she'd threatened to expose him if he didn't pay her more money. It had really been delightful knowing she had been on death's door, so he'd been generous. He'd given her the cash and he'd agreed to organize and pay for her funeral and burial. The owner of the funeral home had a few dark secrets and had been more than willing to eliminate the bill in exchange for Lund's silence. He hoped the services had been a sufficient farewell, a final act of gratitude for the financial gain she'd unknowingly given him.

Knowing he was free of Donna and her threats, he allowed himself to relax. He should have known she'd been playing him all these years. Thinking back, he realized he liked the little bit of danger that she'd posed; she'd cost him precious little, only enough money to survive on while she was on the run, only sufficient warning that her husband was tracking her down, and enough misinformation about her husband watching the border to prevent her from leaving the country. He'd told enough lies to keep her right where he could keep an eye on her. And she always bought that he'd sent a cheque to the last address and if she hadn't cashed it, someone had. How did he know she wasn't scamming him? He'd played her so well. He'd been fairly confident she'd never have followed through with making the photo of him public. Besides, she'd given him more crooked federal politicians, doctors, lawyers, judges, and too many others for him to keep track. Some of them still had a guilty enough conscience that they continued to pay, even though they were no longer in the public eye.

He sipped at his scotch, his eyes glancing at the door through which Bailey had left. He wondered what the little snot would do if she knew he'd forged her birth certificate. The thought of letting that cat out of the bag was tempting. The fun he could have withholding her true identity. He didn't know her true identity but neither did she and never would. Donna had never said where she'd gotten the baby and frankly he hadn't cared. Smiling to himself, he slowly drank the rest of the exorbitantly priced Scotch.

Since no one had found out about him in over forty-five years since his first 'experience', he didn't know why he'd worried so much. It really was a blessing that Donna had that picture and not her husband. He would have blackmailed him for every dime he had and then made it public knowledge, gloating in his ability to bring him down.

Uh, but they lost.

He smiled the first genuine smile he'd had in a very long time.

He was safe.

18

Rising from his crouched position beside a house a few doors down from Bailey's, Payme watched the guy he'd run into finally drive away. He stood and moved along the shadows of the building. Since the girl had left and he'd already looked through her place to no avail, he may as well get his other career back on track. He walked around the house and onto the deck to peek through the patio windows. The house was spotless and on the table he could clearly see a note. There was something about the personal touch of a handwritten letter that tempted him to reconsider what he was going to do, but his need to find alternative methods to bring in money won. Mr. L would be cutting him loose soon, especially when he found out the girl had gotten away from him.

He snuck off the deck, found a rock in the flower garden and within seconds he'd broken the glass and had climbed in. The note let him know he had plenty of time. The residents were out of town for a few days and the message was for their neighbor. Crumpling it, he chucked it on the floor before heading upstairs to the bedrooms. They were always the best places to start. Snooping through the house, he'd forgotten how much pleasure he derived from peeking into the lives of others, of taking from the lives of others. He found jewels, valuable coin collections, cash, credit cards—all that he was looking for and more. Since time wasn't a factor, he took his time searching.

After he had his pockets and a nice leather duffle bag full, he headed out the back door. Slithering into the darkest shadows, he clambered over the fence and scampered through the yard to the next one. The back alley had proven once too often to be the place he'd be caught. Instead, he chose to scramble over fences and dash through yards, only having to hide when the early morning partiers drove by.

His phone rang.

He immediately dropped to the ground, scrambling to grab the damn cell before it went off again. Since he wasn't used to carrying one, he hadn't thought about the noise it would make. As he answered it, he fleetingly realized that Mr. Lund would want it back.

"Make sure she leaves the city. Once she's gone, call me."

Payme didn't bother to tell Lund he was across town and not on her tail as he was being paid to be.

"That's it. What about them pictures?" Payme scratched at his prickly stubble.

"It's done. You'll get a nice bonus for your work. Call me later." There was a distinct click as the call ended.

Payme stared at the phone. Something didn't feel right. He was to get her out of town and then what? Was he being hustled? He could be identified; it was uncertain whether the man he'd run into had seen his face, but the woman definitely had. It was time to eliminate her, regardless of Mr. L's orders.

He'd called the girl earlier to scare her. With her gone, he knew he could look freely.

He'd wanted to get that picture, but not to simply hand it over. It just might have been his retirement ticket, but now she'd run to Lund and now he had the damn picture.

Payme slugged back several gulps of the cheap whisky he'd swiped from the last house, shuddering as it hit his empty stomach. He pulled out his pack of cigarettes and holding it below his nose, he took a long whiff. It had been a while since he'd had a fresh pack of smokes. Thankfully, bumming and smoking butts would now be on hold for a while. He reached into his shirt pocket to get his matches but they weren't there, despite patting down all his pockets. Swearing, he looked around. He'd left his car a few blocks away. Since no alarms had sounded, he was emboldened to take the alley. He was returning to his vehicle, smoking a few cigarettes, sleeping a bit and then he'd call Mr. L to tell him the girl was gone. He'd then grab Bailey when she returned to the house. Once he had her, he and Lund would renegotiate their agreement—after he'd had a bit of fun with her, of course.

Lund seemed way too eager to keep tabs on her, so there had to be some serious money to be made.

19

Bailey drove back across the city, wondering if it was safe to return to the house. A couple blocks away from her mom's, she pulled over to draw in several calming breaths and steady her frayed nerves.

She tried to make sense of all that was going on. First, there had been the intruder and then Lund with all his lies, and she wasn't sure which one was creepier. Lund had been good, slimy but good. He'd almost had her believing he was genuinely sad her mother had passed away. But she knew better. Living on the street had taught her a few things. She hadn't acted the victim since she was about fourteen. She'd perfected the role of the naïve, innocent schoolgirl yearning for a little bit of cash to buy a new outfit. Would the nice gentleman please give her twenty dollars?

That had been her scam for a long time and it had worked, at least until her mom had found out and put a stop to it. It was just another of her mom's many major disappointments in her. Her stomach clenched at the memories of what she had done just to survive.

Leaning back, she slid her hand into her pants pocket and pulled out the USB keychain she'd lifted from the false bottom of Lund's desk drawer. She was confused by some of what her mom had doodled on the envelope to her but locating and getting that jump drive had been clear.

She started to chuckle. He'd been so easy. Talking about women's menstrual cycles always seemed to freak guys out; they didn't dare question a fifteen or twenty-minute absence. Of course, when she'd returned and given a detailed biological explanation to Mr. Lund on menstruation cycles, it had been his undoing. He had hustled her right out the door.

With her free hand, she reached to her hair to tug out the elastic from the ponytail. She liked the ease of it when it was pulled back but she also knew it made her seem more like a teenager than a woman pushing thirty. The effect on men was the same, they strutted their stuff like they were groomed peacocks.

Without warning, her door was yanked open. She jerked sideways, her arm rising to shield herself, her foot lifting to lash out. Before she could make contact, a body pinned her and a hand reached across her, ripping out the keys. The scream that formed in her throat was swallowed as she met a steely pair of blue eyes. He moved back but not before redirecting her foot to the floor mat. Her hand instinctively wrapped around the flash drive and slipped it into her pocket. Feeling faint with relief, she slumped back. Her door slammed and her would-be thief was soon around the car and opening the passenger side. Sliding into the seat, Guy closed the door, leaned back and glared at her.

Too tired to move, she rolled her head sideways to meet the glower, but neither spoke. She waited him out. After a moment, she raised her eyebrows.

He folded his arms across his chest and turned to look out the window. "Who was the guest at your house?"

"What?"

"Don't ask me, '*what?*' You heard me."

"What were you doing there?"

"Looking for you."

Since he wasn't looking at her, she took the time to study him. He definitely had the cute bad boy down pat; all dressed in black with his leather coat and his windblown hair falling over one eye. The scruffy beard was almost going too far.

"I don't know who he was. I thought maybe he was a friend of yours."

That brought his piercing gaze around to hers. His jaw clenched. "Aren't we funny? I never sent him but someone did. Any ideas?"

That had been her thought as well, but that didn't mean she had to play nice. The lack of knowledge scared her more than she cared to admit, and a shiver began as a fine vibration shimmying down her spine. "What makes you think he wasn't just a random burglar?"

"Too much that was ransacked was left behind for him to be a burglar. And before you say he could have been looking for drugs, I met your friend at the door. Since I got up close and personal with him, I would agree that he was the slime of the earth. But I don't think that getting high, was what motivated that break in."

"How'd you find me?"

"I've been following you ever since you left Lund's. Didn't know I was behind you, did you?"

Fear shook her body as though she were in arctic weather. Without questioning the cause, Guy smoothly slid the key into the ignition and started the car, turning the heat on full.

"Thanks." She rested her forehead on the side window, staring out at a black night the muted streetlights vainly tried to penetrate. A dark shape, crouched low, before shooting up and scrambled over a fence and then reappeared climbing over another one as he traveled through one back yard after another. Startled, she sat up but strained to keep her focus on where she'd last seen him.

"What's wrong?"

Not bothering to look at him turned out to be a mistake. His warm breath brushed the back of her ear as he looked over her shoulder. She suppressed the shiver of excitement that tickled her nerve endings as she pointed off to the right.

"Someone is running through yards. Watch, you'll see him in a moment between the gray house and the blue one. He'll scramble over the hedge between the yards."

A few seconds later a person did exactly that. A thin strip on the neck of the hood glowed in the dark.

"The guy who visited you tonight had on a hoodie, right?"

"Yes." Forgetting he was so close, she whipped around and they literally ended up nose to nose. She froze.

"I figured we'd end up like this."

Trying not to breathe in his tantalizing male scent, her eyes opened wide.

"Nose to nose that is. You like to get your way and I like to get mine."

Exhaling slowly, she eased back. "Are you suggesting that's the guy who was at my place?" She inclined her head in the direction of their night crawler.

Guy nodded.

"What the hell's going on? My life was normal." She ignored the twinge of guilt her remark elicited. "Until you barged in, telling me I'm someone else." Her hand flipped up to stop his quick retort. "What you've said doesn't make sense. Please don't. I don't want to hear it again."

"You do recognize that you're in trouble?"

"As dense as you may think I am, yes, even I get that. I just don't understand why. Except that, back to my theory which I never got to finish, until you barged into my life I never had people chasing me down. So when I put two and two together they add up to you." Glaring at him, she crossed her arms. "Or add two and two and you get… oh my god."

The man they'd been watching jumping fences emerged from the back alley onto the street. Once he was under the street lights, she immediately recognized her burglar by his long, greasy hair and grubby clothes. "That's the guy…"

A black car zoomed around the corner. Tires squealed and the vehicle swerved, the myriad sounds of a crash blending together. She gasped as the man they'd been watching landed on the hood of the car, only to be shot forward when the man slammed on his brakes. The vehicle spun around.

Bailey reached for the door handle, ready to help when Guy grabbed her arm and pulled her back.

"What the hell's your problem?"

He jammed the gear into drive, his leg straddling the console as he stomped on the gas pedal. As they screamed away from the curb, he cramped the wheel, so they did a U turn.

She slapped at him, fighting for control.

"He's got a gun."

She never saw it but the sound of gunfire was unmistakable. "Give me the wheel and move your damn foot. I know what I'm doing."

He promptly removed his hand. "Turn right." After they squealed around the corner, he removed his foot, letting her take control.

"Where did that driver come from? Did he kill the other guy?" She barely slowed as she whipped down a back alley, gunning it on the straightaway.

"I don't know. I don't see him anymore. Keep going."

She snapped, "The other man, what happened to him?"

"I think your guy—"

"I don't claim ownership."

"Your guy—"

She glanced at him.

He smiled wanly. "Might have gotten in the way of our shooter. Know who or why either of them would be chasing you?"

Her gaze automatically went to the glove compartment. The letters from her mom were in there. *No, but I have a feeling I know who might be able to tell me.* "Where am I dropping you off?"

"You're not."

After zipping down another avenue she slammed on the brakes. She spun around to face him. "Then get out."

"No. You and I are joined at the hip, so to speak. If it's because of me that these goons found you, then that's my responsibility."

"I can take care of myself." She clenched her teeth.

"I'm sure you can. However, I will be along for the ride. Besides, if you ever want to see your family, you need me."

Slowly shifting to face forward, she stared out the front window at the deserted street. *Aaaah yes, my one lifetime dream. Family.*

"Where are we going?"

"I can drop you off at any time." She put the car in drive and eased forward. Taking several back roads that took them another hour, she then headed west on Highway One. She drove for a while before turning north. Silence was something she was used to. Driving with a partner was not. Refusing to let herself be intimidated by him, she ignored him as she drove. When her back started to ache, a sign she'd been in one position too long and she realized they needed fuel, she pulled into a service station.

"Would you like something to...?" She looked at him slumped sideways across the seat. She wondered if he'd been shot but then she saw the gentle rise and fall of his chest. Her hero had fallen asleep. Before she forgot, she pulled out the envelopes from their hiding place in the glove box and stuffed them into her back pocket.

Quietly getting out of the vehicle, she filled up. Since she had no idea how long it was going to take to get where she was going, or exactly where she was going, she purchased an Alberta and B. C. map because she wasn't sure her cell phone would always work in the mountains or if she'd have time to charge it. She wanted to be prepared. She also loaded up on junk food, a 12 pack of lemonade and a 12 pack of water. Since he was now in the back seat, she set everything on the seat beside her, eased into hers, put on her seatbelt and pulled back onto the highway.

"Not a smart thing to do."

"Aaahhhh." Her head almost hit the roof and the car swerved before she was able to still her reaction. "Jesus."

"No, but I do get mistaken for him."

She frowned as she looked at him in the mirror. Then the joke hit her. Her laughter started as a giggle, then a chuckle. It sounded off-key which just made her laugh even harder.

"Pull over."

Too far gone with laughter to question his command, she pulled off into a tree-covered campground. Gasping for breath, she was finally able to bring herself under control. Completely drained, she slumped over the steering wheel. "Thank you."

Guy climbed out of the back seat and stepped up to the driver's side, opening the door. "For what?"

Too exhausted to move, she rolled her head sideways but didn't lift it. "For making me laugh, for keeping me company, for feeling safe enough to fall asleep."

His cheeks became a nice shape of apple red, which got her attention. She sat up and faced him.

"Tough guy, embarrassed about that?"

His face became ruddier as he swore. "Let's just say it's an issue." He turned away, his shoulders shaking slightly.

Surprised, Bailey got out of the car. Placing her hand on his back, she bent over to see his face. "Hey. I wasn't making fun..."

He was laughing. Confused, she stepped back.

"I'm sorry. The insanity of this just hit me." Scrubbing his hand down his face, he yawned.

"Where are we headed?"

Contemplating how much to share with him, she finally replied, "Near Jasper."

He looked pointedly at her. "Your turn to sleep. I'll drive." He opened the driver's door.

That shot some pep into her. She squinted, trying to block out the glare of the interior light as she faced him. "I'm fine."

"What the hell?" He moved so quickly that she had time only to stiffen at his gentle touch against her swollen cheek. "Your intruder?"

Affirming his suspicion with her eyes, she found she couldn't pull away from his concerned gaze or break the contact with his hand.

"That bastard."

Realizing she was enjoying his attention way too much, she stepped back and stiffly walked around the car. She opened the passenger door and reached in.

"Want a bottle of water or lemonade?"

"Lemonade please."

She tossed him the bottle over the top of the car which he snatched out of the air.

"You have bags under your eyes. Since I've already had a good nap, it's your turn." He looked at her. "Unless that look is vogue right now?"

Arching his eyebrow, he didn't wait for her to respond. "Seriously, if we're going to figure out what is going on, we need to work together. I have information you need and I believe you have some I need."

Breathing out slowly and without another word, she climbed into the back seat and lay down, curling onto her side. A few moments later, he climbed into the front, downing his drink.

"Where are we headed?" He pulled back onto the road and headed north.

"Jasper. For now."

He didn't ask why; he just drove. Reaching into the seat beside him, he ripped open a bag of chips and grinned over his shoulder at her. "My kind of woman."

She tried to stop it but the warmth of those words went well beyond the joke he'd intended. She tried not to allow that simple statement to make her sit up with pride but it did. Her mother had never doled out any praise and it now seemed the slightest amount made her want to strut like a peacock. Then she found herself drifting off to sleep as if a curtain was descending, something that had never happened to her before.

20

Da-da-dum, da-da-dum, da-da-dum. Charge.

Scrambling, Guy yanked his cell phone out of the case strapped to his belt. He hit the talk button as soon as he realized it was Graham.

"I've got something interesting."

He peeked over his shoulder to see if the noise had disturbed his passenger. Bailey's hair had fallen across her cheek, hiding her face. Her chest rose and fell like someone in a deep sleep. "What time is it there?" Guy looked through the windshield into the black night. Every now and then he'd pass a forlorn vehicle along this stretch of road. Glancing in the rearview mirror, he spotted a set of headlights but they were a long way behind them. He was confident they weren't anything to worry about, but he'd been keeping constant watch.

"Too early for the sun."

"Did you get any sleep?"

"When there isn't work to do, I will. How about you?"

He'd often wished he'd had Graham's stamina. The guy could stay up for twenty-four hours, sleep a couple and then off he'd go again. It exhausted him just thinking about it.

"You've got company?"

Guy smiled. "In a matter of speaking. So yes, I'll be talking quietly."

"All right here goes. Mrs. Donna Saunders came into existence August of 1983—"

"She was born in 1952."

"Hold on my dear friend, I'm not finished. Mrs. Donna Saunders *came into existence* in August of 1983. There is no information regarding a Miss, Ms or Mrs. Donna Saunders prior to that time."

Guy rubbed his forehead. "It can't be a coincidence that it happened so close to baby Cassidy's abduction."

"I don't think it is, either. I have lots of information but can't find a thread to tie it all together yet. I'll keep working on it."

"Thanks Graham. This case is turning out to have more surprises than either of us could have predicted." He proceeded to fill him in on what had happened so far.

"Holy Toledo. Are you sure you don't want to go to the police with this?"

Glancing over his shoulder at his passenger, he knew that he might pay for his decision. "No. But I do need you to run a license plate. I'm sure the car is rented but not legally. Of course, I can always hope."

"By the way, your grandmother, the next coming of God, wants to know where the report is that you promised her. She scares me."

He chuckled. Graham loved to make her think that, but he also knew she was a big marshmallow on the inside.

"I haven't really had the time or place. So I'll tell you

what to write. Then fax it to her private machine." He dictated the details.

"Got you boss. Hyuuh. Hyuuuuh. Hyuuuuh."

He clicked off the phone, on Graham's sad rendition of Goofy's laugh but couldn't help chuckling at his friend's odd sense of humour. Yawning incessantly, he followed the highway that led him to Jasper. It would be another hour or two before the sun was visible but the horizon was already growing lighter, making visibility much easier. The mountains in all their majestic beauty were now in view. He couldn't help but gaze in awe as he drove into the town limits. Not knowing Jasper, he drove around until he found a motel off the beaten path, where he rented a room. Bailey might not be pleased but she was still sleeping and he needed a few hours. Besides, he had no clue where exactly they were going.

Pushing the motel door open, he stepped back as an old, musty stench jolted him. Leaving the door open to air out the room, he returned to the car to get his travel mate. After a moment of trying to figure out how to best get a sleeping Bailey out of the car without waking her, he decided there wasn't really any graceful way. Worst that would happen, he thought, was she'd wake up and give him hell. Thinking that was as bad as it would get, he wasn't prepared for what happened when he reached in to lift her.

Her fist punched him in the chin as her foot clipped his knee. Next thing he knew he was on the ground writhing in pain and she was standing over him, ready to kick the crap out of him.

"Stop!" He rolled out of her reach. Her stance didn't change much but the crazed look in her eyes dissipated even as her chest continued to heave. He slowly got to his feet, his hand automatically going to the lump he could feel growing on the side of his face. His jaw still moved easily enough but not without pain. Standing up, he realized his knee didn't feel all that great either.

"I should have awakened you. My mistake. I thought we could both use some proper sleep so I got us a room." He waved behind him. "Since we're parked on the back side, out of the main stream of Jasper, I figured we'd be okay."

"We're in Jasper?" The intensity in her stare seemed out of place.

"Yeah."

"I slept for three or four hours?"

He shrugged and nodded, trying to let her know it wasn't a big deal.

Bailey stared hard at him before reaching in the car, grabbing her bag and marching past him into the dingy room.

Thinking that a hot breakfast might do them both some good and give Bailey time alone, he headed down the road to a fast food place they'd passed. Fifteen minutes later, he was back in the motel parking lot. Rather than get out, he stared absently out the window, trying to shake the uneasy feeling in his gut. Reversing, he drove down a few side streets and back alleys, almost losing her car in the mud puddles and finally parked a few blocks away. He grabbed the food and walked back to the room, barely able to refrain from devouring it all before he arrived.

He knocked and then waited a few seconds for a response. "Bailey?" When there was no answer, he inserted his key and cautiously entered. She lay flat across one of the beds, her left hand dangling off the side, her shoe-clad feet off the other and her hair covering her face. Her stillness except for her deep, even breathing was an unmistakable clue that she was sound asleep. He tiptoed to the small, round table in the corner and started to munch on his breakfast. He opened the curtain slightly so he could watch the area.

"Don't eat all that."

He'd never been skittish in his life and was known for having nerves of steel, but her voice startled him into jerking around and knocking over his chair with a loud crash. He glared at the woman who had so calmly moved from the far bed to drape across the one closest to him.

"Dammit. You're going to kill me."

Bailey shrugged and reached for his food, but he swatted her away. "Yours is in the bag."

"Grumpy, aren't we? Maybe you need some sleep." She kicked off her shoes and socks, grabbed her meal and sat down on the bed.

Growling, he straightened his chair and returned to sitting in it. He vainly attempted to finish his breakfast while ignoring her sitting barefooted, cross-legged, eating like she hadn't had a meal in weeks.

"Oh man. This is the greasiest, tastiest stuff I've ever eaten."

"Slow down or you'll have a gut ache."

She wiped her mouth with a napkin. "You sound like my mother. Only, she would never have let me eat this kind of stuff." She proceeded to polish off the egg, sausage and tomato sandwich.

"Oooohhhhh." Bailey flopped backward. "I ate too much."

Guy laughed. Bailey tried to glare at him but couldn't contain her smile.

"So we're in Jasper. Where to from here?" It was like he'd flipped a switch again. Her face lost all animation and became very somber before turning away.

"I'm going to have a shower. Get some sleep." She stopped at the bathroom door. "What time is it?"

"About 8:00."

Without another word, she grabbed her bag and closed the door behind her.

He needed to figure out what was going on but he needed sleep even more, something he wasn't sure would come easily. He stared at the closed bathroom door. She was confusing and aggravating and made him feel more alive than any woman he'd ever met. The thought scared the hell out of him. He wasn't known for lasting long in a relationship. He jerked out of his crazy thinking. They were running for their lives and he was analyzing whether she'd date him. Silently calling himself all manner of names, he made sure the room was secure, although he doubted the man had followed them. He locked the door, rigged a chair against the knob and moved the table in front of the window before stripping down to his shorts and crawling into bed. Within minutes he nodded off.

⚜

Hit and run. And a shooting. Man killed in residential neighborhood. Well known to police as Payme...

Lund's hands crumpled the paper with such force he trembled as if having a seizure.

"Are you all right, dear?"

Not bothering to respond to his wife who'd come home much earlier than he'd hoped from her sister's, he rose from the table and headed up the stairs to his office. He locked the door behind him before making his way to his desk, where he flopped into his leather chair. Sweat beaded on his forehead and trickled unheeded across his cheeks. His heart thumped wildly in his chest as he clenched his hands into fists. *They'll never be able to connect him to me.*

He removed a key from around his neck and unlocked the second desk drawer. The soft clicking sound usually gave him a little thrill, a sense of control over people he could bring down. Today, though, that feeling didn't emerge. Carefully pulling open the drawer, he removed the few books there as decoys and touched the back corner of the false bottom. It popped up. He leaned forward to satisfy himself that the only copy of all he'd done, of all he knew, was safely in its hiding place.

It wasn't there.

A lightning quick, forceful pain shot through his chest and he flung the key across the room. He clutched at his rib cage, opening and closing his mouth like a fish out of water as he tried to catch his breath. Tremors shook his body as he slumped forward, slamming the drawer closed.

21

After climbing out of a luxuriously long and much needed shower, Bailey dried herself off. The clothes from the day before were dry but felt grungy against her skin as she pulled them on. Finger brushing her teeth, she then detangled her hair as best she could, her mind wandering as she tried to figure out their next move.

She had to assume the guy from the previous night was still after them, though she didn't know why he was chasing them or what he wanted. She knew the answer lay in her past, which meant she had to somehow find people who remembered her and her mom and convince them to tell her something that would make sense. The thought of going back through a maze of places and time made her shiver and goosebumps to cover her arm. A devilish face which had plagued her childhood and many of her adult dreams popped into her mind.

Refusing to allow that nightmare to take hold, she opened the bathroom door. A loud sucking sound as though air and a bit of water was being sucked through an inadequate straw met her, followed by a gentle whooshing. Tiptoeing to the far bed, she stared at her partner. He lay on his back, his head turned to the side. She was amazed with the racket he was making that the curtains weren't fluttering. His bangs fell across his forehead. It wasn't until she felt the heat of his skin on her fingers that she realized she was about to brush them aside and she yanked her hand back.

She sat down heavily on the other bed, confused by her concern and her reaction to him. The last thing she needed to do right now was to analyze her emotions. To avoid it, she picked up the remote and turned on the TV, lowering the volume. She flipped through stations until she found a news station. The anchor was reporting a serious traffic accident in Calgary's south side. Another large company was about to declare bankruptcy and there had been a hit and run.

About to flip the channel, she stopped when they showed the street where the killing had occurred. She pressed her hand to her mouth as she recognized it.

"Payme, well known to police..."

Bailey stared hard at the photograph they displayed. He had a long, lean face, brown eyes, a hook nose and bad acne. She recognized him instantly as the intruder. But who the hell was he and what had he wanted with her? Who killed him?

Her mind raced with one question after another, but the one that would not let go was, *'What did you do, Mom?'*

Without a doubt, her mom had something to do with all of it. As she pondered the information Guy had been trying to give her almost from the moment he'd met her, she realized it could no longer be ignored.

You're not who you think you are.

Bailey hadn't wanted to listen. She knew as soon as she did, she'd have to admit it was true. Just letting the thought loose in her head confirmed what her gut was telling her, leaving her with a strong sense that what her life had been for the last 29 years wasn't what it should have been.

All the frantic moves, the constant picking up and starting over, living in places not fit for four-legged creatures, eating whatever could be begged, borrowed or stolen, the late night disappearance acts, the constant need to hide, all came flooding back. Like an avalanche came the horror that not only had she been alone all her life, now she didn't even know her true identity.

Clutching her chest, she curled onto her side, pulling her knees in tight to her chest. She lay there for a while, trying to stop the images that flew at her at warp speed. At five, there was the mouse that had run across her mattress on the floor. At three, she was staring out the back window of the cab as they drove away. At ten, they ran away to live under a bridge. Faces distorted into frightening Halloween masks.

Enough!

She jumped to her feet, slid on her runners, grabbed her coat, yanked open the door and raced outside. Not stopping to think, she ran. After all, it was what she knew how to do. She pounded the pavement, her heart thumping in her chest, her pulse throbbing in her neck as she gulped what air she could. It wasn't until her muscles tightened and knotted up that she finally stopped. Bent over, heaving with exhaustion, she didn't straighten up for a good five minutes. Her head throbbed, her legs felt watery and her lungs protested the excessive exercise. At least she had something else to focus on, something other than what her life was or what it could have been. Standing up slowly, she massaged her thighs, easing the aching muscles. Her fingers moved over the small but distinct lump in her pocket and reality came slamming back. Fight; that's what she knew how to do.

She hadn't a destination in mind when she'd set out, nor had she paid attention to her surroundings. But looking across the street she couldn't believe her luck—an internet café. She zipped through the steady stream of vehicles headed in both directions. Walking through the door, she stopped as a complex aroma of coffees, teas, spices and herbs assailed her senses.

Nirvana came to mind. Reeling from the overdose of smells and salivating on command, she walked up to the old-fashioned counter with the tall baker window beside it. She refused to look at the delectable selection of sweets. Instead, she smiled at the middle-aged woman.

"Hi. I was wondering…" Bailey's eyes opened wide as she patted down her pants pockets and realized she'd left her money and her bag in the room. "How does it work to get on a computer and get access to the internet?"

"The amount of time you want determines how much it costs."

"Do I book in advance or just show up?"

"It's first-come, first-served."

"So I can get on it now?"

The woman shook her head and waved in the direction of a few crowded tables. "Sorry, that's the line up."

"Fine. Thanks." Spinning on her foot she intended to walk out the door, only to be met by a pair of very intense blue eyes.

"If you came to buy coffee, you forgot it." His tone indicated that he wouldn't believe any excuse she offered.

Ignoring a twinge of guilt, she replied, "Actually, I did want a coffee but as luck would have it I forgot my money."

He eyed her critically before shoving his hand in his pocket and pulling out $20. "Black coffee and two glazed donuts."

"Looking for an early heart attack?" Before he could reply, she seized the twenty and stomped back into the café. Five minutes later she was back, balancing two coffees and a bag of treats.

She handed him the coffee but held the bag out of reach when he grasped for it. He arched an eyebrow at her. She smiled sarcastically. "Uh-uh-uh. I get to choose first and you'll just have to wait until we get back to the room."

As though she was talking directly to his stomach, it growled. They looked at each other and started laughing. The light moment allowed them to walk companionably but silently to the motel, each lost in thought. She almost felt a sense of calm, of just being, a feeling that was foreign to her. She noticed Guy looking over his shoulder and knew she should be concerned as well, but she just couldn't muster the energy. She had enough to ponder.

22

Guy steered Bailey away from the main road and cut through a heavily treed path that he'd taken in search of her. He glanced behind him, immediately noting the slow-moving blue truck and the string of traffic piled up behind him.

After dodging through a few circuitous side streets, they meandered back to the motel. He ushered her inside, briefly explaining that he wanted to scout the area. He walked to the corner of the motel and dialed Graham. When he received his voice mail, he left a message. "I have another vehicle and license plate for you." He rattled off the information. "I'll call later."

The area was quiet. Very little traffic passed by. Guy strolled around the motel and then around the block. Fifteen minutes later, he knocked on the door, announcing it was him before using his key to enter their room. Bailey was just coming out of the bathroom; her eyes met his for several heartbeats, before she reached for the cafe bag. She pulled out two raspberry-filled pastries.

"Speaking of heart attacks."

She shrugged as she handed him the bag. It held two glazed donuts and one blueberry-filled one.

"Okay, want to tell me why you snuck out this morning?" Guy quickly wolfed down a donut and reached for a napkin to wipe his hands. She was staring at his fingers but appeared deep in thought. He'd have given anything to know what had put that defeatist expression on her face. She looked like she needed to say something, as if she wanted to tell him what was going on. Like maybe she was starting to trust him.

Not sure what to do, he casually tossed the paper towel into the wastebasket. When he faced her again, the moment had passed and her chin was thrust out, her shield back in place. Sighing inwardly, he sat on the edge of the bed.

She paced to the window but didn't pull back the curtain. "I needed some air. My life is flipped upside down." She faced him. "And I've got some lunatic telling me to trust him. The only catch is he keeps telling me, I'm not me."

Guy flopped backward and stared at the water-stained ceiling. "I don't know what I'd do in your shoes. I don't even know how to tell you everything I need to." Blowing out his breath, he sat up. "Here's what I do know. You were born on February 2, 1983 to…" He looked away. "Let's just say to a nice couple for now."

She slammed her hands onto her hips. "Are you freakin' telling me, you won't say who my parents are? You want me to believe your bullshit but you won't tell me who they are?" Spinning away, she clenched her fists and shook them before tapping them against her forehead. She turned back to glare at him before grabbing her bag and heading for the door. "You're an ass!"

He was off the bed and had his hand planted over her head before she even managed to grab the knob. She refused to turn. "I know it sucks. But… there are other people I have to listen to. For now. It was devastating for them when you were stolen at just two days old."

"Why was I still in the hospital?"

"You had a cough and the doctors wanted to make sure it cleared up."

"And then, according to you, I vanished." She spun around and pushed against his chest.

For a moment, he didn't budge. He liked the feel of her small, soft hand against his body. Knowing this wasn't the time to pursue that topic, he stepped back. She took a wide berth around him, walked over to the bed and flopped down onto it, only to come to her feet just as quickly.

"Why did someone steal a two-day-old baby?"

He stared at the wall behind her. It took him a moment to answer. "We think it had to do with the black market."

"You're telling me you think I was stolen so someone could sell me to another person?" Shaking her head, she continued, "I get how horrible it is but I have to tell you, there's no way it could have been me. My mom followed the law to the letter. Even though we hid every time we saw a cop car, whenever she saw someone breaking the law, she'd find a pay phone and call in an anonymous tip. She turned people in for speeding, jaywalking, selling drugs. She never broke the law." She stopped herself in time. She'd been about to share with him that they'd lived in shady places, so her mom had plenty to inform the police about. The cops had never known who she was; she'd always said she wanted to remain anonymous so people couldn't retaliate. "There's no way she'd have stolen a baby."

His fingers dove through his hair. Sitting, he rested his elbows on his spread knees and clasped his hands.

"Look, let me lay out everything I know and then we'll talk about what you know. This sucks but there's no doubt as to who you are. You saw the picture yourself."

"Pffffft. It could have been doctored."

He shook his head.

"It could mean I'm related but not kidnapped. Right?" Her eyes opened wide.

He really wanted to tell her yes.

"Who the hell are you?" The yelling came from outside. Bailey and Guy raced to the window. Guy carefully lifted the edge of the frayed curtain. Two men were at the lobby door. One was an older man with heavy lines etched into his face, seemingly in total contrast to the bulging muscles that strained against his tight t-shirt and blue jeans. He was obviously not a person one refused to cooperate with, and he did not look happy when the employee wouldn't tell him anything. The angry man strolled away from the building and climbed into a truck, his head turning constantly, his eyes taking in everything.

It's the same blue truck.

How the hell did he find us?

He watched until the man drove away. "Okay, grab your stuff. We have to go." He turned to address Bailey, only to find she was already halfway out the door. "I didn't mean that fast." This was someone who was a little too comfortable with being on the move.

"Where?"

"That way." He indicated where he'd parked the car.

She paused, looking around before sprinting across the parking lot and then the street. He ran to keep up. Halfway down the residential block, he pulled her down a back alley. Once they reached the vehicle, he unlocked it and climbed in, ignoring her glare and her thrust-out hand. Huffily, she climbed into the passenger seat.

"Going to tell me what that was about?"

He looked at her for a moment and realized he didn't want to tell her anything. She'd been through a lot and he didn't want to be the one to add to it. He wished he could tell her that whoever was after them was really after her. Somehow he was sure this was all connected to the black market ring and her kidnapping twenty-nine years before. Someone wanted her to remain missing.

"I think we should get moving, to wherever it is that you need to get to. I'm assuming it's a place that should give us some answers?"

She shrugged, staring out the side window. "I need to go back to that café. I want to get some food for the road."

There was something she wasn't telling him but he was too preoccupied staring at every vehicle they encountered to drag it out of her. "Fine, I'll drop you off there. Wait for me. Inside."

Her head whipped around. "That guy was after us, wasn't he?"

"Let's just say I want to make sure he didn't see us. Okay? So stay in the restaurant until I get there. Got it?"

"Right."

Before he could answer, she climbed out. After he left her, he circled the block three times to ensure their unwanted company wasn't around. Grabbing his phone, he hit speed dial.

"Graham. I need information and fast." He quickly filled in his partner on the unfolding events. "I need to rent another vehicle now but not in either of our names. How long?"

"Give me ten minutes to hack in and put your paid reservation into their files. Okay? How's an SUV sound?"

"Great. I'm thinking a 4x4 might come in handy. I need to talk to the sketch artist the Ontario Police Services use. I'm hoping he can do a drawing of my guy; then you can run it through the police database."

"Got it. I'll get him to call you right away. Where and when will you be able to look at an email, once he gets a draft done?"

"Unfortunately, she still hasn't told me where we're going. I'll be in touch." Looking out his window, he couldn't help the awe-inspiring sight—the mountains, snow-capped and glistening in the sunlight. He wished they had time to enjoy it. "Cell reception might be an issue though. We're headed west, which means we're going into the mountains. I'll call as soon as I can. Any information on those plates?"

"First vehicle was stolen three days ago from a car rental agency. No suspects yet. Interestingly, the truck was just reported stolen about an hour ago in Calgary. No idea when it was taken. The owner was away for several days. When he got home early this morning, it was gone."

Guy swore. "Thanks, bud. I…" He didn't know how to say thank you. This was very different than anything they'd ever been involved in before. Neither one of them had ever been the target.

"I know. Keep it upright." It was Graham's way of telling him to stay safe and don't get into trouble he couldn't get out of.

"I will," he answered, but he was beginning to realize it was going to be easier said than done.

23

The office was small, nondescript. Two walls of glass, a large counter and a woman who looked like she wished she was anywhere else. As soon as her eyes met his, she pasted on a forced smile betrayed by the cold look in her eyes.

"Hi. What can I do for you today?"

"I'm here to pick up a vehicle for Knight's Associates."

She quickly punched information into the computer. "Yes, here it is. Uh, it's been paid for but I need a password." She looked up. "Usually we ask for ID."

Guy shrugged. "Butler." Graham loved the whole persona of an English butler—the accent, the formality. It was a long-standing joke between them.

He signed for the new vehicle, asking casually what was west of Jasper.

"West? BC," she answered. "Only two ways to go—head south through Valemount or west through Prince

George. Valemount is small; doubt you'd want to go there."

He nodded as he headed toward the vehicle. He had a feeling Valemount was exactly where they were headed.

Flipping on the signal, he was about to pull into traffic when he saw the blue truck heading in the opposite direction. Though Guy wanted to get a good look at the driver, instinct prevailed and he slouched down and averted his face. As soon as it was clear, he headed to the café. He pulled up outside, scanning the area. Nothing stood out. Walking into the dimly lit restaurant, he looked for Bailey. Concerned, he approached the counter to ask if they'd seen her when he spotted her in a little alcove. The angle was such that he couldn't see exactly what she was doing but she was sitting at a computer, intently studying the screen. There was no way he could look at it without her becoming aware of him first.

"Bailey. We have to go."

At the sound of his voice, she jerked as though he'd cracked a whip. Her fingers quickly hit the keyboard, and by the time he reached her side, whatever she'd been reading was gone.

Not meeting his eyes, she said, "Oh yeah. I was just checking emails. I've been out of touch for a while. I didn't have a chance to get any food for the road, though."

He got the hint but he was reluctant to leave, and he was hesitant to tell her about their tail. Her guilty expression didn't do anything to ease his suspicions. "I'll get something but we're leaving now." He walked away but kept an eye on her. She pulled something out of the computer and stuffed it in her jeans pocket.

Five minutes later, they were headed west. "Want to tell me where we're going?"

"Valemount, B.C."

"How do we get there?" He glanced at her to see that

she was looking it up on her cell. After she gave him the directions he needed, the trip was made in silence.

She rested her head against the passenger window. He tried to focus on the beauty of the mountains but his mind and eyes were constantly on the lookout for their tail. A sign indicating they were entering the village of Valemount let him know they'd arrived. He pulled into a service station just off the highway, muttering to himself, "Now where to?"

She jerked upright, her eyes intense as she slowly turned to take in a full 360 degree view. Guy followed her gaze. Pristine white mountains announced its status as a snowmobiler heaven but he was pretty sure that wasn't what was holding her attention. They were surrounded by those majestic mountains, and snow filled the ditches but thankfully the roads were bare and dry. The area was beautiful, the sun dancing off the glaciers almost blinding, yet she was ogling as though it were hypnotic. Sighing, he leaned against the door to wait her out.

A moment later, she was still gaping but he'd had enough. He yanked open his door and climbed out. "I'm going to get something to drink, can I get you anything?"

Absently she looked at him and then away. "A juice."

The chilly spring air caused goosebumps to form on his arms. He zipped up his jacket before entering the building. When he returned, he pulled open his door and slid in. Turning, he went to hand Bailey her drink only to discover she wasn't there. He looked in the back. She wasn't there either. He climbed out, tossing the two bottles on the seat. He did his own 360 spin but saw nothing. Sprinting a short distance back, he came to the crossroads that led into the small town. He didn't see her wandering into the village, so he looked in the opposite direction. A gravel road led into the country. Just where the road curved, he caught sight of her green jacket. Swearing, he ran back to the SUV, jumped in and sped off after her.

The road continued straight for about a quarter of a mile before making a sharp ninety-degree turn. As soon as he made the curve, there she was, running down the middle of the road. Pulling up behind her, he waited for her to move to the side. When she didn't, he lowered his window and yelled, "Bailey." No response. "Bailey!"

She flinched but kept on running. Really worried now, he pulled up to pass her. With the right side of the truck in the ditch, he made it by her. He stopped the vehicle and climbed out. Panting and looking wild-eyed, her brown hair tugged in all directions by the circling wind, she seemed oblivious. When she ran right past him, he really became concerned. Not sure what to do, he got back into the vehicle and followed her.

About a quarter mile later, she turned left. The area was so heavily forested it was like driving into a tunnel. Ten minutes later, she suddenly shot off the road to the left. He slammed on the brakes and jumped out.

"Bailey. Stop!" She either wasn't listening or didn't hear him as she continued to run down a path that looked like it had been made by an ATV. Glancing over his shoulder at the brand new black SUV, he sighed. Not really a bill they could afford but something had spooked her and he needed to go where she went. He climbed back in and plunged down into the ditch. Thankfully the foot-high snow was crunchy and not too eager to hang onto the tires. He drove along the path, ignoring the high-pitched squeals the Douglas Fir, White Spruce and Red Cedar branches were making as they scraped along the sides of the Ford Escape.

She never slowed down nor looked over her shoulder. She just kept going. Then she disappeared. Guy's pulse jumped furiously in his neck. His hands gripped the steering wheel tight enough to snap it. He pushed on the gas pedal. Branches slapped at the windshield, obscuring his vision until he abruptly burst into a clearing. No Bailey but there was what might have once been a beautiful log cabin, but was now weathered as though abandoned. Parking the SUV, he got out and looked around. He wondered if the rutted, overgrown path and the clearing around the cabin had once been properly maintained. If so, it had obviously been a long time. Several animal tracks covered the area.

Wading through the shrubs and tall, dormant grass, he moved through the ankle-burying snow toward the cabin. Seeing it was padlocked, he realized that Bailey hadn't been able to get inside. Moving more quickly, he circled the building. Nothing. He stopped. There was a rushing, gurgling sound. Looking down, he was able to distinguish Bailey's footprints from those of the animals. He followed her path that led toward the sound. Even though the sun was high in the sky, it only penetrated enough through the thick forest to leave a murky light. The snow quickly soaked his feet and ankles.

A few minutes later he stepped out of the trees into another clearing. A creek with the hint of winter ice still clinging to its banks, rippled by. And there was Bailey perched on a large flat rock, hugging her knees to her chest. Tears streamed down her face. She looked stunned and spooked at the same time. Not wanting to add to her distress, he sat on a smaller stone nearby.

"I don't know how I found this place."

Guy consciously stared at the river, making sure he didn't look at her. She was scared.

"But you know it."

"Yeah. I came here as a kid. I think. I remember running and playing and a man chasing me. I was laughing. I sat here a lot and tossed pebbles into the stream."

He gave her the time she needed to gather herself. They sat in silence for a long time, the frigid air enveloping them. His mind wandered to all that he hadn't had as a child. There hadn't been much joy in his life until Dorothea and Joseph had taken him in. They'd tried to make him happy. He'd worked awfully hard to be a good boy, to follow all the rules, to never be in their way. They soon convinced him that they wanted to hear him, they wanted him running, laughing and having fun. He'd been fifteen or so before he'd really felt comfortable living with them. It had taken six years for him to accept that their mansion of a house was actually his to call home. They'd made his life good but he'd still never quite trusted that it wouldn't disappear one day. Comparing his life to Bailey's, he realized how great he'd had it. He'd been saved but she hadn't been. It dawned on him that he'd been running for a very long time. Running away, he was scared of losing what little he felt he had.

The never-ending musical notes of the babbling creek, not to mention the stress of the last few days had Guy alternately widening his eyes and blinking them to get rid of the grit. *Surely no one could have followed us here.* The peaceful sounds, the warmth of the sun and exhaustion, all pulled at his eyelids. Giving in, he closed them for just a second.

24

Bailey looked at her shining knight leaning against her rock, his head at an awkward and uncomfortable angle. He was going to have a few kinks when he woke up.

Rubbing her face with her hands, she tried to remove the tracks her tears had left. Here, she'd been happy. The flashes of memory were of her smiling, giggling, running, playing. Those were not things she often associated with her childhood and until she'd found this place, she'd not remembered she'd had such moments. The pictures on the walls of Lund's office had started it. They had opened the floodgates. With no idea what she'd find, she knew she had to find this place. The sketchy details hidden in his office files had sent her to Jasper. The jump drive had provided directions. Now that she was here, however, she was left with more questions than answers, including who owned this place and why they had stopped coming here.

"Bailey, get back from the water."

"Momma, baby fish."

"Yes there are lots, Bails. Now come back from the edge."

"Shiny, Momma."

"Yes Bails, they're shiny."

"Catch some."

"We've got to go, Bails."

"Noooooooooooooooooooo. Momma." She cried and she screamed and stared out the back window of the car as they drove away.

It had become her childhood routine, except eventually she'd learned to stop screaming—at least, audibly. Wiping her hands over her cheeks, she removed any traces of her emotions before quietly sliding off the rock to avoid disturbing Guy. He had his eyes closed though it was difficult to tell if he was sleeping or simply enjoying the quiet solitude. She walked to the edge of the stream. Scooping up some water, she splashed it on her face. The chill of the recently thawed stream penetrated her dulled senses.

As she stared down, a memory flitted at the edge of her thoughts like the quick vibration of the hummingbird's wings, fleeting and elusive. Placing her hand on the edge of the rock, she used it to keep her balance as she stepped around to the other side. Treading carefully over the snow so she wouldn't skid on the hidden stones and slippery moss that lay underneath, she headed back to the cabin. Its magnetic pull had been undeniable when she'd passed it upon first arriving, but she hadn't been strong enough to enter. Instinct told her she'd find answers there; she just wasn't sure she was ready for them.

In the brief amount of time she had spent looking at the jump drive, it had been enough to know that hours would be required to study all that Mr. Lund kept on it.

There was no file for anyone named Donna Saunders, but there had been something about this cabin. If Guy hadn't arrived at the cafe when he had, she might have discovered more. The directions to the cabin had been laid out fairly clearly. And though Bailey hadn't recalled the precise location, her memory of the place was very strong. No distinct pictures, just a sense of fun, of safety... and then of something bad.

You lied, Mr. Lund. He'd told her the cabin was in Alberta and he no longer owned it.

As she looked at the padlock, watery images flitted through her mind, too indistinct and fleeting for her to quite catch them. Without the key, she couldn't get in. She checked obvious hiding places around the door and window frames, her fingers poking into every nook and cranny. She came up empty. There was nowhere else on the old log frame for her to check. Looking around, her attention was snagged by the SUV. As if her memories were coming alive, she saw two cars parked in the cleared area and a man whose face remained in the shadows. He had walked away briefly and then he'd returned to open the door.

She knew she was looking for a pine needle in a forest but she had to try to find the key to the cabin. She headed back to the water. Guy was nowhere in sight. His footprints in the snow indicated he was following the stream. A huge yawn caught her off guard. Not ready to give in to the fatigue that was weighing her down, she continued to scout the area.

Where would someone hide a key? Why do I think it's here?

A few minutes later and after flipping over every stone, looking around every bush, she realized she'd been wrong. Slumping against the same rock upon which she'd sat earlier, she slammed her fist against her thigh in frustration. "It has to be here, dammit!"

"Weren't you the one giving me a lecture about swearing?"

"Jesus." She jerked around to face her wandering tag-along.

"No, actually I'm not but I can see how you could make that mistake. Again."

She peered at him for a moment before his joke clicked for her. She laughed and once it began, the laughter took hold of her. Finally, she wound down and sank bonelessly to the ground.

"Uhm. I'm glad you found that funny."

"I…" She burst into tears. Horrified, she glanced at Guy before scrambling to her feet in effort sudden urge to run. But he was faster. He grabbed her and pulled her to his chest. At first she was rigid, refusing any comfort. But since he wasn't going away nor letting her go, she gave in and sagged against him.

She cried like she was a child again, before she realized moving and loss was a fact of life. When she finished, she felt as wrung out as a rag put through an old ringer washer. Trying to find strength to stand on her own two feet, she weakly pushed against his chest. He didn't budge. Instead, he guided her to sit on the stone and with his arm still around her, sat beside her. He left it to her to decide how much she took from him. Feeling comforted by his strength, she leaned against his side.

"Tell me about this place."

"I don't know much, except the few times I came here as a little girl, I was happy."

The picture in Mr. Lund's office flashed through her mind and she made the connection. Jumping up, she tore through the trees. Guy was soon crashing behind her. Coming upon the clearing, she stopped for a moment. It didn't look quite right. She moved around to study it from all angles. Finally, when she reached the road and looked back at the cabin, she was sure that was where the picture had been taken. Time had made many changes; the cabin no longer looked new, the ground was no longer cleared, and stacks of firewood were missing. Though trees now partially obscured the view, it was the place. "Mr. Lund."

"What about him?"

Startled, she glanced at him. *How much do I tell him?*

"He…" She realized she was tired; tired of constantly hiding, habitually telling only partial truths, being perpetually on guard. That had been her whole life and look where it had gotten her. "Mr. Lund, my mother's lawyer, has a photo of this view in his office. I'm guessing this was his place, but I remember a different man, a happy person, someone other than Mr. Lund."

A bird chirped, catching Bailey's attention. "The bird house." She jumped to her feet and ran through the trees before stopping to listen again. The robin cheeped again. She looked to her right and then up.

"There." She pointed high in the tree. "How are you at climbing?"

He leaned his head back. "Is there a good reason I need to get up there?"

Smiling, she said, "Yep. The key to the cabin is up there."

"You're sure?"

She nodded.

A short time later and after a few scrapes and several curses, Guy shimmied down the tree with the prize which had been tucked away in the tiny wood structure fifteen feet off the ground. Bailey eagerly grasped it. Returning to the front door, she stuck the key into the rusty lock. Taking a deep breath, she tried to turn it but it wouldn't budge. She tried again, jiggling it and then pulling it part way out. It was not moving. It wouldn't turn at all. In frustration, she kicked the door.

Ignoring her protests, Guy reached around her and took it out of her hands. He jimmied the lock a few times but to no avail. She had a sinking feeling it wasn't going to work. Swearing, she couldn't believe that a tiny piece of metal was going to keep her from entering the cabin and finding the answers her mom had wanted her to find. Suddenly, an idea popped into her head. She took off but was back within a minute.

"Move!"

Guy pulled back just in time as she slammed down the tire iron she'd taken from the rented vehicle. The first hit connected but the old lock didn't do more than groan. She attacked it with a vengeance, lifting the iron up and bringing it down as hard as she could.

"Stop. Stop!"

It took a moment for Guy's yelling to get through to her. With surprise she realized not only had she managed to get the lock open but she'd pretty much pulverized it. Blowing out her breath, she dropped the tire iron and grabbed the door knob. A feeling of trepidation caused her to pause for a moment before she turned the handle and pushed. It didn't move. She tried again, this time leaning more of her body weight into it. It did little more than groan. Beyond frustrated, she bent to pick up the tire iron.

Guy grabbed her wrists, stopping her. "Let me." Dropping his shoulder, he slammed it against the solid access which scraped heavily against the floor, moving only a few inches. He grabbed the edge of the door, lifting and pushing at the same time. It opened another six inches.

Bailey took a deep breath, suddenly fearful of what she might discover.

25

Late day sun filtered in through two grimy windows, highlighting the dust-laden air. Cautiously, Bailey stepped through the opening. There was a '70s style maroon couch, a rocking chair, a stand-alone fireplace, a bookshelf totally covered in filth and sparsely lined with books. The kitchen had a sturdy wood table and six wood chairs. Everything might have been neat and tidy underneath the layers of dirt and mouse droppings. It looked as if someone had left with the intent to return soon but that day hadn't come. It all looked foreign but normal to her. She had hoped it would trigger more memories but she couldn't even picture herself inside; outside playing, yes, but in there, no.

Walking across the open space, she entered one of the other rooms. A four poster, double bed was pushed against one wall while a dark mahogany tall boy hugged the opposite wall. Neither grabbed her attention. She turned, almost colliding with Guy. After only a moment's hesitation, she sidestepped him. She glanced into the bathroom as she passed, noting the standard toilet, pedestal sink, shower and open shelves before heading into the kitchen. She had no idea what she was searching for but she had a strong sense that there was something. There had to be; why else would her mom insist she go there?

There was nothing out of the ordinary about the kitchen either. In the cupboards, she found a set of china dishes, not very practical but probably very expensive at one time. There were a few pots and pans and some utensils but no glasses and no food.

"Bailey, come here."

Sighing, she returned to the bedroom where Guy was snooping through the drawers. As she approached, she peeked over his shoulder. Captivated by an item in the drawer, she reached for it. Her hand shook as she took a closer look. Weakly, she sank onto the bed. Guy knelt in front of her.

"Are you okay?"

She couldn't answer. She just shook her head, her eyes glued to what she held in her hands. *It's here.* She had been sure it was gone forever. At one time, it had been her constant companion but then one day it just wasn't there. Her mom had told her she'd lost it.

"She's so ugly, she's beautiful. Her dress is a little worse for wear and her hair needs a good cleaning and combing." It was a filthy matted doll that had meant the world to her. The pug nose on Miss Piggy looked like it had been pulled one too many times as the snout stuck out like a twisted and dented cone.

"This was yours."

"Wh-what? Oh-oh yeah. I thought it was long gone." She couldn't ignore the excitement that was building. "What did you want to show me?"

He reached in the drawer and pulled out a packet of papers, rifling through them before handing a small square one to her.

"A picture? Of who?" She stared hard at the photo. "It's me. Oh my god. It's a picture of me." The girl of about four or five had long brown hair that looked like it hadn't seen a brush in days. A pink, muddied ribbon hung limply down one side of her face. Mud dotted her forehead and one cheek but a huge grin minus a few teeth was what grabbed her attention. The little girl looked happy.

"Are there more?" Bailey sat up straight, reaching out.

"I'm checking." He flipped through the blank pages but found nothing else. "Sorry. That's it. What were you hoping to find here?"

She studied her younger face before answering. "I don't know. I just know I had to come here." Meeting his gaze, she held up the two items. "I can't believe this is all there was to find."

"Does anyone else know about this place?"

"I didn't know about this place."

He looked at her dubiously.

"Okay, well not consciously. So I don't know. I know my mother never talked about it. Mr. Lund told me he'd sold it. I don't know." As she went back in time to the few memories she had of the place, she had a sense of peace and of fun. And just as quickly, she felt herself tense; something dark had happened. Had it just been because it was another move?

Suddenly, she wasn't in the past anymore and that same sense of doom was growing stronger. Something bad was coming. She jumped to her feet, startling Guy, who waddled backward to get out of her way. He put his hands on the bureau to brace himself.

"We have to leave. Now. Don't ask." Stuffing the picture in her back pocket, she clutched the pig in her hand as she hustled her way through the cabin. She raced across the open space, not waiting for him, and climbed into the SUV, started it and turned around in the tight space. Guy jumped into the passenger side just as she was moving forward again.

"What's going on?"

She hit the gas pedal. If there had been any paint left on the side, it was soon in the process of being scraped off. They hit a rut so hard the vehicle slammed forward, only to send them flying in the next moment. She held tight to the steering wheel but still couldn't stop her head from pitching forward and hitting the top edge of it. Guy, she noted, grabbed the door and the dashboard as the seatbelt didn't seem to be keeping him in place either. She knew it was crazy but she also knew she had to get out of there quickly. Easing up slightly, she maneuvered through the tight, overgrown laneway. Finally, they broke through the brush and were soon back on the road, spitting gravel as she gunned it. Backtracking the way they'd arrived was no problem, as a map of the area was as clear to her as though it was sitting in front of her. When she hit the T intersection to go right, though, a half ton truck barreled down on them. It felt personal. Going with instinct, Bailey turned left.

"That driver either has a very heavy foot or we've got company."

He looked out the back window. "Where exactly are we going?"

"I don't know but out of here." Slowing only slightly, she turned once more to the left, keeping a close eye on the vehicle that was fast gaining on them.

"It looks like a truck from the motel." Guy glanced at her but she was too busy concentrating on the road.

"Did you ask questions about northern B.C.?"

Guy's silence was telling.

"Could he have put a tracker on the car? Followed us to Jasper and asked questions, like what we traded the car in for?"

"Dammit. He obviously has connections just like I do."

She frowned at Guy's comment but didn't break her focus. She slowed enough to let the truck get within six inches and then stomped on the gas pedal. It wasn't quite soon enough but it did change the impending impact to a glancing blow. The vehicle fishtailed but before she was able to do much more than straighten them out, the guy rammed them a second time. The seatbelt cut into her shoulder as she flew forward after thumping back against the seat. She shook off the bile that was crawling its way up her throat. This was life or death. Her hands gripped the wheel tightly as she cranked it, trying to pull out of their wildly skidding vehicle. The rear end snapped from side to side. It took all her skill and strength to keep it from taking them into the ditch or from sending them spinning right around.

"He's coming again, Bailey."

She had to make a move. Glancing in the mirror, she noted that the vehicle was rapidly moving toward them.

"Hold on." Going with the natural swing of the vehicle, she turned the wheel to the left and gunned it just as the rear end of her vehicle hit the far right of its skid. They zoomed into the ditch, bouncing their way through the rough terrain. Between that and the snow sucking the tires into a path, the SUV straightened out. They slid down the incline and entered a narrow passage between Black Spruce trees. Branches slapped and scraped the sides of the rental, sometimes giving such a high pitched sound it grated on her nerves like fingernails on chalkboard. It made her cringe.

Too occupied to see how Guy was handling the ride, she was thankful he wasn't giving her instructions or yelling at her. She hoped he wasn't knocked out cold. Turning sharply to the left, the rear end slid sideways, wiping out two young trees. In the rearview mirror, she could see the half ton was no longer behind them but forging its own path from their side. She focused on zigzagging through the trees, driving through spaces that looked like a compact wouldn't fit.

"Look out!"

The snow was no longer their friend. She cramped the wheel but not in time. The deep pocket they'd hit grabbed the SUV, sliding it sideways into a large poplar. She flinched but didn't stop, punching the gas pedal instead.

"Duck."

She did and slammed on the brakes at the same time which was all that saved them. The half ton zoomed past which also luckily moved the aim of the gun pointed at them. The shot went high, skipping off the top of their vehicle. Cramping her wheel to the right, she gunned it. The tail-end fishtailed to the left, slamming into another tree and stopping them. The wheels spun but they weren't moving. Looking around frantically, she was glad to see their company had run into much the same problem. He was shoving his truck into drive and then reverse, rocking back and forth, trying to get unstuck as well.

"Dammit. Let's go." Bailey slammed her hand on the steering wheel as she mimicked the other driver's actions. A mixture of snow, dirt and grass flew up behind them but they weren't going anywhere.

"Stop. STOP!" As soon as she lifted her foot off the pedal, Guy jumped out.

"What the hell are you doing?"

"Getting us some traction."

He grabbed some branches from the evergreens and proceeded to break them off. She had a moment of guilt about the damage they'd done. Shaking that off, she pulled away just in time to see the truck grill aiming right at them—and coming fast.

"Guy!"

"Go." He dove in, yanking the door closed behind him.

She hit reverse. They spun. She slammed it in forward. They got enough traction to move a few inches. She hit reverse and then drive again. She glanced sideways. The emblem on the grill was very clear and getting closer. It was the evil smile beyond it that scared her senseless. Shoving into low gear, she pushed on the gas pedal. The tires caught, shooting them forward like a slingshot. But it wasn't quite quick enough. The truck hit the rear left corner, sending the SUV into a spin and then into a tree. The jolt of the sudden stop sent Bailey slamming backward and then sideways. A bit dazed, she shook it off as she looked for their assailant. The crash had sent him sliding down a knoll. It was the break they needed.

Bailey stomped on the pedal and they surged forward, grinding and scraping as they pulled away. The SUV gained speed as they went. A quick look in the mirror showed the truck wasn't moving. He was stuck, but that didn't stop him from firing off some shots. Bailey drove like a madwoman with no idea where she was going, simply relying on instinct to get them out of there. Ahead, the road peeked at them between the branches. With her foot hard on the pedal, she headed straight for it. It was so close. She was so focussed on getting onto it and getting out of there, she didn't see the mound until the Ford Escape climbed the sharp incline and shot through the air, narrowly making it between two poplars, nearly stripping them bare. The landing slammed them down hard. Bailey flopped around like a rag doll in a clothes dryer. Instinct caused her to hit the brakes. Shaking off the shock that loomed at the edges of her consciousness, she didn't waste time thinking but relied again on instinct. The tires spun, spitting snow, dirt and grass as they bounced out of the ditch and finally made it onto the route of escape.

Guy sat back in his seat, facing forward. "That should slow him down."

"What?" She didn't take her eyes off the road.

"He tried to follow us but he went a bit sideways and hit an evergreen head on."

Continuing on instinct and what she hoped was a reliable sense of direction, she zigzagged down country roads.

"Back to Jasper?"

"No."

She wasn't clear at all where they were going but knew she had to listen to her gut. She had to follow her past.

26

"What's going on? I expected to hear from you already. Tell me this has been resolved." Geoff straightened his tie as he looked out his office window. The expanse of the orchards, the leaves gently fluttering in the wind, reminded him of all he'd fought for. This was his life, his legacy. No one would take it away from him, no one.

"Listen, asshole. I did you a favor twenty-nine years ago. Not the other way around. You came to me. I'm handling this situation."

You damned well better be. Or we all pay.

"Tell me you know where she is." The silence was so long and tense, he feared the man on the other end of the phone might be plotting more than just the girl's death.

"For your information and in case you want to come and take care of the problem yourself," there was a pregnant pause, "she's in Edmonton. You know, the capital of Alberta."

Geoff ground his teeth but didn't respond to the jibe. This man would soon be out of his life forever. The last link they had to each other was Cassidy. If this man couldn't do it, he'd find someone who could.

"I've got to go."

The phone went dead. Geoff looked at the receiver in his hand for a moment before setting it down. He might need someone else anyway.

"You seem stressed, Geoffrey."

His head snapped up, his eyes narrowed. "What the hell do you think you're doing, sneaking into my office, Dorothy?"

"Ah, we're going to play those games, are we, Geoffrey. My name is Dorothea. Your memory seems to be going. Maybe it's time I stopped you from being my right hand person. Hmmm." She walked in as though royalty and sat at his desk, in his chair.

The rage rushed through him so quickly he was barely able to stop himself from grabbing her cane and beating the living daylights out of her. Again. It had been so long since he'd reacted so strongly to her.

Does she know it's because of me she's carried that cane around for 50 years? That did bring a smile to his face.

"Aahh. I'm glad to see you're going to be sensible, Geoffrey. I need to talk to you about some concerns I have regarding the contract negotiations with that small winery in Southern California. It seems we're paying an exorbitant fee."

Oh, you have no idea, my bitch of a sister. He felt elated and sad almost simultaneously. He wished he could be there to see her expression when she put it all together, when she found out there was no winery. There was no money. Sighing, he glanced outside. It was almost sad that this amusement was coming to an end. He'd have to move on. He took a deep breath, smiled and walked to the straight-back leather chair he kept for guests. He sat down and explained to his sister what made the fictitious California winery worth every penny they were putting into it.

27

"Okay, I didn't ask questions all the way here." Guy sat up and looked around.

"Huh?" Bailey pulled her unfocused gaze from the slow moving traffic in front of her to glance at Guy.

"Where are we?"

"Edmonton." They had driven in silence the entire way, her mind preoccupied with what she needed to do.

"And we're here because?"

Frowning, she glanced at him. *What the hell was he talking about?* "I'm tired. I need some answers. I figured this was the best place to get them."

"Oh, what's here?"

My past. "A library—one that can hopefully show me old footage of a baby being stolen from a hospital in Quebec twenty-nine years ago." She glanced in her right hand mirror then zipped into the other lane. "Right now, we're going to find a hotel. One that is nice, warm and odor-free." She arched her eyebrows at him.

"Hey, I was just trying to find us an out of the way place. I never thought to ask the guy if they'd fumigated." He slouched in his seat and crossed his arms.

Ignoring him, she headed downtown, parking in a centralized garage. "Let's get a room." She got out, raised her hands over her head and arched her back, groaning as she did so. And as she did everything else, when she was ready, she went.

He scrambled out of the vehicle, slammed the door, his footsteps echoing in the garage as he raced to catch up to her. He fell into step beside her. When they walked into the lobby of one of the most expensive hotels in the city, she wished she had a camera.

"What in the hell are we doing here?"

"We're staying here. And you're paying for the room." Walking up to the counter, she smiled at the desk clerk, who seemed a bit hesitant to take her information.

"May I help you?"

"Yes, I'd like a room with two double beds."

"We are not staying here," Guy whispered harshly into her ear.

Tugging her arm out of his grasp, she smiled at the desk clerk and whispered out the side of her mouth, "Oh, yes, we are. You've dragged me all over the place. You've uprooted my life. You tell me someone wants me back after all this time. Well, someone's gonna pay. And it ain't gonna be me."

"We have two rooms available both with two queen size beds; one has a Jacuzzi, the other doesn't."

"Jacuzzi."

"No Jacuzzi."

The desk clerk maintained a professionally tolerant expression.

"Get out your wallet."

"I'm not…"

Bailey smiled openly at the woman and winked like it was a girls' problem. "Give us a moment." She grabbed Guy's hand and pulled him a few feet away. "You owe me. My life was fine until you entered it." She ignored his dismissal of her claim. "You're going to continue to screw up my life until we figure out what happened when I was a baby." She patted his cheek. "So be a good boy and get out your damn credit card. I'm sleeping here, after I soak in the hot tub."

"Wait. It can't be in our names."

"Why not?"

"Because, in case you've forgotten, we have a friend or two tailing us. Do you want them to find us?"

She knew her cheeks paled to a pasty white. It must have worried him because he wrapped his arm around her and escorted her to a plush leather chair. He fanned her face with his hands.

"Then what…"

"Give me five. I have a friend who can get us in here under assumed names."

She didn't have the energy to question him or really, even care how he was going to do it. She watched as he walked a short distance away and made a phone call. If his hand ripping through his hair was a sign of how the call was going, it didn't look good. He walked back to her while clicking off his phone.

"Sit tight for ten minutes and we're in."

She hadn't moved from her slumped position. Exhaustion rolled over like a steam truck, leaving her limp and drained.

His phone rang almost exactly ten minutes later. He didn't answer or even look at it; he simply tapped the screen to stop the ring. He reached out his hand. She shifted her coat to her left arm and allowed him to pull her to her feet. Within minutes, they were being escorted

to the elevator. Bailey wondered if they did this for all
their guests or if they were getting special treatment
because they had no luggage or because all of a sudden
they had a reservation which they'd forgotten they'd
made. Acting had been something she'd become very
good at over the years.

In an attempt to appear normal to the hotel employee,
Bailey had whispered to her that she couldn't tell her
husband she'd booked a Jacuzzi room, he'd never have
gone for it. But by embarrassing him, he couldn't back
out of paying for it. The hotel clerk appeared to accept
the excuse but continued to look at them strangely. It
hadn't really dawned on Bailey until then how disheveled
they must look. Then Guy told the woman they had no
bags. The fact that she gave them a list of all the shops
downtown and even a few coupons for discounts was a
broad hint that they weren't looking their best. Bailey
hated the feeling of being judged like when she was a
kid living on the streets, always feeling like she didn't
belong or wasn't good enough. Biting her tongue she gave
an abrupt nod.

The woman would certainly tell all her friends about
the scraggly looking couple that showed up at one of the
swankiest hotels in Edmonton. Bailey just hoped she'd
never have to see her again, a feeling that was probably
mutual.

Once they entered the luxurious room, they both were
drawn to the view out the window; from twenty floors
up, they had a spectacular view of the river valley and
the Hotel McDonald.

"Okay, shower and get out."

Guy gaped at her and spluttered, "W-what?"

"I'm getting in that hot tub." At his look of interest,
she qualified, "Alone. You'll go shopping for some clothes
and then I'll go. Hmmm. I guess you'll have to come

along since you'll be paying for those too. Now go." She made a pinching motion at the end of her nose.

"Are you suggesting I smell?"

Her eyelids opened and closed as she twisted her head away as though there was a horrid stench coming from him.

He tossed a pillow at her. "I wouldn't be talking too loud there, missy. Pew, Pew, Pew."

She chucked the pillow back at him. "Go, dammit."

"Bossy woman. I happen to be paying for this place," he grumbled but headed into the bathroom.

She waited for him to get in the shower before she put a few inches of water in the hot tub. Stripping off her shirt, she washed quickly, aware that at any moment he could come out. Finishing up, she drained the tub and sat on the bed flipping through TV stations. She was watching the shopping channel when he finished.

Rubbing his hair with a towel, he strode into the room and glanced at the television. "How long do I have to be gone?"

"An hour and a half. Two, if you want to be a gentleman." He pulled on his t-shirt grimacing as he did. She tried not to notice how it stretched taut over his well-muscled chest that had just enough hair to let her fingers play in. Her breath hitched as she stared hard at the television.

"I'll meet you right here. Okay?"

"Of course." She shoved him out of the room, leaving him in the hallway. She checked her watch and waited five minutes, then opened the door and peeked out, checking both directions. Seeing no one, she quickly made her way to the elevator. Once on the ground floor, her steps quickened as she left the hotel, keeping a watchful eye out for Guy. Sprinting across the street, she entered the building that she hoped held answers.

The library was large and spread out. What she needed was situated in the far back corner. Sitting at a computer, she glanced around before plugging in the flash drive. She rifled through folders, cognizant her time was limited. Associates—she clicked on it. All the files were listed by initials. It didn't look right so she got out of there. Aperture—no idea what that even meant. Cabin— opening that file, she glanced at all the subfolders. None of the initials made sense. Choosing at random, she started to open them. It wasn't until she noticed there were two similar folders—D. Z. and Do. Z.—that a strange feeling washed over her. Clicking on D.Z., she started opening files.

Doug Zajic

– Paying $12,000.00 per month – cabin fees.

That was all it said, except for the number 345 in the top right corner. Not having a clue what any of it meant, she closed it and opened the other file – Do. Z.

Donna Zajic

– Pay out $8,000.00 per month – cabin fees

There was nothing else. *People renting the place? A little pricey.* Closing out those files, she saw one labeled, My Legacy. She clicked on it. Several subfolders listed by initials were listed in alphabetical order. She clicked on the D. Z. file—it came up as weird letters and shapes. She tried the Do. Z. file—same thing. It looked like they were ruined or something. She wondered if carrying them around in her pocket had done that. *Crap!*

She clicked on other files at random, most displayed shapes similar to hieroglyphics or had one readable line containing an amount and a cabin fee. Lund had done well with that little place in northern B.C. But it was all very confusing. *Why did I need to get this, Mom? Is this one of our tail chases?*

At the age of twelve that's what Bailey had dubbed their sudden moves – tail chases. There had never seemed any rhyme or reason to when or why they'd relocate. They'd just up and leave, sometimes ending back where they'd started like a dog chasing his tail, going round and round but not going anywhere at all.

When she found yet another scrambled file, she banged on the desk, flinching at the loud sound. She glanced around and was relieved to see that no one was watching her. She propped her elbows on the chair arms and dug her fingers into the sides of her head as she tried to make sense of it all.

A cabin… where her mom had hidden a picture and her favorite stuffed toy. Was that the only reason she had needed to go there? It didn't make sense. None of it did but she couldn't shake the thought that she might not be who she'd believed she was all those years. She may not have even belonged to the woman who raised her and she may actually have relatives, people who were looking for her, wanted her.

Her nostrils flared as she struggled to block the sob that threatened to rip through her chest. Closing her eyes tightly, squeezing her ribs firmly with her arms and taking several deep breaths were enough to impede the flood this time. She felt like she was being split in two. *When will it make sense?*

Frustrated at not finding what she wanted, she closed all the files and folders. Maybe the internet would give her some answers. Having no idea how to find what she was looking for, she typed into the search engine—newspapers from twenty-nine years ago.

28

Guy hid behind the bookshelves, watching Bailey. Seeing her so distressed was almost enough to make him rush to her aid. That, however, was not going to help him figure out what was going on. Instead, he made his way to another computer desk, keeping an eye on her from behind the high walls of the cubby. He had to find out what she was up to and why she felt the need to ditch him. In fifteen minutes, all he learned was she was fidgety. Every few minutes she would shift—she'd lean forward and then back, sit up and then slouch, put her leg under her and then set both feet flat on the floor. No matter what she did though, her shoulders started sagging more and more. She was fighting the exhaustion that had to be dragging her down. He knew he was feeling it. Her elbow soon found the desk and her chin found her hand. After the third time of her head bobbing sideways and then jerking to keep herself upright, she finally gave up and left.

Tempted to follow her and make sure she was okay, he first needed to see what she'd been doing. He sat down at her computer. The search bar showed she'd been trying to find some newspapers from a long time ago, twenty-nine years to be exact. She didn't seem to know what she was doing, though he conceded that being overly tired might have played a part in it. Not wanting to spend too much time as he wasn't sure she'd make it back alone, he was about to log off when he noticed the jump drive sticking out of the computer. He quickly scanned the folders on it. Clicking on several of them, he discovered they were encrypted. Intuition told him this had been what she'd been trying to look at.

There were some answers there but first he had to check on Bailey. He logged off, took out the USB drive and hurried out the door, following Bailey back to the room. He made sure he remained far enough behind to keep an eye on her without being detected himself. At the hotel, he gave her ten minutes to play out her hot tub ruse before he showed up.

Entering the room, he realized immediately he hadn't needed to wait. She was zonked out, lying across the bed fully clothed. Being a gentleman warred with the knowledge she would be pissed. It was going to get him in trouble but he knew she would be much more comfortable out of her clothes. He unzipped her pants, the slight tremor in his hands surprising him as he slid the jeans down her long, slim legs. Tossing them aside, he reached for the hem of her shirt and slid it up slowly, trying not to jar or awaken her—or stare at the soft smooth skin he was uncovering. He tried to keep his eyes averted or at least his mind but it was a losing battle. His hands shook and his pulse pounded as he the edge of the bedspread over her. It was difficult not to notice the sexy cut of her underwear nor the fact that it wasn't silk, something he felt she should have been wearing all her life. Guilt was eating at him. He knew he wasn't responsible for her being taken, yet he had been able to live in luxury while she hadn't. Even though she'd been the one on the streets, everything about her reminded him that those were really his roots. They weren't really meant to be hers.

With a last glance at her, he slipped into the hallway and called Graham.

"Hey, good to hear from you. Where are you?"

"Edmonton. Is Stanson done with that sketch?"

"Yup. Check your email. Since I hadn't heard from you, in twenty some hours, I went ahead and ran the sketch. No hits yet, so it might not be all that accurate. What else have you got?"

Guy quickly ran through all that had occurred since they'd last talked.

"Holy Christ, man. This isn't fun and games any more. Time to bring in the police."

Guy's hand scrubbed down over his face. He shook his head, trying to erase the tiredness wrapping around him like a weighted cloak. "I know but…"

"I know you don't know what to tell them right? Let me call Bean."

"He's still on the police force?"

"He might be old but he's a good detective. I'll fill him in and see what he wants to do."

He wasn't the person Guy would have chosen but he was good friends with Graham's family. Detective Holstein felt he owed them for Graham's dad having saved his life a couple of times. "Have him call me before he includes anyone else in this circus. I don't know who I can trust."

"Will do. Check the email. Keep in touch every couple of hours. Okay?"

"Yeah. I've got something else I have to do right now. I'll call you later." Clicking off the phone, he wasn't sure why he hadn't shared the jump drive. Holding it tightly in his hand, he crossed the street and entered the library.

An hour later, he was yawning so much that he felt like his face was permanently morphing and he still couldn't figure out how the guy had encrypted the data. None of it made sense. He was about to go back and get some sleep when a moment of clarity hit him. Within ten minutes, he'd broken the code. Flipping through files, his eyes widened. There were very interesting and incredibly damning information. A yawn caught him off-guard, almost splitting his face. And as always seemed to happen, where one yawn went, several seemed to follow. He realized he wouldn't be able to get through all the folders so he took to copying and pasting, emailing several for Graham to look over along with how to break the code, knowing full well Graham probably would have gotten in faster than he had. He then sent all the ones he'd read and reviewed in an email to himself just in case.

If it was all true which he feared it was, many people were going to be embarrassed, some charged and maybe even killed if this information fell into certain hands. The one thing it didn't do, however, was tell him how this all tied in with Bailey.

As he sent the last email to Graham, he realized he hadn't looked over the police sketch of his suspect. As he scrolled through the five he'd received in his email, he picked out what he thought was the right picture and where he needed to make changes. He cc'd Graham to start searching when he got the new sketch.

It was time for bed. He'd put it off too long but he had one more phone call to make. After leaving a message for Graham to find him one more piece of information, he propped his elbows on the desk and rested his chin on his palm. He just needed to close his eyes for a moment...

"Excuse me. Excuse me." Someone's hand was on his shoulder, shaking him. Annoyed but still in a groggy state of sleep, he jerked away.

"Excuse me!"

He snapped upright as the words were hissed in his ear. A middle-aged woman holding a book like she knew how to swing it was staring at him in disgust. Heat instantly infused his face.

"No sleeping here."

"I'm sorry. I was…"

"Just get out. We don't allow bums in here."

What? Guy shook his head but stood up and moved away from the crazy lady and headed outside. He placed his hands on his back and arched backwards. His spine realigned itself with a ddrrrrr-ddrrr sound. As he straightened, a woman and a man walked by, smiled at him indulgently and slipped something into his hand. Confused, he watched them leave and then looked down. They'd given him a five-dollar bill. He looked at them and then back at his hand. His attention soon slid past and was snagged by the dirt and grime ground into his jeans. He burst out laughing. He hadn't gone shopping and it was now a must. People were mistaking him for a homeless guy or someone really down on his luck. He took a deep breath in, his nose wrinkling as he did so. His clothes even smelled like one. No time like the present to buy some new pants and shirts, if they'd let him in the store.

29

"Hello." Bailey managed to garble out that greeting as she pressed the cell phone to her ear and snuggled back down under the blankets.

"Uh huh... yeah... sure... yeah... bye." She clicked her phone off, clasped it in her hand and let herself drift again. When she was just on the verge of sleep, the conversation she'd just had floated through her head.

"Hello, Bailey. It's Mr. O'Sullivan from CBC. How are you today?"

"We just wanted to confirm that you'll be here this Friday, 10:00 a.m. at our office?"

"Will you need to be picked up at the airport?"

"If you send us your itinerary, I'll make sure a car is there to pick you up."

She shot upright, her mouth hanging open. "Oh, my God. What did I just do?" Swearing, she jumped out of bed and was about to go flying into the bathroom when her awareness expanded to take in where she was and what was going on.

"Good morning." Guy waved at her from the hot tub. "I take it that phone call wasn't good?"

She whirled around, becoming instantly aware she was only wearing a bra and panties but it was nothing more than a fleeting thought as the impact of the conversation hit her full force. She slammed her hands onto her hips. "It's the phone call I've been waiting for. But am I ready for it? No, I'm half asleep. Why? Because I've been traipsing all over the place, trying to find out who I am. Not because I'm lost but because some nut job thinks I am."

"You're not really a morning person, are you?"

"What?" She marched to the edge of the tub. "Listen. I've had just about all I can take from you and this BS you've been spouting. That call was my real life. They want me on Friday of this week. Am I going to make it? Jeez, I don't know. Let me see it's now… What's today?" Looking down, she realized she still had her phone in her hand. She looked at the date and time.

"Great. This is just great." She walked across the room and back. "I have four days to fly back to Vancouver, pack my apartment, fly to Toronto and be ready to start my new job." She shrugged and made an exaggerated face about how that wasn't impossible. Her eyes zeroed in on him. "And who do I have to thank for this?"

Walking over to the curtains, she flung them open. *My life's gone to hell and nobody asked me what I wanted.* She pressed her hand to her chest as her churning emotions weren't sure which direction they were going to go—laugh until she peed, cry until she peed, or punch the daylights out of anyone or anything that got in her way.

"You have a new job?"

She felt like someone had just stuck a pin in her. She dropped down into a chair as all her energy fizzled out.

"Yeah." *I'm supposed to have my own TV show. Or at least that was the plan.* She'd worked so hard at not only being a top interior designer but also at getting this show. Ironically, she hadn't known how she would tell her mom about it. Now she didn't have to worry. The pain of that was too much to think about. She gazed out the window to stare at the blue sky and skyscrapers.

"Want to tell me about it?"

She jumped as she realized he was right beside her. She turned to address him, only he was right there, all of him. Her heart started to thump wildly as her gaze tracked the lone trail of a water droplet coursing slowly down his well muscled chest over a flat stomach, to be absorbed in a thick, white terry cloth towel.

"Hmmm."

"Care to do something about that?"

"Huh?" she said, absently. Her hand slipped up to rest against her throat.

He bent down in front of her, catching her gaze. Her eyes opened wide as she met the spark of interest in his.

"Oh, no. No." She moved to stand behind a chair.

"Hey, I'm not the one who started this."

"Started what?"

"Running around naked."

"I'm not naked, dammit. You're the one who stripped me." She glared at him.

"Excuse me all to hell."

"Besides you're the one who's just hot out of a steaming bath, dripping water all over, looking like you stepped out of *Playgirl.*"

"Read that a lot, do you?"

She thrust her nose in the air and sailed past him. "I'm going for a shower. You do whatever you need to do."

She almost made it but his hand snapped out at the last second, grabbing her forearm. He pulled her close.

The steam from the two of them would have fogged her glasses, had she been wearing any. This wasn't a good idea for either of them, yet she didn't seem to be able to fight it. His lips gently touched hers before pulling back. Her heart galloped as she blinked several times to bring the room back into focus. It took her a few moments to realize she was free.

"This conversation isn't over." He looked at her pointedly, his nostrils flaring slightly. His pupils were large and black and revealing emotions she wasn't prepared to handle. Dazed, she made her way into the bathroom, closed the door and fell against it. She gulped in air.

He knocked.

Her heart leapt into her throat. She spun around and braced her hands against the door, not sure if it was to keep herself upright or to keep him out. "What?"

"I thought you could use this."

She opened the door just enough to see what he was talking about. Two white bags emblazoned with an upscale company logo dangled from the end of his fingers. She snatched them, closing and locking the door before she did something crazy like invite him in. She proceeded to open the packages and immediately burst into tears. Rarely had anyone ever purchased anything for her and no one ever bought her clothes before. She flipped on the shower, stripped and climbed in, hoping he couldn't hear her blubbering.

Trust. Where does that come from? What makes one person trust another? Is it the way they talk? The things they do? Who they help? She wasn't any good at any of that. Her mom had taught her well, never to trust anyone. *I'm alone. Damn you. I'm alone.*

Leaning her arms against the wall, she let the water pound her as the tears flowed. She didn't know what to do now. Should she run or stand and fight? She wasn't even sure what she was fighting for anymore; too much didn't make sense. She wondered just how much of what her mom had told her was a lie. *I'm not who you told me I am. The question is did you steal me?* The tears flowed unheeded down her cheeks.

Thirty minutes later, absolutely drained of energy, she dressed and returned to the room. Guy was sitting at the table by the window reading the morning paper, drinking from a mug.

"I made some coffee. Help yourself."

Grabbing a cup and filling it gave her the moment she needed to clear her mind. She sat opposite him. "I'm sorry."

He carefully closed the newspaper and set it down before meeting her gaze. She tried not to flinch nor look away but the compelling blue of his eyes offered her something she'd never experienced before: understanding. "Tell me about your job."

"I…" Sipping her coffee, she sat back. "I've been offered a job as an interior decorator. It's what I've been doing for a while. It's really all I know. I accepted the job. It's good money. I said no a few years ago and that almost killed me." She waved her hand at the inquiring expression in his eyes. "Long story. Anyway I almost declined again for the same reason. But I couldn't this time. I want it but…"

She stared out the window. *But life has a funny way of happening.*

"But?"

She shrugged. "I guess I won't take it now."

"Why not? You just said you wanted it." He leaned forward.

No one had ever asked her what she wanted or why. She'd always been told what she needed or didn't need.

"My mom." He sat there looking as though he was genuinely interested, and that was all she needed to talk.

"She had this weird set of rules. Don't lean on anyone. Don't expect others to do for you. Don't get your picture in the media. Don't talk to strangers. Don't move east. Clean up after yourself, you're not a princess." Heat crawled up her face as she realized all that had spilled out of her mouth. "She didn't want me to take this job."

"Why not move east?"

She shrugged.

"We need to talk about everything. Are you ready to hear all that I have to tell you? And to answer some questions?"

She wasn't sure. She knew she was tired, tired of running, of being alone, of having nothing that was truly hers. She needed to know who she was. *Am I ready? No.*

"Yeah. Where do you want to start?"

"Tell me about your mom."

"I thought you said she wasn't my mom?"

He sighed heavily.

"All right. My mom, or should I say, the woman I thought was my mother."

His steady gaze never wavered.

"I don't know what to say. She was the constant in my life. We moved a lot. She was paranoid about everything. I assumed for a long time that it was just being a parent. But other parents weren't like her. She'd pick me up at school in the middle of the day and I'd never see it again. Sometimes we'd leave in the middle of the night." She stood and went over to her bed, flipped back the covers and pulled out the tattered Miss Piggy.

"I cried for a month when I thought I'd lost her. My mom told me to get used to it. I'd lose lots in my life. Why? Why did I have to give up everything?" Her voice became thick with emotion. She hugged the doll to her chest. "There were only two things I ever asked for in my life—this," she held up her doll, "and a home. You know I was such a good kid. I did everything she ever asked of me. I was loyal to a fault. I worked every scheme. Everything she wanted. And what the hell did I get in return?" She started to pace.

"What do you mean by schemes?"

"Oh my god. My mom was a master at getting what she wanted from people. I'd play nice to old men and they'd give me money."

His hand fisted around the cup. "What does 'playing nice' mean?"

She waved it off but wouldn't look at him. Some things weren't meant for sharing. "Nothing. Enough that they'd smile at me and give me money. I was darn cute ya know." She knew that joke had fallen short when he didn't even blink.

"Look, I've come to realize my childhood was maybe not the norm but it really wasn't that bad." Unaware of what she was doing, she started slamming her right fist into her left hand as she paced. "My mom fed me. Clothed me. Housed me. Okay not always but…"

"If she's not my mom, how did I end up with her? Where would she have gotten me? It's not like you can pull off the side of the road and dial a baby." Her eyes narrowed as she considered the possibilities. "I don't even know where to start. I know nothing about my mom— not where she was born. Grew up. Relations. Nothing. So how…?"

"Your mom came into existence in 1983."

She whirled around to stare at Guy. "She was born in 1952."

"That may be true but we can't find any information on a Donna Saunders prior to July 1983."

"And you think that has something to do with me, right? But how could you make that leap? If I disappeared in February, what happened until July? And how did I end up with her? In Alberta? You want me to go along with your half-baked ideas. What else do you need to share with me?"

It was his turn to look away. He seemed awfully focused on the view outside the hotel. Slowly he turned to face her. "Sit down."

She pursed her lips.

"Please."

Detecting his serious tone tinged with reluctant displeasure and genuine sadness, she complied. He reached into his pocket and with his hand closed, he extended his arm across the table.

"I think this is yours."

She placed her palm under his. He dropped something into hers. She knew even before she looked what he'd given her. "How the hell did you get this? You stole it out of my pants. What do you think you're doing snooping through my stuff? Dammit. I knew I couldn't trust you. My mother was right, don't put faith in anyone." She stood and was about to storm off when he spoke.

Very quietly he said, "You left the flash drive at the library last night when you were supposed to be in this hot tub relaxing."

She dropped into her seat, heat flooding her neck and face. "I…"

He put up his hand. "Don't. Just let me tell you what I found on it."

"I checked it out but it was all in a foreign language or something. Or it's wrecked, I think."

"No, it's encrypted."

"Spy stuff?"

He shrugged. "Encryption is pretty common, actually. And I was able to crack the code."

A tingling sensation cruised through her body. "Oh my God. Really? This is so cool. Like you really had to figure out the code and then apply it to get it to unscramble."

"Yeah, more or less. Look, here's what I found. Your friend Mr. Lund was into a lot of illegal activities."

"What?"

"We'll discuss the details later when we have more time. He has files on anyone he was in contact with. And it seems he collected dirt on a lot of important people as well. There are quite a few he could have had locked away."

"My mom. What did he have on my mom?"

"That's the funny thing. There was nothing on a Donna Saunders but—"

She sat forward in her chair. "But..." She gestured for more information.

"But there was information regarding a Donna Zajic."

"I saw that but I've never heard of her."

"She was born January 5th, 1952."

Bailey gasped. "No. No." *Jesus, she even used a fake name. So who the HELL am I?*

Jumping out of her chair, she sailed to the door but before she could open it, a tanned, nicely muscled forearm inserted itself under her nose and Guy's hand landed beside hers, effectively keeping her from opening it.

She held herself rigid for several seconds but when he made no move, no sound, she gave in. It was like pulling the plug on the tub; all the energy was sucked out of her. Lethargy invaded her body and her mind. She just didn't give a damn anymore. Couldn't take anymore. Giving in, she rested her forehead on his arm. Taking several deep breaths, she let go. She tried to tell herself the emotions rolling over her were nothing more than a fresh, clean scent akin to aromatherapy, but she knew in her heart of hearts it was the healthy male redolence that confidently surrounded her without smothering. She tried to tamp down the feelings but she was powerless to stop the sentimental, secure warmth that enveloped her as two strong arms wrapped around her.

For the first time in her life, she knew she was safe.

30

"What do you have for me, Graham?" Guy shoved his hand through his hair as he watched the sun wink at him over the top of the high rises. A cool wind whipped around him as he made his way around Churchill Square, careful to ensure no one was within listening range of him.

"Not as much as I'd like." There was the sound of clicking keys on a keyboard. "Donna Zajic married to Doug Zajic, disappeared June 30th, 1983. Never heard from or seen again. There was speculation that her husband killed her but it was never proven because they never found her body. There were allegations of abuse but all charges were dropped. Another thought is someone helped her vanish. I talked with the police chief who was in charge back then; he said they had a hunch someone hid her and then set her up with a new life, but they could never prove it. He said Doug Zajic was a politician through and through. He was as plastic and authentic as a Ken doll."

Guy chuckled. "Police Chief, a good guy?"

"Yeah. Dedicated and a straight shooter. Liked him. Retired now. Enjoying the simple life. At least so he said but he sure was willing to do some leg work for me, if I need it. He was mad as hell the case had never been solved. He was sure Zajic was dirty but could never make anything stick. He's says it's not too late to take him down. I didn't have the heart to tell him Doug Zajic died several years ago in a hit and run."

"So we've got birthdates that match. First names that match. There's a good chance our Donna Saunders was Donna Zajic. And it looks like Mr. Lund, an esteemed lawyer with some very dark secrets of his own, might have been her accomplice."

"Yeah. I went through some of his files." He whistled, long and low. "Looks like he was blackmailing a good number of people. He was blackmailing Doug Zajic and maybe Donna as well. I haven't gotten through them all. I'll let you know what I find."

Guy shook his head as he listened.

"The guy is as dishonest as the devil's disciple. Oh crap! Guy, that Mr. Lund is in the hospital."

"Did someone he screwed over exact revenge?"

"No, hang on. It sounds like natural causes, heart attack. I was just googling his name to see what I could find and here is an article written… just a sec… Sunday, April 26th."

"That's the same day that Bailey was there. Shit."

"Are you saying she might have had something to do with it?"

"You do the math. He goes into cardiac arrest some time either while she's been there or sometime after. She just happens to have some confidential information that I'm sure he would have gone to his grave protecting." He placed his left hand over his stomach as acid poured into his gut. He sat on the cement bleachers and hung his head. "Now what?"

"Don't know, man. Buddy, this is the biggest doo-doo you've ever landed in, eh? 'Ol boy, you sure know how to pick 'em," Graham said, in his charming but imperfect old-boy English accent.

Guy smiled. "Thanks, man. Can always count on you to find the good in it. How about my sketch guy? Any leads? I'm getting nervous."

"Check your email. Stanson sent you three revised sketches. I've already got them running through the police files of known criminals. Hoping we'll get a hit. Detective Bean was more than happy to take this on. He wants that mug shot as soon as we get it done."

"You want to know who it was before you hand it over to him. Right?"

"Of course. Bean wouldn't have any problem using you as bait to catch this guy. And we'll assume he's not a very nice man, so I'd rather you knew who was chasing you before I give Bean the opportunity to nail him."

Several people were crowding the Square. Most seemed to be cutting across the cement park, while others had come to loiter. A few appeared a little too interested in what he was doing. "Gotta go, Graham. Keep me in the loop."

"You keep your neck out of the noose."

"Gotcha." Guy strode down the street when less than a block from the hotel the hair on the back of his neck suddenly bristled. He thrust his hands in the pockets of his leather jacket and hunched his shoulders while he casually looked around. The streets were busier now that it was afternoon. He'd been there longer than he'd planned. Walking past the Westin Hotel, he headed west along Jasper Avenue. There didn't seem to be anyone following him but he couldn't shake that sense of unease.

Turning down 101st, he followed it to 102 Ave. When he got to 100th Street he raced across the middle of the road, ignoring cars honking and tires screeching. When he reached the opposite side, he noticed someone retreating into the shadows of the other building. It couldn't have been a coincidence. Not waiting to see who it was, he raced down the street, turning before the hotel and coming in from the other side. As he entered the lobby he headed for the escalator, taking it up one flight. Then he climbed the stairs another two flights. Once he was on the fourth floor he took the elevator to the 20th. He knocked gently before putting his card in and opened it.

"Bailey, it's me."

Silence. The table was still covered with the morning paper he'd been reading. The hot tub was drained. He peeked into the bathroom; Bailey's dirty clothes, still scattered on the floor, were the only sign of her. His gut tightened. He checked out the room more closely, hoping for a note or a clue as to where she'd gone. On the pillow of his unmade bed as they'd asked for no housekeeping, there was a folded piece of paper which blended with the white pillowcase.

Opening it he read, *'Some things, I have to figure out on my own. Bailey'*.

Swearing, he crumpled the paper in his hand and threw it. It landed gently against the other bed, right beside Miss Piggy. Reaching down, he picked up the ugly toy. Her hair was tangled and twisted so badly, she looked as if she had a nest on her head. He touched the deformed nose that resembled a bird's beak. Smiling, he clutched it between his hands. He pressed more firmly. There was something inside her. She was lumpy and misshapen but when he pressed hard enough, he could feel a long, hard object. Flipping her over, he dug his fingers along the seam in the back of her head and pulled. The old tattered material ripped, not as neatly along the seam as he would have hoped but across the back. After rooting around for a few seconds, he grabbed onto something. It took only a moment to identify it even before he saw it. The hum of excitement started to course through him.

His eyes widened as they lit upon the cassette. If it had survived the intervening years, he knew it had to hold valuable information. He called Graham.

"You won't believe what I found. A cassette tape."

"Jolly happy for you, 'ol boy."

Guy rolled his eyes. "I mean I found a tape that I think is related to this whole shmoz." He filled Graham in on where he'd discovered it. "So my question now is where do I find a cassette player? Do they even make them anymore?"

"Hmmm, good question. I think so but they're not very popular. Find a second-hand store or go to a garage sale."

"Right! Like I've got time to hunt down garage sales. Any news on your end?"

"No, ran into a bit of a glitch with my computer. I think someone almost detected me accessing the police files. I must have been sloppy. Won't happen again. I should have something for you by early tomorrow. What are you up to now? How's your roomy?"

Guy looked around the messy but empty room. "Gone. I'm not sure where. Oh, and I think our guy has found me. I'd appreciate it if you could send Bean in this direction."

"Got ya. No problem. Now get out of there."

Guy didn't need to be told twice. A chill pressed itself between his shoulder blades. He opened the door and peered in both directions. Just as he took a step, a man got off the elevator. Their eyes connected. It was unmistakably the man who had played smash up derby with them the day before. Guy didn't wait but dashed the other way, heading for the exit. With his hand on the railing, he was able to slide down, barely touching any steps. The door echoed above him. His assailant was coming after him. Ripping down five flights, he opened the door and ran the long hallway to the other end. He raced down several more flights. At ground level he headed out the door to the parking garage. The SUV stood out like a train wreck with its bashed-in side. Digging in his pocket, he pulled out the keys. But he couldn't leave Bailey to deal with this nut by herself. He headed back into the hotel, carefully scouting the area. There was no sign of his follower. He dashed to the desk.

A young, smartly dressed man smiled at him as though it was perfectly ordinary to see a mad man run across the lobby. Guy described Bailey to him and asked if he'd seen her. No; but he'd check to see if anyone ordered a cab. Guy was breathing hard, his nerves on fire by the time he returned. Yes, she'd ordered a Yellow Cab. No, he didn't know where she was going. Guy spun around intent on leaving, only to stop suddenly. His 'friend' was standing at the elevators. The way his eyes opened wide, Guy was sure he'd recognized him at the same time. He ran for the front door and shot onto the street. He had no real plan; he just knew he didn't want to get any innocent people in the crosshairs. And there was no way he could fill out a police report, accusing this man of attempted murder. Did he have proof? No. He ran south. Half a block later he was at Jasper, a main avenue. He headed east. When he could, he entered stores through one door and then zipped out through another, onto an adjacent or parallel street. He took side streets and back alleys. Twenty-five minutes later, he made his way back to the parking garage at the Westin Hotel but not before he'd hidden in doorways, peeked around structures and then snuck his way back to get his vehicle.

He started it and then raced out of the parkade, not sure where the guy was hiding nor where he might pop out. Shooting out on to 101 Street, Guy headed north. Grabbing his cell phone, he dialed the cab company. The guy was nice enough to tell him that no, he couldn't give him the location of his friend. Frustrated at being unable to convey the seriousness of the situation, he jammed his phone into his pants pocket, then thumped his fist on the dash.

"Temper, temper."

Jerking in surprise, the vehicle swerved as his hands tightened on the wheel and his foot slammed on the brakes. Horns honked and several people flipped him the bird as they maneuvered around him. As he looked in his rearview mirror, a pair of black eyes stared back at him above the barrel of a gun.

31

"Drive." The words were softly spoken but there was no denying the steel woven within his tone.

Easing forward, Guy drove to the end of the block. He stared up at the CN Tower which loomed over him.

"Don't even think of ramming that building. It'll be the last thing you ever do." The muzzle of the gun was jammed into Guy's head right behind his right ear. "I want the girl."

He was tempted to say 'what girl?' but didn't think the guy had too much patience left, not considering his dark, angry expression. Breathing deeply to calm himself, he flipped on the signal and turned left onto 104th Ave. Acting like he had some place specific to go, he maneuvered through the downtown traffic.

"What do you want with her?"

"Come now, Mr. Turner. You're the one who found the woman. If it hadn't been for you, I would have continued to believe that she'd died in that plane crash with my sister."

"I'm curious how you know my name."

"You'd be amazed what I know about you. You'd be amazed by what I know, period."

Guy's mind was on rapid-fire. The guy did have good connections. Thoughts were swirling like a tornado, the vortex ripping apart all the flickering recollections he was trying so desperately to pull together into something that made sense.

"Your sister died?"

"A long time ago. And now I can tie up the final loose end so she can rest in peace."

"So your sister's the one who stole Bailey." He glanced into the rearview mirror, locking onto the hard black glint of his eyes. They were akin to looking into a coal mine. The message was clear. His days were numbered.

The man snapped forward, clamping his hand onto Guy's shoulder. "She was doing right by that baby. My sister was a good woman." He emphasized his last statement by squeezing with the force of a vice.

Guy tried not to wince but struggled with it when his fingers tingled and then went numb.

"I have more strength in this hand than you do in your entire body. Care to test that?"

The man looked like he'd just stepped out of a body-building gym. Though the gray locks tinting his black hair belied his age, he was definitely in much better shape than most men half his age. Gritting his teeth, Guy stiffly shook his head.

The man chuckled and leaned back, though he kept the gun pointed at Guy's head. "We found a loving couple who would have been good to her."

"And they paid you a lot of money."

He laughed maniacally like it was the best joke he'd

ever heard and causing a shiver to run up Guy's spine. "Ah, but that was the whole point of it. To get rich."

Guy turned right onto 109th St. He still had no clear destination but a few ideas were beginning to surface. Go where it's busy.

"So, how many infants did you borrow?"

"Borrow, I like that. Funny man. Funny." He leaned forward. "We had something good going until that baby messed up everything. Too much publicity. Had to sit tight for a long time. Then when we do move the squalling infant, the damn plane crashes. Go figure. We should have held her for ransom."

"Where was she going?"

"What?"

"Where would you have sent Bailey? Where was the family she was supposed to go to?"

"Diamonds. A girl's best friend you know. Let's just say she'd love surfing and have a nice tan now."

"I don't understand."

"You're not meant to. Enough with the nice chat. You know all you're gonna know. Where is she?"

Guy stopped at a red light. He glanced toward a large mall situated off to his right. There was something there but he just couldn't figure out how it would help him. The tip of the gun was shoved into soft tissue of his neck. He lifted his hands in surrender.

"I'm headed there. Just hold on a minute."

He eased forward as the light changed to green. His eyes darted from left to right and back again, desperately searching for a way to escape. Approaching the north end of 109th, he realized it ended in a T intersection and he would have to turn. This may be his only chance. He slowed making sure there was no one ahead of him at the intersection. Then he slammed the gas pedal. They surged forward, throwing them both back against the seats and then just as quickly he hit the brakes. He floored the vehicle once more as he opened the door, hit the lock button and jumped out. It all happened in the blink of an eye. He tucked as he flew out of the SUV and landed hard on his shoulder. He flipped onto his back into the screeching oncoming traffic. Even though his first instinct was to nurse his injuries, there was no time; instead, he leapt to his feet and trotted with a limp and a dangling right arm across the street of honking vehicles and astonished drivers toward Kingsway Mall.

Too concerned that 911 would trace him, he dialed 411 instead for the non-emergency number at the Edmonton Police Department, where he left a brief message about the accident. Then he hit speed dial.

"Graham. Graham."

"You've reached the man. Leave me a message."

"Dammit. I need you to get Detective Bean. He can catch the guy at the corner of 109th St. and Queen Elizabeth Ave. He's locked in a smashed SUV with another car sticking out of it. Call me."

He entered a store that in turn led into the mall, cutting through clothing racks, dodging around the perfume counter, coughing as he did so and finally shot into the main part of the busy building. The odd looks he was getting piqued his curiosity but it was the throbbing in his hand that forced him to stop long enough to look down. Blood dripped off the tip of his index finger. The trail behind him was a perfect dotted path leading right to him.

Crap. Nothing like giving him a map to follow.

Zipping into a pharmacy, he lifted a box of bandages and quickly wrapped the scrapes on his wrist and hands as he continued to race through the long building through a serpentine hallway. A large department store would have hidden him better but would also have slowed him and right now he wanted distance between them. He glanced over his shoulder to spot anyone in pursuit but the crowds were thick and as swiftly as he parted the way, it closed up behind him. He rocketed out a side entrance. Hardly believing his luck, he spied a row of taxis. He jumped into the first one.

"Westin Hotel."

"All right sir." The driver flipped his meter, adjusted his mirror and cautiously pulled out.

"I'm in a hurry." Guy looked out both side windows and then the one behind him, the sound of sirens growing in the distance. The cabbie pulled into an intersection, signaling to turn left. Guy leaned forward as the sound grew louder and more insistent. An ambulance flew past with lights flashing.

He sat back, turning to the side. The cab meandered down the street, keeping up with traffic.

"What will it cost me for you to floor it? I need to get there now!" He pulled out his wallet and leaned forward, showing him two twenties. The driver sped up a bit. Guy took out another twenty. He was slammed back against the seat as the cabbie hit the gas, swerving in and out of traffic.

"Without getting a ticket." The cabbie slowed marginally but Guy couldn't complain when they pulled up outside his hotel in record time.

Paying him and then adding a twenty to get him to wait, Guy climbed out and carefully took full stock of the area. There didn't seem to be any strangers interested in him. Not sticking around, he raced into the hotel, up the escalator and took the elevator to the 20th floor. He shoved the card in the lock and flew into the room, slamming the door behind him. He'd barely gotten it closed when he found himself spun around, punched in the gut and flattened on the floor. Flipping quickly, he was ready to retaliate when he realized who his assailant was at the same time she did.

Her eyes wide, her breathing hard, she had her fist in a position to give him a short but quick and he was very sure, effective punch to his nose or throat. Rolling away from her he jumped to his feet. "Hi, honey, couldn't find anyone else to kick the crap out of?"

32

Bailey spun on her heel and grabbed a backpack she'd picked up to hold her meager belongings. "By the way, thanks for the clothes." She didn't bother to look at the torn knee and filthy pants. They looked nothing like the new duds he'd bought her less than ten hours before.

"I forgot to say that this morning. I appreciate what you did for me." She couldn't believe he'd not only bought her jeans and shirts, but that he'd bought clothing that had fit her—and had purchased not one set but two. Since she'd just returned to the room after a terrifying escape through the downtown core, she hadn't had a chance to change. Actually, she'd planned to be gone before he came back. Some ugly people knew her mom and believed she owed them, even twenty years later. Unfortunately, one woman named Anna Marie that Bailey had hoped to find was gone had either moved or was deceased; her neighbors had never heard of her. Bailey stuffed her things into the backpack before slinging it over her shoulder.

As she reached for the door, she was snapped back to the present when his hand grabbed on to her forearm.

"Where are you going?"

"Where I need to." She tried to grasp the door handle but stopped when she realized he hadn't let go. Facing him, she crossed her arms over her chest. "Look, I appreciate what you've done." A frown marred her brow as she considered that. If he hadn't found her, she wouldn't be in the mess she was now in. She gave him a half-hearted smile. "I need to do this on my own. I'll figure out what's going on. When the time is right, I'll get hold of you and we'll see about meeting the relatives. That really was what your job was supposed to be, right?"

She'd had plenty of time over the last six hours to think about this crazy relationship. The guy was in over his head. Yes, he'd been helpful in getting them vehicles and places to hide but he really hadn't signed on for the kind of life she was used to. Besides, she was a pro at disappearing. If she didn't want someone to find her they wouldn't; it was but one of the many useful skills her mother had taught her.

"Don't start giving me a lecture about what my role is or isn't. I'm in this with you. You think it's my fault that we're being chased, right?"

It was her turn to feel the heat crawl up her face.

"Well, I do too. If I'd left you alone, you wouldn't have guys trying to kill you."

With what she'd learned that day, she couldn't let him take the sole blame. "I'm sure at some point someone would have come looking for me. My mother was not exactly a person who endeared herself to people. She used them, spit them out and left. I found several of those people today and since they can't retaliate against her, it appears I'm the substitute."

"Care to tell me where you went and what you did?" He looked pointedly at her torn and dirty clothes.

She shook her head. She was tempted to consider the day as a total flop, albeit a frightening one, but that wasn't totally accurate. She'd found people who remembered her and her mother; people ready to take revenge for her mother tipping off the police on a myriad of illegal activities, including drug trafficking and felony theft. A few had tried to exact payback they had wanted to bestow upon her mother. Today Bailey could have added to their long list of crimes—assault, threats and attempted kidnapping. Her eyes widened as she realized that was the flavor of her life. She almost laughed sardonically at the idea she could have been stolen again. Fearing that she wouldn't be able to control her hysteria, she pushed it away. "I need to go."

"Not by yourself. I picked up our friend again. Or he picked me up. He wants us both dead, and I'm not sure he's acting alone." He grabbed the doorknob. "We need to go. I'll go first but stick with me. Got it?"

He turned suddenly. She stopped but not quickly enough. The width of her hand was all that separated their faces. She didn't even have time to form a coherent thought before his lips pressed down on hers. It lasted no more than a heartbeat and was over before she could blink but the power of the magnetism behind it was going to take a while to forget.

He shot out the door. "Come on."

It was time to move. There was no need to discuss what had just occurred between them because it was not going to develop into anything further. She wasn't a virgin but she also had been selective about whom she'd slept with—selective enough to get out without getting scorched and she was sure Guy would leave a blackened, burnt-out mess when he left.

Running fast, she caught up to him on the stairs. So far, she agreed with his precautions but she wasn't confident he really knew what he was doing. She wasn't one to put all her trust in anyone else but as long as her instincts agreed, she'd go along with him.

It wasn't until they were in a cab heading across the river valley that the change in transportation hit her. Then she noticed his appearance.

"What happened to you?"

Looking her over, he replied, "Not much different than I'm thinking happened to you. Care to share your story?"

The city scenery was a blur as she stared out the cab window. Anna Marie, her last hope, seemed to have vanished and several even thought she was dead. Bailey struggled with a profound sadness. Anna Marie was the first person that had been like a mother to her. She'd dried Bailey's tears when she'd fallen, talked to her about life and let her know in so many ways that she didn't belong in that world. Ironically, she'd been the reason Bailey had become an interior decorator. People would have laughed at that. Anna Marie had lived under a stairwell in a dilapidated building. Grimy, tattered drapes were both her protective veil and her doorway to the world. A shredded blue duvet, no doubt pulled from a dumpster, covered her concrete bed. An eclectic hodgepodge of beads was strung together to form a gateway to the world and her decorations. The colors, the fabrics, the minutiae that Anna Marie had assembled had made her feel like she had a home. She'd been a remarkable woman living in an impossible place yet she seemed invincible. She'd lived each day with love and laughter.

Bailey tried to shake the melancholy that washed over her. Whatever opening she might once have had to her past appeared to slam shut like a steel metal door; a prison door locked from the outside and now no one seemed to have the key. Anyone who might have had answers wasn't talking or had disappeared. Guy seemed to be the only one with a link to her past. But what if trusting him cost her everything? Huddled against the door, she stared at the scenery. Twenty minutes later, they arrived at the Edmonton International Airport. Vehicles were maneuvering three deep in the drop off zone as they struggled to exit the cab amidst the turmoil.

She was transfixed by the chaos. A beautiful woman with long blonde hair climbed out of a sleek sports car. A gentle breeze caught her hair, fluttering it across her face. Chuckling, she leaned into the car, her short skirt displaying a considerable amount of leg, stopping just shy of flashing all that was hidden beneath it. The woman straightened, had a porter fetch her bag from the open trunk and proceeded to follow him on stiletto heels into the airport.

The woman reminded her that she'd had that vision of herself when she was fifteen. Her knight would arrive to save her, taking her away from her reality; then she'd awakened with the realization that knights didn't exist in the real world—at least not hers.

"Any time you need a taxi, call me."

Bailey pulled herself back to the present. Guy accepted the driver's card and shook the hand of a very happy man. After seeing the amount of money he was stashing in his pocket, she could understand why. Once in the airport, they checked out the departures.

"There's one to Toronto, leaves in two hours. Perfect." Guy hustled off toward the ticket counter.

Bailey watched him leave and then perused the list again. She headed in the opposite direction. She hadn't gone far though when a familiar hand clamped onto her. She barely reacted, like she knew who it was, like she knew she was safe. That frightened her and angered her.

"Where the hell are you going?"

"Why thank you so much for asking. That's so sweet that you give a damn what I want."

Yanking away from him, she continued on her way.

He ran in front of her but instead of stopping her, he ran backward, facing her. "Okay, I made an assumption we're going east. We're not?"

She shook her head emphatically and moved to get in line.

"We're going to your place, aren't we?"

"I've had it. I'm going home. If I'm done, then this has to be over, right?" She tried to sound as though she was pleading but she knew she'd failed when he retorted in a curse. Several passengers turned to look at them. He stared back. Bailey couldn't help but giggle.

"Not funny. We need to discuss this." He started to pull her out of line.

"Don't let him bully you, honey. I can blow this." A short, elderly lady retrieved a referee's whistle from her neck chain and put it to her lips.

Bailey's eyes opened wide. As much as she'd love to see that play out, she knew they didn't need any more attention. She forced a smile. "Thank you. He's a good guy, just a bit rough around the edges. Don't worry; I'll keep him in line."

The lady nodded her head sharply, her purple hairdo bobbing drunkenly before returning to its original lacquered shape.

Bailey allowed herself to be led away. She bit her lip. She thought about all that had happened in the last few days. Her lips twitched. She tried to focus on anything but what had just occurred. When Guy pulled her into the lounge, she couldn't hold back any longer. She started to laugh. She flopped into a chair, clutched her stomach and continued to howl. The waitress gave her an odd look but smiled, then took the order from Guy and moved away. Several people had given her cursory glances but when she didn't stop, they openly stared. Normally that would have been enough to end any attention seeking behavior but for whatever reason, the giggles just wouldn't go away.

"Care for a sip?" Guy was holding a glass of water in one hand and a beer in the other.

That just set her off again. Gasping, she tried to catch her breath. Small vibrations started at her core and spiraled outward as she shook with uncontrolled hilarity. Her heartrate jumped to that of a marathoner's—her hands became clammy, her eyes opened wide. She wasn't certain whether she'd asked for help or Guy had observed that she was out of control and frightened. He came around the table and pulled her up, forcing her to stand. He wrapped his arms around her, pulling her as physically close as he could. Then he began to softly hum. His deep baritone melodic voice reached through her defenses and soothed her frayed nerves. It was so comforting that she never wanted to leave that space. If only it could last. He had given her more than anyone had in her lifetime; he could be all she had ever wanted.

When she felt strong enough, she reluctantly pulled away and sank into her chair. Staring at the beer in front of her, she grabbed it and downed half of it. As she returned it to the table and played with the label, a warm hand caressed hers.

"It's okay. I know you're not used to accepting help, but I'm not going away. It's nothing to be embarrassed about. You've had more happen this week than many have had in an entire lifetime. Give yourself a break." He smiled reassuringly. "I know you want this nightmare to end. So do I. But I need you to trust me."

She couldn't quite meet his concerned blue eyes that looked as enticing as a blue sky on a clear day. She nodded and then drank the rest of her beer.

"Are you okay?"

Never one to shy away from responsibility for long, she allowed her gaze to meet his. He smiled. It contained warmth and genuineness she wasn't accustomed to seeing. It zipped right past her defenses and sucker-punched her in the chest. She gasped.

Immediately, he was out of his chair and kneeling beside her. "What? What's wrong?"

She didn't respond but just pushed him away.

"You're all right?"

She nodded.

"I'm going to get us on a plane to Toronto. I know you'd rather go home, but will you be able to get any answers there?"

She shook her head.

"Then we need to go my direction. That's... that's where I hope we'll get some information that will hopefully unravel all of this. Okay?"

She half-heartedly smiled.

"I have a few things I need to check out. I think there's some surprises even I couldn't have guessed. I'm going to make a call and get us on that flight." He headed out of the lounge, stopping just outside the entrance.

Without him beside her, her thoughts invaded once again.

The woman she knew as her mom wasn't. She wondered if that was why she'd never really felt connected to her or if that was just an excuse. Many kids didn't connect with their parents. She was really no different. Someone wanted her though. Why? Neither of them had ever had any money. The house and store were owned by someone else. Donna Saunders had left letters that had encrypted information in them. Her doll hadn't been lost.

All of it meant... what?

What kept playing over and over in her mind was the number of people her mother had potentially used and abused. She thought she could find people from her past that would have answers, who would have been able to make sense of a senseless life. The grungy hangouts and the homeless shelters had whisked her back to the various times they'd sought refuge in similar places. It had reminded her of what a belly swollen with malnourishment felt like. Memories flooded in: getting in line for food, begging, lying and stealing, all in the name of survival.

33

Bailey shuddered at the memories that flooded back. There had been no answers, only more questions. Thankfully, Guy chose that moment to return. He sat heavily, propped his elbows on the table and rested his head in the palm of his hands. His fingers got lost in his shaggy brown hair. He breathed deeply several times.

She couldn't take her eyes off him. Three bandages covered the outside of his right hand from the wrist to the base of his pinky. Surprised she hadn't noticed it before she reached out and barely stopped herself from touching him. She looked at her outstretched fingers and then at him. She had nothing to offer him. Slowly, she lowered her hand to the table in front of her. It didn't stop her from wondering what kind of day he'd had. She was guessing it hadn't been all that dissimilar to hers.

When he didn't raise his head after a few moments, she realized his breathing was a little too even, too deep. She glanced at the clock over the bar. They had just over an hour until the flight left if he'd managed to get them on the one he wanted. Reaching toward him, she placed her hand on his leather clad, scuffed shoulder and gently shook him. "Guy."

No movement and no change. She tried again but was a little firmer in her shake and in her voice. When that didn't work she nudged him a little harder but she got little more than a grunt. A woman jabbing her husband with her elbow caught Bailey's eye. She realized again they seemed yet again to be attracting unwanted attention. Besides the fact she didn't like being in that position, they needed to be more inconspicuous.

Getting up, she smiled at the people staring and rounded the table. Once she was beside Guy, she leaned down and whispered in his ear, "Time to get up, sleepyhead. We're attracting attention and our flight is leaving soon."

Another unintelligible sound. Hissing through her teeth, she drove her tongue into his ear, pulled it out and said, "Let's go, big boy. Now. Or you don't get any."

His head snapped back. She snorted in mock disgust and headed to the exit. He blinked several times but soon stumbled to his feet and followed after her.

"Where's our tickets and boarding passes?"

"We have to pick them up from the ticket counter." He swiped his hand over his stubbled jaw. "Slow down. We've got time."

She maintained her stride until his hand halted her.

"What the hell is your problem? I'm sorry I fell asleep. I'm tired. All right?"

She thrust her chin in the air and turned her face away. "Get our tickets, okay?"

He grabbed her arm and pulled her into line with him. "All right. What's got you upset?"

"I could use some slumber too. Uninterrupted slumber."

"Then what's the problem?"

"You. You wake up as soon as there's a sexual suggestion. Nothing else would open your baby blues."

He groaned. "Since I'm not a hundred percent sure what you're talking about, did it ever occur to you that maybe you tried several things that started waking me and it was the fifth or tenth thing you said and not the mere suggestion of sex that was successful?"

Two young women blatantly ogled Guy. He leaned close and whispered in Bailey's ear, "I don't know what sex you were offering but I'm saying yes. And no, I wasn't thinking of another woman. Baby blues, huh?" He moved to the open counter.

Stupefied, Bailey stood there until she heard one of the women say, "Wow, is he hot." Then she joined Guy. Not quite daring enough to slide her hand into the crook of his arm, she leaned in close so the two chicks would know he wasn't available.

34

"Why'd you come after me?"

"I wasn't going to let you go wandering off by yourself." Guy wanted to heave a sigh of relief now that they were finally in the air, but he couldn't quite shake a well-founded paranoia.

"I meant, why did you come and find me in the first place?"

"Oh." He looked at the newspaper he'd purchased before boarding the airplane. *I owe my grandmother, well really my step-grandmother.* "I…I guess you could say I was doing a favor for someone. I was intrigued. Of course, this becamse so much more than I figured."

They shared a commiserating smile. Now that they were en route to Toronto, they both relaxed a bit. Guy felt safer heading back to his own territory, but he wasn't confident it was the right decision for Bailey. What if he was taking her back to where it all began thirty years before, only to find the same threat was still there?

"Excuse me, would you like a beverage and snack?"

They both took the offered juice and cookie, wolfing it down before the flight attendant had even moved forward. He caught her looking at him as guilty expressions morphed into amused ones.

"Well, that ought to knock off the twelve-hour hunger."

He looked out the window at the darkening sky and the black clouds. He thought of his attacker and wondered if they'd shaken him at last. Graham hadn't heard back from Detective Bean yet, so neither knew whether he'd been arrested.

Guy shoved his hand through his disheveled hair, dropped his head back and breathed a sigh of disgust. *This is crazy!*

He closed his eyes and recalled his conversation with Graham just prior to getting their tickets.

"Where the hell are you and what's going on? Are you all right?" Graham had demanded.

After Guy had assured his partner he was okay, Graham had continued, "The guy you wanted me to track down, John Denori, has a long rap sheet. He's a con man—theft, fraud, assault, outstanding warrants for questioning on three attempted kidnappings occurring in 1978, 1979 and 1980. Sound familiar?"

"Attempted?" Guy had answered.

"It appears that in each case, a family member was behind the abductions. He was fingered as the guy they'd hired. Sick."

"No wonder he wants Bailey. Maybe she's the last link to his nefarious career with the black market. I'm assuming that's what his gig was?"

"I suppose. In each case, it appeared someone's inheritance was threatened by the person they wanted abducted."

"Jesus, there are some sick relationships. Makes you wonder." Guy had stared off into space, his mind trying to fit the pieces of the puzzle together. "Before we go too far with this, I need two tickets to Toronto. There's a flight leaving in about an hour and a half. Can you get us on it?"

"Yes. But you need to fill me in on what's happening."

"Did you get hold of Bean?"

"Yeah, that ungrateful s.o.b. He acted like he was doing me a favor instead of the other way around. Dick. Anyway, I haven't heard back from him. Doubt I will, so I'll hack into the Edmonton Police files later to see if they arrested Denori. Sorry I can't give you a definite."

After he had filled Graham in on all that had happened, he'd asked him for a favor.

"Graham, I need you to do some research for me. It may take you a while and I need everything kept so silent, there's not a whisper of it anywhere. Okay?"

"You know me, I don't share spit with anyone."

"I know that Graham, but no one can trace you. And before you tell me you never leave a trail, I need you to make sure. These are some serious people and the person I want you to do some checking on may have connections and be into something that no one will believe."

"I'm taking it you know this person. So before I let you tell me, is this going to put my life in danger?"

"It might. Want out?"

"Hell, no. I just like to be prepared for excitement if it's coming my way." He'd sighed. "I live such an exhilarating life that this will feel like a walk to the washroom. I look forward to this trip. Thank you, my friend."

Guy had laughed. "You are so odd, Graham. Must be why we're friends. Thanks. The person that I need a complete history on is Geoffrey Caspian."

A long slow whistle had met that announcement. "Oh, really? Well the good old chap is showing his true colors, eh? I'll get right on it. Be careful. I don't like the fact that family might be involved in this dirty stuff."

"Me neither."

His conversation with Graham left him feeling like the ride hadn't even started. All that they'd been through so far was the warm up.

What are you going to do about it?

"What are you doing?"

Startled that Bailey was asking him the same question that was going through his head, he frowned at her. "What?"

"You're twisting that package like you're trying to make a rope."

Looking at the mangled snack box, he said, "Just thinking."

"Care to share?"

No, because all I have are hunches. And I don't want to scare you away from your family.

"Just that this week's been crazy."

She snorted, reminding him if he was finding it nuts, she had to be just about certifiable with what she'd gone through.

"I should have asked before now, how are you holding up? With losing your mom and all?"

She glanced at the newspaper he'd stuffed beside him. Seeing the direction of her look, he pulled it out and offered it to her. She shook her head.

"No. I… it's just my mom had an obsession with the news. I always thought she was just a control freak, but now I wonder if there could be something more to it. Any ideas?"

"I don't know. Any particular part she used to read?"

"Cover to cover. And every major newspaper she could get her hands on. The weird thing was when I was throwing them away, the ones from years gone by, I remembered where I was on some of those dates."

"Oh."

Turning, she faced him. "Yeah. Like where we lived. I learned to connect where we were at to a date. It gave me something to do. It kept me from thinking about what was going on in my life." She twisted her hands together. "Every time we moved, every time we screwed someone over, every time we did something that made my stomach feel like it was full of battery acid, I can tell you the date. Ask me to remember when something good happened and I... don't know. Sad, eh?"

"It had to be tough being on the go all the time." Guy restrained himself from reaching out to touch her, knowing she needed to keep talking and any sympathy on his part would shut her up.

"You have no idea. But at some point it became an expectation. You never really unpack. Never get too excited. Too attached. Because it will all change." She knocked her knuckles together. "Okay, enough about me. Tell me something about you. Did you move around a lot?"

He couldn't look away from her questioning gaze. He shifted several times in his seat.

"Ants in the pants? Guess I hit a nerve. Easy to talk about me but you don't want to follow a pathetic life story, huh?"

"No, I probably can't beat your story but mine's not so pretty either. Let's just say I was the result of a bad situation."

He ignored her arched brow for a moment before giving in. "My mother was a maid for a wealthy family, she was said to have been raped. It was hushed up and she was given the boot. Until I was nine, I lived with my mother and grandmother. Then my mom was killed in a car accident. My grandmother was a bit nuts and devious. She was blackmailing the rich family, telling lies and slandering them. She wanted money. My step-grandmother, the matriarch, basically bought me. She paid the old woman and next thing I knew I was growing up in a beautiful, old monstrosity of a house where I was treated like gold."

"So your real grandmother didn't want you and figured you were a good way to get rich? How long did you live with her after your mother's death?"

"A few days."

"Your step-grandmother put up money right away for you, even though you weren't related?"

"Uh. No."

"Okay, I'm confused."

He met her compelling gaze. He'd never told anyone about his upbringing before. "The day after my mom died, my real grandmother put me in the foster care system. It took my step-grandmother over a year to find me and to stop the old bat from screwing with my life."

He didn't realize his hands were clenched into fists until he felt her soft palms gently caressing him. Taking a deep breath, he allowed her soothing touch to calm him. "So can I compete with your upbringing? No. Do I know what it's like to be shipped around and unwanted? Yes. Do I know what it's like to be a pawn in an ugly game? Yes."

"I'm sorry." It was a simple statement but it didn't hide her depth of emotion or the tears that threatened her voice.

It almost choked him up that she could feel empathy for him when he'd only had it bad for a short time. She was still living her hell. Opening his hand, he flipped it over and clasped hers. They sat in silence for a long time as they both stared off into space, enjoying their shared camaraderie.

A long time later, he looked down at the long, disheveled brown hair spread across his shoulder. Her breathing was heavy and constant. She was sleeping hard. He covered a yawn; he must have snoozed a bit too because he didn't remember her leaning against him. Not wanting to wake her, he settled back against the seat and carefully adjusted her head, so it rested more snugly against his chest. His arm slipped around her. It felt too comfortable. Too natural. Getting involved with a client was a big taboo and had never been an issue for him before. But he was coming to the realization this was no longer just about keeping her safe so she could reunite with her family.

He stared out the window, watching the gray clouds below them. The fact he was headed home gave him a moment of reprieve. The tightening in his gut started to ease slightly, to gently unwind. Then his mind shifted to all that had happened, to all still to come and to all that needed to be done. He must figure out who was behind it all. The acid rolled and clawed his insides like a cat climbing a tree to escape a predator. If what he suspected was true and with knowing what Bailey still had to learn, he was going to hurt the one person who had saved him. And he was going to drown Bailey in the hell of who might really have been the one behind her abduction.

35

The pitch blackness caused her to stumble and slam her shin into the low coffee table. A flashlight flipped on.

"Where the hell have you been, Bailey?"

"Mom, it's only 9:30. I was studying for my language arts test tomorrow. I was at the library. I told you that this morning."

"What's that?"

"Mathew bought this for me for passing the math test. Isn't it beautiful?" I twirled the flower in my fingers and smelled it. I couldn't hold back my Cheshire grin.

"Let me see it."

I didn't want to. I put it behind my back. Her long claw-like arm snaked around me and snatched it away. Her razor-sharp nails sliced it into tiny pieces.

"Mom. What are you doing?" I clamped my hand over my mouth as she tossed the stem at me.

"That young boy wants something from you. And let me tell you now young lady, he won't get it. He's not going to be sniffing around you."

"He's my friend. That's all. He got this for me because I passed the math test and I wasn't sure I would. He's nice. What the hell's wrong with you?"

Her hand connected with my face, her nails scraping over my skin. A tiny drop of blood, like that of a tear, slowly trickled down my cheek and dripped off my jaw.

"Don't you ever talk to me like that again. That's what that young man has done to you." She stood, her dark robe billowing around her as she raised her arms. The light silhouetted the white, death-like color of her skin and eyes like black orbs.

Then the image changed. I was being pulled backward by the seat of my pants down a long dusty road. I reached for the white light flickering in the distance. As it died away, the picture changed. Miss Piggy was sitting high up on my dresser, laughing down at me with maniacal laughter.

"I've got your secrets, Bailey. Oops Cassidy. Ooops nobody. Ha-ha-ha-ha-ha-ha."

"Noooooooooooooo."

❦

"Bailey! Bailey! Wake up."

She jerked upright, her head snapping around, her eyes quickly scanning the area. She was alert and ready to run. The lady in front of them twisted around to peek over her seatback. The couple across the way had owl eyes which they quickly diverted when Bailey caught them looking at her.

"Are you all right, Ma'am?"

Her eyes peeled wide open, Bailey looked up at the flight attendant before turning to Guy.

"It's okay. It was just a dream." He reached for her hand.

She pulled back. Taking a deep breath, she pasted on a smile. "I'm fine, thanks. It was nothing. Really. Sorry for any disturbance I caused. I'm just a little overtired."

"That's okay. Is there anything I can get you?"

Besides a strait jacket you mean? Bailey shook her head.

She waited until the flight attendant moved away before asking, "Uh, what exactly did I say? Do?"

"You cried out a couple of times. Want to talk about it?"

"I'm not sure." Brushing her hand back through her hair, she grimaced at the ratty, tangled mess. It reminded her how grubby she felt. Not even twenty-four hours of running around the streets of her old neighborhood and she felt like she needed to be hosed down. She barely controlled the shudder that threatened.

I wonder if I chase down the stewardess and tell her I'd like a bath, what she'd say. That might have been what she wanted to suggest.

"Guy. We need to talk. There's something I'm missing in all that's happened. There's some clue somewhere. I…" She reached down, opened her backpack and pulled out Miss Piggy. He gasped. Frowning, she looked at him.

"I swear I forgot. It's been a crazy day. That nut that wants to kill us took me for a crazy ride; I crashed the SUV getting away from him. And I swear it just slipped my mind."

"Care to explain what you're trying to tell me?"

A light flush crept over his face as he slipped his hand into his leather jacket and pulled out a cassette. Laughing, she reached for it.

"This is what you forgot to tell me about. Oh my God, I haven't seen one in years. I'm not even sure they make cassette players anymore. Do they?"

He shrugged. "I don't know. Graham told me to go to a garage sale or find a secondhand store."

"What's on it?" She flipped it over but it contained no label.

"I was hoping you'd know."

"How…?"

Pointing at the stuffed animal, he said, "It came from her."

"Really? That's why you tore her apart. I thought you were angry."

Tugging on his ear, he replied, "This morning after I discovered you were gone, I picked up the Pig, not sure why and I felt this unusually hard object. So I kind of pulled her apart to find it."

Flipping over the toy, she showed him the ripped head. "I was sure you'd done this to her but I couldn't figure out why." Staring hard at the two things she held, the cassette and the toy, she tried to make a connection.

"I had Miss Piggy until I was six or so. Then she disappeared." Holding up the cassette as if it could reveal answers, she said, "I'm not sure I've ever seen this. I think Mom was the one who hid it there. But why?"

"Did she ever send you secret messages? Or did you ever have a code or something?"

Bailey snorted, thinking about the two letters her mom had left her to decipher which in turn, reminded her she hadn't figured out the second one. "She was the master of codes. Of espionage. She used to write nursery rhymes but she'd change the characters or the story and I'd have to figure out what she meant. She made up her own language. She drew pictures. She'd have made a good coder for countries who wanted their secrets kept."

So what haven't I figured out, Mom? The first letter led her to Mr. Lund and the hidden jump drive. She flipped the cassette over and over in her hand, distracted by what might be contained on it. "What did you find on the jump drive?"

"Uuhh." Grimacing, he replied, "I didn't find much. I sent it to Graham to decode. Sorry."

"We're approaching Toronto Pearson International Airport. Arrival time twenty-two minutes. Please put your seatbacks in the upright position…"

Bailey only half-listened to the captain as he went through the routine of preparing for landing. She glanced out the window but immediately pulled back.

"Don't be scared. It's safe."

Averting her face, she replied, "Don't know what you're talking about." She stuffed Miss Piggy into her backpack and shoved it under the seat. She looked at the cassette in her hand, reluctant to let it go but knowing it would be a while before she could listen to it.

"So what happens when we get off?"

"A friend is meeting us. We'll go to my place."

She cocked her head as she studied him.

His hands flew up. "It's just the closest and easiest and hopefully the safest place to take you for now. If you don't like that, I'll book us into a hotel."

She frowned.

"I'm not letting you out of my sight. I might not be the best at protecting you but whoever wants you will have to go through me."

A thrill of excitement ran through her. Perplexed because she enjoyed the strange emotion, she turned away from him.

Silence ensued between them. The plane landed. Bailey and Guy waited patiently while everyone stood and grabbed their bags from the overhead compartments. Guy stepped back so Bailey could get in line in front of him. Walking into the airport they followed the long confusing miles of hallway and escalators to finally emerge in the baggage claim area.

Guy started doing his owl imitation, scanning the crowded area. Bailey couldn't muster more energy than it took to give more than a cursory glance around. People of all shapes and sizes were anxiously looking through the stream of passengers for their loved ones. A blonde disheveled haired guy that reminded her of Scooby Doo's sidekick, Shaggy, waved. Since Guy smiled and waved back, she had to assume that was his buddy who'd gotten them all the deals.

The two men clasped hands like they were going to arm wrestle and slammed their shoulders together. Bailey stood back and let them perform their male bonding ritual. Looking around, she noticed all the hugs and tears that were being shared, the genuine missed you looks, glad you're here. It was such a foreign sight to her that she couldn't help but stare. It was while she was watching a couple racing into each other's arms and practically start making out that she noticed a man with an old deerstalker cap staring at her. Something didn't feel right. He had a hard look in his eye as if he hated her. She glanced over her shoulder to see if anyone was standing beside her. No one was close and no one was looking in his direction. Turning to look at him again, she was surprised that he was gone. Her stomach, her radar system, was clenching. Confused, she looked around.

"Bailey, come here. I'd like you to meet my friend and partner, Graham—the man who can accomplish anything."

He bowed very formally before reaching for her hand. Not sure what to make of him but sensing he was harmless, she allowed him to hold her fingers in his palm. "Enchanté, my dear. You are much more beautiful than my esteemed friend would have had me believe."

Bailey looked past him to catch Guy's eye, only to see his smile and his head shake. Not sure what to do or to think, she stood there stunned as Graham planted a kiss on the back of her hand, then tucked her fingers in the crook of his elbow and proceeded to walk with her out of the terminal.

"Oh no, you don't." Guy slipped between them, easily extricating her from him. "Okay, where's the car?"

Graham made a woebegone face, sniffed a few times before bowing regally and stepping back. Bailey giggled. He winked at her. His face became serious as he faced Guy again.

"Parkade. I need to talk to you first." All joking was gone.

Guy turned to Bailey. "We'll be right out this window. Stay right here. Okay?"

She nodded, trying to convince herself they'd be safe. After all, who could possibly have known that they'd flown to Toronto? It wasn't like they'd given a whole lot of notice. The two men stepped outside the building; still sheltered by the cement overhang protecting them from the pouring rain, they moved off to the right, still within sight of Bailey. Guy kept glancing at her every few seconds.

She considered following them but decided to stay inside where she was warm and dry. She watched as Guy really seemed to be getting into their conversation. He'd finally stopped looking her way. She would love to know what they were discussing. Something jabbed into her side. Due to the overcrowded area, she assumed it was someone not paying attention to where they were going. About to turn and give them a piece of her mind, she was jerked from behind.

"Keep your mouth shut and step behind this column."

36

Fingers bit into Bailey's arm as she was pulled backward and slammed up against a hard body. She tried to turn her head but he squeezed her elbow hard. "Don't waste your time trying to figure out who I am, you won't be around long enough for it to matter. Keep your mouth shut and move." He held her tight to his body, walking right on her heels. She tried to break his strong hold but every time she moved or made a sound, he threatened to slice her throat. Biding her time, she tried to attract attention—she blinked rapidly, and rolling her eyes from to the side. She frowned. She glared. She made faces.

No one even gave her a second glance.

Bailey was sure there had to be a mistake. "Who are you?"

"Your worst nightmare. And you're mine. Shut your mouth or I'll use this gun to solve my problem right here and right now." His gravelly, acid-filled voice sent shivers down her spine. He peeked past her. "Go." They moved forward going deeper into the terminal, against the mass of people that were heading out.

Taking a deep breath, she stuck out her left foot. It was quick but sufficient. A tall man stumbled, kicking her, sending shooting pain and then numbness up her leg. Off-center, she took advantage of it and threw herself sideways, pulling her assailant with her. At the same time, she kicked out, connecting with her captor's shin.

Already off balance, he cursed as he threw out his arm to block his fall, loosening but not completely abandoning his hold on Bailey. She shot off in the opposite direction, the chain reaction causing more people to fall.

A teenager plugged into an MP3 player stumbled into the path of another man pushing an overfull cart, tumbling as he took several people down with him. Luggage scattered. As the crowd began to dogpile, it quickly degenerated into a crowd fight with some swearing while others shoved.

Other victims of the melee screamed, while still others wiggled and squirmed in an attempt to get untangled from the mess. Their efforts only resulted in more unsuspecting travelers toppling, making it impossible for those at the bottom, including Bailey, to rise. She braced her feet against an unfortunate man's backside and shoved with all her might. Her captor, who was trying to hold onto her while keeping himself from getting trampled, couldn't maintain his grip.

She yanked her arm out of his grasp and dove over the pack, climbing over the sprawled bodies as though they were lifeless debris. She didn't bother apologizing; no one would hear her over the commotion anyway. She slapped away hands that either threatened to dislodge her or were vain attempts at their own rescue. Bruised and battered, she finally reached the edge of the heap. She jumped to her feet and plunged through the crowd.

There was utter chaos. People were pushing and shoving, tripping over one another, swearing at each other. Bailey plowed through the crowd like Rambo in the jungle with a machete. Never having been in that airport before, she raced down the long open baggage claim area lined with conveyors and masses of people, all waiting to retrieve their suitcases from the black belt. Using the confusion and the ever-thickening crowds as camouflage, she glanced over her shoulder but did not spot her assailant among the commuters and visitors that were moving in all directions. She shuddered at the thought that if what she'd been told was true, that was the second time in her life that someone had attempted to abduct her. Well, third actually, if she counted the guy on the street earlier that day who had wanted to turn her into one of his junky whores.

She crouched low, weaving amongst other passengers to race outside. Her head pivoted like a hawk hunting prey as she hurtled along the outside of the building, using the masses as a shield. Graham and Guy were standing in the same place. Relieved, she charged up to them, grabbing each by the arm as she made a beeline for the parkade.

The two guys laughed. "What's going on?"

"Get moving. Now."

Guy stopped, forcing her to face him. Feeling his eyes burrowing into the top of her head, she looked up. Her breathing was still labored. She had no idea what he would see in her eyes but she was doing her best to hide that she was spooked. He brushed a stray hair off her cheek, pushing it back over her shoulder. She tried to lower her eyes but was caught by the mesmerizing look in his. He blinked once, stepped back and set a pace just short of a run. Not sure what he saw, she was thankful he didn't ask any questions but hustled them toward the parkade. In fact, it was she that had to hustle to keep up with the two men. At the car, Guy opened the door, grabbing and tossing a hodgepodge of clothing and books into the back seat. Though it was relatively clean, it looked like Graham might live in there. She climbed into the back and was surprised to find Guy climbing in from the other side. He crouched down and encouraged her to do the same.

"What happened?"

She shook her head, hoping he would just leave it alone but she should have known better. In the next moment, he'd slid across the back seat, shoving the books, wrappers and clothing onto the floorboard to sit beside her. He gently cupped her chin and forced her to look at him.

"Why were you limping?"

"Let's say there was a bit of chaos inside. Let's get out of here while I fill you in."

She forced herself to meet his questioning gaze even while she focused on her breathing to calm her nerves. Clasping her hands tightly in her lap, she pasted on a forced smile.

"So nothing serious? It just scared you?"

You have no idea. She glanced at Graham before replying. Guy might trust him but she didn't know him. "Yeah, just a little too crazy busy for me."

"Welcome to Toronto."

She slouched against the door. At this point, she didn't care where they went or what their final destination would be. She'd seen all she wanted to see. *Who the hell attacked me?* She found it implausible that the man from B.C. had followed them to Toronto, but the prospect of a second assailant frightened her even more. How many people were out to get her?

Turning, she was surprised to meet Guy's unwavering gaze. And for the first time in a long time she felt concerned about her appearance. Not sure how to read his expression, she found her hand rising almost involuntarily to rub her cheek as though she had dust on it. She was tempted to finger-comb her windblown, tangled mass away from her face but knew that wouldn't change anything. Certainly not the smell as she became aware of her own odor. She comforted herself with the fact that some of the strong stench could be Guy's.

Not wanting to explain what had happened, she stared straight ahead, refusing to acknowledge him. Besides what could she tell him, *'some guy I didn't even see tried to accost me'*? He finally gave up and leaned forward to talk to Graham. Snippets of their conversation drifted back to her.

"—he's wanted in several provinces. Looks like Bean will get the bust."

"What did you find out?"

"Some very interesting stuff. He's not who we think he is..."

Their voices dropped too low for her. She knew she needed to hear what they were talking about but it took too much effort. Her eyelids dropped, her mind let go.

❧

"Looks like your lady friend is out."

Guy looked behind him. He slid back over to his side of the car. Reaching for her, he gently moved her away from the door and eased her down, resting her head in his lap. When he looked up, he couldn't avoid Graham's raised eyebrows in the rearview mirror.

"It's not what you think. She's just had it rough these past few days."

"Yeah and then some. Hey, it's okay, you know, to get attached to someone. I'd say it's about time." He grinned from ear to ear. "And you picked a hot one." His eyebrows bounced up and down like Groucho Marx.

"Just get us home." Guy stared out the window for a while but it was futile. He allowed his gaze to be pulled back to the woman he held. He smiled as he took in her dirty, wrinkled, torn clothing. He reached out his right index finger and slid it into the tear in her shirtsleeve.

A thin line of dried blood lay hidden beneath.

From whatever happened in the airport?

He knew he shouldn't have left her alone but he had gotten caught up in all that Graham found out. Besides, he figured they were free and clear—at least for the moment. It bothered him the way she'd looked when she'd come out of the terminal. Had something else happened she hadn't shared? She had a wild look in her eyes akin to a trapped animal.

He didn't buy that it was confusion and chaos. Settling back, his hand resting on her shoulder, he allowed himself to recall all he knew. Tension roiled in his gut as he thought about what he'd have to do, what he must share and at what he suspected was true. It was going to change his family in ways he couldn't predict. His step-grandmother may regret bringing him into the family after all.

"Let's go to your place, Graham."

"It's not that different to my car, you know? It'll need tidying up before company comes over." He nodded his head toward Bailey.

"Your mom would be so proud that you're concerned." Guy knew Graham was trying to take his mind off their circumstances. They may be opposites when it came to cleanliness but he also knew that Graham's place had state-of-the-art security. Besides, his family didn't know where Graham lived.

37

"You're late for our Board meeting, Geoffrey. Couldn't you have changed before you showed up? You look like you've been dragged around by your coat tails. Who is she this time?"

Geoffrey pulled himself to his full six-foot two-inch height, reveling in how he towered almost a foot over his sister. He ignored the twinges of pain that radiated from several bruises and aches. He'd never suspected the girl would know how to defend herself. Not a mistake he'd make again, once he found her; and that shouldn't be hard. He knew who she was hanging out with.

"For the record, Dorothy." He liked that her spine stiffened at the use of the informal name. "I lent assistance to an accident victim on my way here. That's why I'm late. Why I'm a bit dirty. So excuse me for stopping to help my fellow man."

Her eyes opened wide with remorse for her swift judgment. Her look of dismay was enough to put him on Mount Olympus.

"I'm sorry, Geoffrey. There are some things happening that need straightening out. There are questions about that California winery that you've been negotiating with. And you recall the European winery you negotiated the purchase of last year? Our treasurer has run into some major problems there." She placed her hand on his forearm. He barely restrained himself from jerking away. He needed to play it cool and move up his plans for a permanent vacation. Yes, there were many problems but they were all virtual, and it's hard to have real problems with places that didn't exist.

"Fine, I'll get my files." He pulled away.

"I'll hold the meeting for fifteen minutes for you. Come when you're ready."

He knew that meant she wanted him to clean up and change into the spare suit he always kept in his office. Giving her that one small concession, he walked away as an ill-concealed smirk curved his lips.

Yes, many things are happening. Most of which you know nothing about.

He entered a plush, dark mahogany office that was larger than most houses. Strolling past the leather sofa, he opened the cabinet at the far end of the room and pulled out a bottle of Ladybank Single Malt Whiskey, poured two fingers and downed it. He set his glass on the table before stepping into his fully equipped bathroom. He stripped down, glaring at the dust that marred his suit and the rip that scarred the right pant leg.

It's all her fault.

All his clothes went into the wastebasket before he stepped into the shower, allowing himself a full twenty minutes to take pleasure in the heat. His plans had changed. He should have known not to call John. He'd bungled the abduction thirty years before. What had made him think the man would clear it up now? That was his second and last mistake.

Anger infused his body. His hands clenched. His face distorted, filled with hatred and the need for violence. Wasting energy punching inanimate objects was not his style; he needed to inflict severe damage. It created such a high to feel another's soft tissue compress until he hit bone; it's cracking had a distinguishable sound—like the snapping of a twig in a still forest—seeming to echo right along with the victim's screams. He recalled the last man he'd beaten—some homeless bum he'd found on skid row. The feel of the man's body fracturing under the power he'd inflicted sent shivers of excitement coursing through Geoffrey's body. He groaned in ecstasy as the distinct sound of bone splintering played out in his mind, sounding like music to his ears. Lust grabbed hold of him, making him hard. He reached for himself, then stopped.

No I'll save this for Lula.

Thinking about one of the latest whores he frequented and the wild and raunchy things she always did to him, with him, almost made him come. For a brief moment, he immersed himself in that physical pain and discomfort, the thoughts of what she could and would do to him and for him. It would help keep him centered and focused, allowing him to control his anger throughout the board meeting. He knew rumors had been flying about new business deals and new partners with regard to their legitimacy, and most especially why no one on the board—particularly his dear sister, Dorothea—had been apprised of them. He was ready though. He had the carefully crafted, detailed set of books that showed the winery was doing exceptionally well, all set up in a fancy presentation for those who thought they were in charge. The real books were nicely tucked away in his suitcase and the real money already waiting for him in an offshore account. He'd show them fictitious possibilities of taking on partners, prove why it was a great idea, all the time knowing he'd already set them up to fail and had taken their money.

The thought of how much they'd have to clean up when he was gone made him instantly hard again, nearly to the brink of ejaculating. He couldn't help but smile; everything was working to his advantage.

Except the damn girl.

He instantly went limp. His anger boiled over and he punched the shower wall, ignoring the broken tile that clattered to the floor. It wasn't his to worry about anymore. Taking several deep breaths, he allowed the water to cascade down his body, washing the blood from his scraped knuckle. This wasn't the time to lose it. He had a show to put on and no one could guess what he was up to, not yet, not until he was gone. Not until they found his badly broken and burnt but unrecognizable body, identified only by an expensive garnet ring and gold lighter with an engraved eagle in flight—things people knew never left his person.

His funeral would be befitting a king. He'd made sure in his will that every detail was spelled out, how the ceremony was to honor him and his wonderful contributions. And of course the beautiful letter he'd left his sister would ensure her guilt, meaning she'd pay handsomely for his eternal rest.

While they mourned he'd be in the tropics sipping exotic whiskey with as many naked, lusty women as he could find. He laughed so maniacally that anyone listening would have questioned his sanity. The guilty pleasure he felt was so divine he couldn't ignore it and realized he didn't have to.

Eyes closed.

Deep breath in. Slowly breathe out. Deep breath in. Slowly breathe out.

Because it was such a ritual, his mind immediately went quiet, loving the darkness and the stillness. He waited, readying himself like a caged tiger who knew the doors were about to open. Concentrating on the darkness, the stillness, he held himself there.

Breathe in. Breathe out.

Now!

Images flooded his mind, some real, some not. Bodies twisting together and apart, writhing in ecstasy, moaning, rubbing against each other, finding pleasure. Their skin humming with that sexual tension, that titillating awareness of what was to come, like an electric shock arcing through the air but not quite making the connection. Throwing his arms wide, he placed his chest so the water could beat down upon it to drum against his front.

"Aaaaaaaaaahhhhhhhhhh," he moaned. In his mind, the crystal clear droplets turned to a crimson red that poured over him, wrapping itself around him like a cloak... accepting him... inviting him... begging him for more. The writhing bodies still meshed together, now screaming in terror, crying out his name, begging to be released. The crescendo was building, was reaching higher. The feeling coursed through his body with the force of a locomotive, firing all his nerve cells. Humming like a perfect note plucked with precision from a harp, he lifted the knife skyward and plunged with all his might. Screams echoed. Fresh blood washed over him. Filled him.

"Yeesssssssssssssssssssssss," screaming, for he knew no one could hear through his soundproof room, he allowed himself the finale. Power surged through his body, filling it, stretching it.

He grabbed himself, pumped a few times and saw not the white milky substance that slid from his body but a white power so pure, he vibrated with the release.

Finished, he leaned limply against the shower wall, allowing the water to cleanse him, to rejuvenate him, for he felt reborn.

38

Guy looked at the caller display, took a deep breath and answered his phone.

"Where are you?"

"Uh, what's up, Grams?" Guy looked wide-eyed at Graham.

"I just had… I was at the Board meeting…"

Guy straightened every nerve in his body alert. "What's going on?"

"I, uh… I may need to hire you for some more investigative work."

"Oh?" He stared into space. He'd never heard a hesitant word out of Dorothea's mouth. Ever. "Are you okay?"

"Well of course I'm okay. I don't need some young pup questioning me. I'm simply telling you that I have…"

He let her ramble on. One. Two. Three. Four. Five. Six. Seven.

Guy took a deep breath. "Grams, why did you call?"

There was silence.

"You had your board meeting right?"

"Yes."

"So you called me because of something Geoff did or didn't do?"

"What makes you think it has to do with him? Just because there's been issues between you two—"

"Gram."

"All right." She huffed. "Something's not right with the South Shore Winery we acquired. I've been staying out of it but…"

"But something isn't sitting right which means Geoff is up to something."

"I think he's being framed."

"Geoff?"

"He was late for the meeting and he looked rattled. He said he'd stopped to help at an accident, but he wasn't acting like himself. He was dreadfully late. I had to apologize to everyone. I—"

"So you think someone is what? Setting him up? Maybe blackmailing him?"

"Yes."

He snorted with laughter. His uncle was a jerk and it wouldn't surprise him if he was a crooked jerk as well. He doubted very much that anyone would have the nerve to extort anything from Geoff, at least not if they wanted to live.

"Don't laugh at him. He had enough of that in his lifetime. I think someone is trying to smear his name and reputation but he won't talk to me."

It was a good thing she couldn't see his eyes rolling; he never understood why his grandmother protected the man. He was pure evil. There wasn't an honest bone in his body. There was no way he'd allow anyone to smear his name. If there was something going on, he was behind it.

"I'll look into it, Grams. I've got to go." He ended the call.

"Geoff screwing the old lady over again?" Graham swiveled in his chair.

"I think there is much more going on. Expand the search into his background. Look into that South Shore Winery we started acquiring several months back—and anything else that has Geoff's name on it."

"We? I thought there was no way in hell you were going into the family business as long as Geoffrey, my dear boy, was involved?"

Guy frowned at him.

"All right, oh masterful one. And what will you be doing?"

He sighed heavily. Graham looked at him quizzically.

"I'm sorry, man. I didn't mean…"

Graham waved him off.

"I think Geoff is behind something bad. Something big. Who else hides their existence? A few more days and we'll figure out what he's up to."

Graham grinned as he spun back to face his computer. "I love your optimism. Wasn't it you who said this situation, finding Bailey, telling her who she really is, would be over before it started?"

39

Bailey drained the tub and refilled it for the third time. If Guy hadn't knocked on the door every half hour to check on her she wouldn't have been aware of time passing. Lifting her foot out of the suds, she used it to turn off the hot water. Her pruny skin also let her know she'd been in there for quite a while. She'd been selfish long enough. Guilt for making Guy wait to clean up was starting to weigh on her.

It was with that thought that she pushed herself up and out. Draining the tub, she refilled it, regretting there was only lukewarm water left for Guy. A quick flash of his naked, lean body lowering into the bubbles not only sent her mind into overdrive at the possibilities that could bring, but a thrill of excitement zipped through her body, leaving goosebumps in their wake.

She dried off and then wrapped the towel around herself, realizing she hadn't brought the new clothes they'd stopped and bought on the way to Graham's.

Slipping out the door, she walked toward the guest bedroom that doubled as Graham's computer room. She stepped into the room, only to stop as two heads swiveled to ogle her. Her eyes opened wide as both sets started at her shoulders and ended at her long, barely covered legs.

"Eek." Spinning, she ran back the way she'd come. She'd almost made it to the bathroom when a warm hand landed on her shoulder.

She spun around. "I just wanted my clothes."

Guy lifted the four bags to her. "I know." His gaze held hers. Embers blazed deep in their depths. An insane thought of jumping into his arms and wrapping her legs around his waist flashed through with the clarity of a movie. Eyes wide, she grabbed the packages and stepped back with the intention of closing the door. Only he didn't let go. He moved closer. Their bodies brushed against each other.

She inhaled sharply.

This is wrong. This is so wrong.

His lips met hers. The bags hung heavy in her hands as he let go and placed his fingers on her naked shoulders, his index finger tracing the line of her collar bone. A hard shudder wracked her body. Nothing had ever affected her so quickly or so fiercely. The parcels slid from her fingertips as she wrapped her arms around him, her hands immediately sliding underneath his t-shirt to massage, knead and experience the muscles that rippled under her fingers. Heat coursed through her blood, thrumming with intense excitement.

His fingers slipped down over the front of her towel, gently rubbing the already erect nipples. Her first thought was to rip off her covering but she sensed he was enjoying the torture as much as she was. His mouth continued to ravish hers in a way that she had never experienced before.

This is right. Oh God, is this right?

Guy's cell phone rang.

They continued to explore each other's bodies, pushing so far yet refraining from that next step, one they knew in which they couldn't, or wouldn't turn back.

The phone rang again.

The sound broke them apart. Bailey was sure her eyes mirrored the confusion she saw in Guy's.

As if to make sure they heard it, the cell chirped again.

"Shit!" Guy pulled it from his pocket. Reading the caller id, he swore again. With a reluctant expression, he backed out, closing the barrier between them as he answered his phone.

Sinking weakly on the edge of the tub, she bowed her head, not in prayer but because she had no strength to hold it up anymore.

Bad. Bad. Bad. Bad. Bailey. She kept reminding herself that she couldn't get mixed up with this guy. She didn't even know who she was. He had no idea who she was, though he might think he did. Of that she was sure. And for all she knew, he was one of those guys thrilled to save a damsel in distress, only she was no damn damsel.

The mere thought that he could view her as such was the catalyst she needed to get moving. She stood to pull out her clothing. He'd bought her two pair of jeans, two t-shirts, two blouses, a pair of dress pants and even lingerie. He'd been insistent about the dressier clothing which she couldn't understand. Grabbing a pair of jeans and a t-shirt, she quickly pulled them on. Once dressed, she walked down the hallway to the guest bedroom.

Graham was still clacking away at the keyboard. He looked up when she entered. She couldn't help but smile because she wasn't sure which of them was more embarrassed.

"I'm sorry..."

"I didn't mean…"

"You first."

"No, you."

Bailey returned Graham's smile and realized they could let it go. Carefully weaving her way through the stack of papers and boxes, she climbed onto the bed behind him.

"What are you doing?" Bailey asked as she looked over his shoulder.

"Uuhh." He quickly shrunk whatever he'd had on the screen.

She leaned her back against the wall and stretched her legs out. "Am I bugging you?"

Graham spun around in his chair. He looked at her as though stumped. "You're not. But you are. How does that grab you, my dear?" he said in a very bad, stodgy English accent.

She replied in kind, "Jolly good, my man. Jolly good."

He laughed with her. "You can joke. I like that." He spun back to the computer and started tapping away again. Bailey frowned but didn't interrupt him nor ask any more questions. She didn't want him to think she was snooping so she tried to keep her eyes averted from the screen, but less than five minutes later she could barely sit still—she crossed her legs, uncrossed them, leaned forward, sat back… She didn't want to be rude and snoop through his house but she'd had enough. Graham was working and Guy hadn't returned from his call. She was about to get off the bed when Graham chose that moment to spin around. She jumped backward, whacking her head against the wall. She gently rubbed the tender spot.

Graham looked at her with a silly grin. "Oops. Sorry. Didn't mean to startle you. But I think I've found something. Something brilliant."

"Oh? What is it?"

His eyes flew to the door. "Uh, where's Guy?"

"On the phone. Why?"

"Just, he's taking a while."

Her eyes opened wide. "Damn. I left him a tub full of water that has to be cold now. Sorry. I'll go drain it." Racing to the bathroom, she pulled the plug and headed back. Since the bathroom was only two doors away from the computer room, she could hear their voices clearly. Tiptoeing a little closer, she stood outside the door.

"You won't believe what I found."

40

Bailey moved closer to the open door.

"Did you tell her?"

"No." Something was mumbled she couldn't make out, then, "…let me worry about that."

"What's happening?"

"Donna Saunders aka Donna Zajic, married to Doug Zajic, a Member of Parliament. Donna disappeared in July, 1983. There was suspected abuse; several calls to police but no charges. She disappeared on the early morning of July 6, 1983. He was even suspected of murdering her, but since no body, no blood, no sign of foul play was ever found, they had to drop it. Her car was finally recovered in southeast Calgary; apparently, she gave the keys to the parking valet. No evidence she ever bought a ticket, though. I think that's where Mr. Lund comes in. I'm guessing he's responsible for getting her a new name. I'm just not clear why. Nor do I understand this next part."

There was silence except for the clacking of computer keys. "It seems our Mr. Lund was playing a bit of a nasty game. He was getting twenty thousand dollars for territory fees—don't know what that means—and another twelve thousand for cabin fees from Mr. Zajic and was paying Donna eight thousand dollars. So he pocketed at least twenty-eight thousand dollars a month for himself. Haven't found an agreement of any sort so I'm guessing it was blackmail. The man was a pro, on the payroll of a wide range of folks from police officers to lawyers to judges to members of parliament. Nasty man. He had to be responsible for Donna's name change. I just don't get why."

"There's no way in hell my mom was getting eight thousand dollars a month. We lived like sewer rats most of the time."

Two guilty pair of eyes swiveled to face her. Guy stood from where he'd been perched on the corner of the bed. Bailey stepped back, putting her hands in the air, halting his forward motion toward her. She stepped around him and over a pile of papers to lean over and look at the monitor. Graham looked at Guy but he didn't change the screen.

"What proof do you have?"

Graham showed her the files from the flash drive, how they were encrypted and the amount of detail. The records definitely indicated her mom had been paid each month. Eight thousand dollars would have made a huge difference in her life. They could have stayed in one place.

"It didn't happen." Looking beseechingly at Graham, she asked, "Is it possible he recorded cheque payments that never existed?"

"Yes. But I don't have any proof."

"What would you need to find it?"

"Access to his bank accounts, any other accounting records he might have maintained."

Pursing her lips, Bailey stared into space, mentally retracing her visit with Mr. Lund. "I might know how to get that." She grabbed her backpack from where it had been chucked in the corner and pulled out her bag. Opening it, she took out the two letters that had been given to her. Her name, written in her mom's meticulous handwriting, stopped her. Tears flooded her eyes. Her index finger traced her name as the craziness of the past week started to crash in on her. Nothing made sense and she was tired of looking like a blubbering idiot. "I need some time." Stuffing the envelope in her pocket, she raced from the room.

She didn't stop until she'd unlocked the four deadbolts, flung open the front door and was soon four blocks away. Gasping for breath, she quit running and bent over, bracing her hands on her knees. She stood like that for a few moments, not paying any attention to the people who walked around her. It wasn't until she raised her head that she realized she wasn't alone.

"I…"

"It's all right. I think you're entitled. Let it go. How about we go for a walk? There's a park about another two or three blocks from here." Guy gestured to his left.

She nodded and fell into step with him. It was the most normal thing she'd done in a long time, one that helped compel her to talk.

"My mom… or the woman I knew as Mom…"

"Don't. It's okay to call her Mom, still. That's what she was. Right or wrong."

Pressing her hand to her chest, she continued, "She was always conservative with our money. It's just not possible that she was getting a cheque for that much each month. If it's true that kind of money was exchanging hands, I think Lund was keeping it and we were his tax evasion. On paper he'd give the money to others when really he'd keep it for himself. There were times we'd all of a sudden have some cash but it never lasted; there were long stretches between those tiny jackpots."

She turned to look at Guy and waited until he looked at her, "I don't know where that money came from. Maybe Lund. But there's no way she got it every month. She did some questionable things to earn enough cash just so we could eat. I always knew where the cash was, how much we had and where it went. She wanted me to know about the evils of our monetary system. She wanted me to know how to save money, because she was always scared I'd be taken advantage of."

Though they walked in silence, Bailey's mind was anything but silent.

"Do you think her husband, Doug Zajic, could have done that to her? If he abused her would that be why she was running? Was he what she was scared of?"

Guy stepped onto the park path, stopped and put his arms around her. She couldn't help but stiffen.

"Relax. I'm not going to do anything. I'm here for you. That's all."

His hand rubbed circles on her back, bringing up a strong memory.

"Oh Mama. That feels soooooooo goooooooooood." Bailey tried not to squirm while her mom rubbed her hand over her back, beginning softly and gently before becoming firmer, then softly once more. She loved when her mom touched her. "Don't stop. Please don't stop."

"I won't, sweetheart. I won't ever stop. I love you, Bails. Don't forget that."

"She loved me." Startled by the revelation and the fact that she'd laid her head on Guy's shoulder, she pulled back.

"I'm sure she did. Let's sit down." They sat on a park bench , thighs touching.

"You said you could get the information on the bank accounts. How?"

She dug into her pocket and pulled out the crumpled envelopes. Without looking at them, she handed them to him. He studied the pictures, doodles and designs.

"She was quite talented, wasn't she?" He started to open one of the envelopes but stopped when Bailey's hand landed on his.

"The answers are right there."

Turning it around and around and around, he finally gave it back to her. "All right, I give up. I can't make any sense of it."

"That's the whole point." She smoothed out both envelopes side by side. Pointing to some drawings, she explained, "This is a law book and this is a police badge underneath it."

"Let me see that." Guy studied it for a moment. "Wow. I see it now. It's like the Rorschach tests; you know—inkblots. This is cool."

Bailey smiled. "Yeah, she was talented. It took me a while but I learned to read her doodles. This one," pointing to the one they'd just been discussing, "means that someone thinks they're above the law."

"I don't get it. Why would the law book be above the police badge? Shouldn't …"

"Sorry. It means that someone in the judicial system thinks they are above the law."

"Lund?"

"Yeah. See this wormlike thing on this fishing hook? That stands for Lund." She didn't explain that was how she'd figured out the cabin. She wasn't sure why her mom had chosen that symbol for him, though. She knew it meant something more.

Guy chuckled as he studied the pictures. He put his hand to his chest. An image of Lund doing that same move flashed through Bailey's mind.

She clapped her hands. "Oh my God. Oh my God. I missed it. Dammit." Jumping to her feet, she paced back and forth in front of the bench.

"Do you want to share?"

She stopped and looked at him but couldn't quite pause her thoughts long enough to focus on him. "Uhmm… he said to me, 'your mom said you'd be full of questions'. How would he know that unless he'd known Mom was dying? For Mom to say something like that she'd have been very stressed. He knew. That pig, he knew. She had to have been in his house. That's how she knew about his jump drive and she wouldn't have trusted anyone but me. What else did Graham find?"

Guy met her gaze briefly before looking away. "You know most of it. Lund was blackmailing a number of people. He has written files, recordings, pictures… He was running a scam; he'd use his skills as a lawyer to get certain guys off in exchange for them getting dirt on powerful people. He'd pay them a pittance and my guess is he also kept them out of jail. He made hundreds of thousands of dollars off other people. Great retirement fund, I'm sure. It would take months to unravel it all. We just looked through the basics."

"I can't believe we lived like street urchins damn near my whole life and that son of a bitch was making money because of us. I'll kill him." She looked at him and then away and then back. "Look, I need to tell you what happened at the airport today. I'm sorry I didn't tell you sooner but… someone tried to grab me. He snatched me from behind and was forcing me to go with him."

The sound of something zinging past caused Guy to dive to the ground, taking her with him.

She yelped in surprise, "What the hell?"

A few feet away, the dirt sprayed up. Someone was shooting at them. Guy grabbed her hand and nodded toward a grove of trees several feet away. Simultaneously, they ran, half-crouched, behind them as several more shots followed. Grass and gravel bounced up, missing her leg by mere inches, so close it was as if the bullet whispered to her as it passed by. Not waiting to see what Guy did, she sprinted, running for all she was worth.

Huffing, he caught up. "This way." Winding their way through the park and out the other side, they raced down serpentine streets, passing through back yards and crouching low behind anything that could serve as a barrier. Finally, they stopped to catch their breath.

"Okay, that word is off limits."

Beat, she dropped her head back against a weed-infested fence for a second, wondering what it would be like to make it through an entire day clean. Memories of her childhood came flooding back; dirty, grimy places. Places where they were lucky if there was enough running water to drink, let alone bathe and wash clothes.

As his statement penetrated her thoughts, she looked at him.

"What word?"

"Kill. I don't think it's the first time you've mentioned it and someone has taken offense to it."

She almost smiled, but since her lips were too tired to move, she soaked up his humor instead.

He punched a button on his phone. "Graham. Call the cops. Report a shooting at Tennessee Park. Okay? Don't mention us."

"No, we're fine. No idea. Come pick us up. We're in the back alley..."

Bailey stopped listening. Her life had gone to hell and she didn't know how to make it stop. It seemed the nightmare of having to flee, to always be on the lookout, the horrors of her childhood, weren't over yet. There always seemed to be a price to pay.

Is there always going to be someone after me? Someone who wants to right some wrong, just because I was born?

She recalled a movie about the Devil's child. Lowering her head to her bent knees, she wondered if that child was her.

41

I think it's time we used your grandmother's connections," Graham said as soon as his two passengers climbed into his Hummer.

"Nice vehicle." Bailey settled back in the roomy, clean back seat, the exact opposite of his car.

Guy was busy typing messages to Graham and then holding his phone for him to read it. Bailey, thankfully, was too awed at the view the vehicle's height afforded. He'd been like that the first time, too.

Did you find the information I asked for?

Graham casually nodded.

Is she part of it?

Graham pursed his lips but shook his head.

Fact or opinion?

Graham put up two fingers to indicate the second option.

No evidence though.

He shook his head sharply.

Sinking back, Guy felt relief struggling against the queasiness roiling in his stomach. He couldn't shut his mind off to the thought that this was going to get uglier.

"We all need a good night's sleep and then we'll set up a meeting tomorrow. Any ideas?"

Bailey leaned forward between the seats. "I thought you said we'd be safe at Graham's."

"I thought we would be. Obviously, someone found us. My mistake."

"Who do you think it is?"

Guy was aware of her intense stare but refused to meet her eyes. He shrugged. She turned to Graham. When he glanced back at her, Guy caught his attention and very slightly moved his head side to side.

"Uh… not sure…"

Guy jerked upright. "What are we doing here?" He looked at the large wrought iron gates before his gaze slid off to the stone guard house on the right.

Graham sheepishly looked straight ahead. "I couldn't think of anywhere with better security."

"Dammit, Graham. We can't stay here."

"Better to den with the lion than have him chase you through the jungle."

"May I ask who's calling?" the guard bent to peer into the vehicle.

"Well, hello, Mr. Turner. We weren't expecting you. My apologies; I'm not sure what happened to the notice informing us of your arrival."

Guy sighed heavily. "There wasn't one." He'd learned a long time ago to call ahead to let them know he was coming. It saved him a lot of anguish and a lot of lectures. "In fact, Jim, there isn't one. We're gonna go. Grandma's probably busy with one group or another. So we'll just-"

"No need sir; I've just informed her of your arrival." The guard snapped to attention and smiled.

Guy crossed his eyes, giving Graham a fierce look. "Thank you, Jim." He should have recalled Jim's efficiency borne of twenty years of working for his grandmother. The large metal gates with its design of intricately woven vines and leaves soundlessly swung open.

"This is where you grew up?" Bailey leaned forward, her eyes wide.

Graham's head swung sideways, giving him a questioning look. Guy glared back. Graham's eyes widened in comprehension as guilt landed on Guy's shoulders like an immovable boulder. When was he going to tell Bailey who her family was? Better question was how.

Following the tree-lined winding cobbled road for a quarter mile, they suddenly burst into a clearing. Bailey gasped. Her left hand covered her mouth as her right hand fumbled to unclasp her seatbelt. She scooted as far forward as she could without climbing into the front seat. "Oh my God, are we at the White House?"

"What?"

"Isn't this what you'd imagine the White House to be like?"

Guy gazed at the white stone columns that flanked the front of the three-story house, balancing a huge balcony on top, as if seeing it for the first time. Vines cascaded over the sides, wrapping themselves around the ornately carved pillars.

"Oh my God. And if I say that more than once, tough. Oh my God." Her head swung side to side, her eyes peeled wide open.

Guy chuckled. The first time he'd visited had been memorable as well. He'd been so intimidated by the mansion looming over him like a dragon that he'd peed his pants. His hand automatically went to the back of his head where his uncle Geoff had cuffed him for being such a baby. It had only been the first of many such interactions with his uncle.

Shaking off that memory, he tried to see it through Bailey's eyes. In truth though, he couldn't take his eyes off her face as she lit up like Cinderella at the ball.

"This is incredible. Wow. This must have been amazing to play in as a kid. Hide-and-seek would have been fun. I'm betting a kid could get lost for days."

He smiled but didn't correct her assumption that it had always been laughter and fun. He was just glad this place didn't scare the crap out of her, because when she discovered who really lived there, it just might be the last time she talked to him.

Graham pulled in front of the extravagant marble stairs that rose to an open set of massive, double oak doors. Guy was about to suggest they go for a drive and come back later but he should have known better. His grandmother was already hustling out the door, her cane barely clipping the ground as she hurried toward them as though she feared they'd drive away.

Not looking forward to this encounter but knowing it was already in motion, Guy opened his door and jumped out.

"Stay here for a minute. Please." He glanced at Bailey but reinforced it with a look to Graham before closing the door. Turning, he skipped up the stairs expecting her usually demanded hug, but she was busy trying to move past him. Guy stepped in front of her, only to have her cane land against his ribs and shove him sideways. Looping his arm over her shoulder he tried to steer her away but she wasn't having any of it. She slipped around him and made her way toward the Hummer.

"Stop. She doesn't know who you are."

She spun so fast he was sure she was going to topple

over. He grabbed her arm, steadying her. "Come and walk with me. I'll explain."

She glanced at him and then anxiously toward the vehicle. It had been almost thirty years since she'd been able to hold her granddaughter.

"Gram. I can't go into all that has happened but I—"

"Never told her anything. Dammit Guy. I sent you because I thought I could trust you. I thought you'd follow my instructions. You were to find her. Let me know. I'd set up the meeting. What the hell are you trying to do to me? I won't have Gina and Daniel put on that emotional roller coaster again. Do you hear me?"

The shouting wasn't out of character for her, but the emotional wobble to her voice was and it almost did him in. It was the fourth time he'd ever heard it. The first had been when he'd shown up at the age of ten. The second had been when his step grandfather had died. The third was when she'd asked him to find Cassidy.

"Yes, I do. And my intention wasn't to spring her on you." *If I had my way, we wouldn't be here.* "But someone's after her. I think they're trying to kill her."

"What? Why haven't you shared this information with me before now? I'm still in charge. And don't you forget it." Turning, she moved swiftly toward the vehicle, her cane swinging freely in her hand.

He stood by and watched. He really didn't know what to do. The rest was really in the hands of fate. If he was lucky, Bailey's future would have the gold lining that his ended up with.

"Hello, my dear. You must be Bailey. I'm Dorothea Lindell. Please call me Dorothea. Come. Let's get you settled."

Bailey climbed out and took her heavily bejeweled hand. At least four karats of diamonds adorned the fingers of her right hand. On her left, Guy would have bet it was double that. He wondered what Bailey thought. She'd been deprived of so much.

"Thank you, Dorothea. I'm sorry to just drop in on you like this. I don't think—"

"Don't you worry, come, we'll have some iced tea on the balcony."

Bailey's head tilted back as they walked under the portico. Guy stuffed his hands in his pockets, not sure what to do with himself. The sound of a vehicle engine starting caught his attention. Spinning around, he was just in time to catch his buddy's wave as he drove away.

"Damn you, Graham." He knew giving chase was futile but that didn't stop him from looking for a softball-sized rock in the garden to chuck at the receding taillights. The vehicle soon disappeared behind the forest which lined the driveway.

"Guy! Guy, are you coming?"

He mentally gave his whole body a vigorous shake like that of a wet dog drying himself, hoping it would awaken him from this insane situation. The two women were talking like old friends as they made their way up the stairs. Sighing, he grabbed the backpack and bag that Graham had graciously unloaded in the driveway. He immediately tensed when his grandmother yelled again.

"Guy. You're being rude. Get in here."

He sighed, feeling like things were almost normal for the first time in a long time. He followed them inside.

42

How the hell did I miss?

Geoff massaged his arthritic knuckles, the familiar pain like poison gnawing through his joints. It had been several years since he'd shot a pistol; he much preferred the up-close contact of a knife. His Spearpoint Knife gave him all the security he needed. It was broad with a fat belly and sliced through muscle and sinew like they were nothing more than butter. Shivers started as gentle vibrations at his core, soon vibrating his entire body with a ripple of pleasure. The high it gave him almost overwhelmed him. Quickly on its heels was the reality of the situation he found himself in. His euphoric feeling vanished like a puff of smoke in the wind. He slammed his fist into his palm.

Dammit, why'd that idiot John get caught?

Geoff knew the man would sell him upstream faster than a bear-chased salmon could swim. He didn't have much time. They'd be coming to question him. He was almost ready to leave. The company jet was ready to go at his command. Everything was going to work out. His thoughts wandered to the board meeting from the night before. He'd attended as if nothing had changed; as though he hadn't just attempted a murder. Maybe he should have said something. Half of the old farts on the board would have croaked, saving him some trouble. They'd all been so easy to convince that he had the winery they were acquiring under control. And yes, he could use the company jet to visit the winery in person to ensure everything was legitimate. He laughed. It was so beautiful. They were giving him a free ride out of there and no one had a clue.

Walking across his newly built suite, he lifted the bottle of whiskey and poured himself two fingers. Downing it, he filled it again. Stepping over to the window, he peered through the telescope and scanned the expansive lawn, the elaborate flower gardens and the exotic ponds at the main house.

He couldn't help but smile every time he looked at them. They couldn't figure out what was killing the expensive fish his sister kept buying. Ah, too bad he wouldn't see her face when she found out. But then that was the least of her worries. He almost couldn't contain himself when he thought about all that had yet to learn. All that would bury her under guilt and shame and just maybe retire that overworked bleeding heart of hers. Shrugging, he was about to turn away when he noticed a vehicle pulling up. He watched as it disappeared from view to park in front of the house. Several minutes later it pulled away. Curious, he walked into his bedroom, opened the door to his walk-in closet, stepped inside and pressed a button. The wall slid apart, revealing a doorway.

Sighing, he walked inside the secret room. He was going to miss all the gadgets he'd had installed. Making his way to the elaborate listening and recording device, he pressed the blinking button. A recorded message played back to him.

Mrs. Lindell, Mr. Turner is here—

That's all Geoff needed to hear. Anger was instant as he thought of the little snot-nose kid Dorothea had the nerve to bring into his house. A maid's kid and God only knew who the father was. She'd taken in the little twerp, raising him like he was her own. The help's brat. Guy would never be more than that, no matter what Dorothea said or did. Geoff had taken it upon himself to make sure the little bugger never forgot where he came from. He'd learned quickly to keep his mouth shut or else.

Almost as fast, a new thought struck him. He smiled. For once, the twit had done him a favor. He was with the woman earlier, so chances were she was still with him. Maybe he'd get lucky and would be able to deal with both of those headaches before he relocated to the Bahamas. He really was tempted to stick around, just to see how extravagant his burial service would be but knew that might be stretching his luck a bit. Too many things were threatening to bring his world down—but not before he vanished.

Everything was in place. Everything was ready. Just to make sure, he did one more check of the C-4 he had strategically placed around the room. The detonator flashed, ready to be programmed.

A feeling of power surged through him. He straightened his shoulders and stood tall. *Time to go visit my dear nephew.*

His heart pounded with the knowledge he was going to serve up his form of justice. A full-blown grin covered his face as he got into his car and drove. Carefully making his circuitous route so that it appeared he'd come from the other direction, he couldn't afford someone finding his precious lair just yet. He pulled over and parked well out of view of the big mansion. Taking a deep breath, he calmed his highly strung nerves.

The time has come.

He allowed a tiny shiver of excitement to course through him before he pasted on a somber expression and walked along the path leading to the big house. The house should have been his, but it never was and never would be. It was Dorothea's.

Everything was Dorothea's.

But not for much longer.

43

Oh my God. Oh my God. Oh my God.

In her work as an interior decorator, Bailey had seen some classy homes but never had she experienced anything like this. The foyer was a massive three story, ballroom-sized area that ended in a domed, glass cathedral ceiling. Silken gold threads wove their way around the windows, flashing in the bright sun that danced across it.

She lowered her gaze when she realized she was not only going to get a crick in her neck but she might trip and break something. With her luck, it would take her the rest of her life and then some to pay it off.

The older, elegant lady wound her way through the house while Bailey tagged along like a gleeful puppy dog. She took in the large oak doors, the ornate carvings, the flower bouquets that filled the house, the priceless paintings and sculptures.

"My dear, you can walk up the stairs if you like but I need to use the elevator. Guy, escort her."

Bailey flinched as she realized she'd forgotten all about him. She faced him with a sheepish grin. He shrugged and smiled back. She wanted to ask him a hundred questions. The decorating inspiration was incredible—not that any of her clients would be able to afford this magnitude but they could manage a less expensive version, she was sure.

Guy saluted his grandmother as the doors to the elevator closed.

"That wasn't nice."

"Please. She can take care of herself. If I didn't give her a little bit of attitude she'd be so high on herself, no one would want to be around her. Staff would quit, no one would visit. She'd be quite lonely here all by herself."

"Why, that's quite a story you've come up with. Nothing like making yourself out to be the hero."

Bowing, he swept his hand in front of his waist. "After you, miss."

Guy and Bailey returned to the foyer to take winding stairs the width of a truck.

"This place is amazing. I don't think I'm going to be able to get my jaw to re-hinge itself. At least not while I'm here. This is…" She spread her arms wide, stopping on one of the steps to spin around.

"I know. When I first came here, I was sure that a hundred people must live here. But it was just her and grandpa—and the staff, of course."

Bailey ran her palm over the smooth, highly polished oak handrail. It would be so much fun to slide down.

"Don't. From this height you pick up so much speed you shoot off the banister like a missile. Only the wall can stop you."

"The voice of experience."

"Yeah. Too much. The older I got the stronger and better I thought I'd be. It's gotten me every time. Many broken bones. And a tooth or two."

Laughing, Bailey skipped up the stairs. The place was so fictionally fantastic she felt like she'd just stepped into a fairy tale castle. Her body was humming with awareness, excitement. She felt like jumping over the second story railing, grabbing a velvet rope that should be hanging there and swinging across to try to make it up to the third level.

"I know this is none of my business but…"

"But you'll ask anyway."

So caught up in her excited state, she didn't catch his dry tone. "How much marble is in this place? I know that's gauche to ask, so put it down to my ignorance but really, this is amazing. Everything seems to be marble." On the third floor she stopped and put her hand against the cool, solid railing.

"Well, it does last forever. I don't know how much, but you don't have to worry about the place collapsing. It's pretty solid."

His response barely registered, because she'd become lost in the view through the large ornate doors that glided open just down the hallway. As if in a trance, she walked toward them and to the edge of a grand balcony. The view was unimpeded for miles.

"It's quite something, isn't it?"

Startled, she spun around to face Mrs. Lindell. She sat off to her left in a large cushioned chair and sheltered by a large umbrella that blocked out the heat of the day.

"Please forgive me for my rudeness but yes, it's amazing."

"Come sit down. Let's talk. Tell me about yourself."

Bailey glanced at Guy who was staring hard at his grandmother. Sensing there might be a silent message being passed between them, she turned back to Mrs. Lindell.

"There's not much to tell. My name is Bailey. I live in Victoria. I'm an interior decorator. Of course, nothing along the lines of the one you hired. Your gorgeous home has given me great ideas for some of my clients. Not on this scale of course but… For instance, that antique Chinese vase in the sitting room just off the entrance, filled with that exotic plumage—wow. It's almost as tall as I am. I'm thinking for one of my clients, she has this large open space in her living room…"

She was not sure what made her realize there was a shift; perhaps it was the small smile on Mrs. Lindell's face or the fact that Guy had moved off to lean against the railing as though exhausted.

She gasped and hopped up from the comfortable seat she'd sunk into. "I'm really sorry. Here I'm babbling on. And I'm filthy." She brushed at the grass still clinging to her knees. It brought back memories of other kids laughing at her for wearing dirty clothes and needing a shower herself. She fought the familiar urge to run; instead, she stood with her hands clasped in front of her despite the fact that her embarrassment over her appearance made her want to dig a hole for herself, through the marble if she had to.

"My dear. You really are a gem, aren't you?" Dorothea glanced at Guy. "It's me who should apologize. I wasn't thinking. You probably want a bath and time to relax. I'm sure you're exhausted after flying across the country."

"Yes, actually I would. So if you'll excuse me, I'll call a cab and head to the nearest hotel. It was really a pleasure to meet you. You're not the ogre at all that Guy paints you to be." She worked hard at keeping the innocent look on her face, even when she could feel Guy's meteoric glare.

Guy's grandmother laughed. It was deep and throaty. It sounded like something she hadn't done in a long time. And by the look on Guy's face, she guessed he'd rarely heard it before either.

"Not true. And not that funny, Gram."

Wiping away the tears of laughter, she smiled at Guy conspiratorially. "Oh, I'm sure it is." Standing, she took the five steps that put her in front of Bailey. Surprised by how close she was, Bailey ignored the temptation to shuffle back a bit. Thin but strong arms reached out and wrapped around her. She went as rigid as the marble she was standing on. Scared to move, her saucer-like eyes looked for Guy.

"You're so much more than I hoped for." Stepping back, Dorothea cupped Bailey's face. "You're very beautiful and I'm honored that we met... finally."

Tears tracked over the beautiful smile, leaving Bailey at a loss as to what to do. She moved back, gently breaking the contact. The beautifully adorned but frail looking hands stayed suspended in air for a few seconds before dropping to her side. It was in that moment that Bailey saw Dorothea's true age. Her entire body seemed to wither and sink into itself. The weight of the world descended in that moment to rest on the shoulders of a woman that appeared as if she'd borne it for a very long time but just couldn't anymore. She'd reached her tipping point. And Bailey couldn't help but feel she was to blame.

Guy immediately stepped forward and put his arm around his grandmother. "It's okay, Grams. It's okay."

Bailey knew he was trying to get her attention but she couldn't quite look him in the eye. She nodded in his direction as he walked his grandmother into the house. Stunned by what had happened, she lifted her hands palm upwards and stared at them.

They look normal. But no, you just couldn't put them around a lonely old woman. Great job, Bailey.

She'd overstayed her welcome. She'd come back later when she was clean and remembered her manners. She hurried down the grand staircase and at the entrance she

paused, before heading outside so she could call a cab.
Guilt seemed to be riding on her tail; guilt for hurting an
old lady, guilt for leaving and guilt for running out on
Guy. But she just couldn't face him after hurting his
grandmother. The demons of guilt chased her right out
the front door. She glanced over her shoulder as she
exited and the man in her path wasn't quick enough.
She ran smack into him. As she tumbled backward, her
first thought had been that she'd run into one of the
pillars.

Until he spoke. "What the hell? Who let you in…?"

Looking up from her sprawled position, Bailey brushed
her tangled hair out of her face. That's when he stopped
talking and audibly gasped, making her feel like he was
looking at someone who was horribly disfigured.

Her first instinct was to scoot backward as fast as she
could. For a moment she was sure she'd seen evil
emblazoned in his eyes. The vision scared her almost as
much as all the times she'd hidden in dark closets waiting
for her mom to come back and get her. She shook her
head to clear it. When she looked again, the man seemed
very contrite and was offering to help her up.

"I'm so sorry, Miss. That was totally my fault. I can't
believe I was so clumsy."

She frowned as she cautiously placed her hand in his.
She doubted this large, elegantly dressed man did
anything awkwardly. He appeared very self-contained,
demanding attention and strong as he pulled her up with
little effort. She stumbled forward into him.

"I'm sorry again."

"No, it's me. I just don't know my own strength. Now
where were you off to in such a hurry?"

"I was heading to the guard house to get a cab." She
could have googled it but she had no idea where she was,
so couldn't have told the cab driver where to come to.
But the man guarding the gate would know.

"Oh, the phones in the house aren't working?"

"No. I just felt I'd overstayed my welcome and that I should leave. It was nice meeting you. Sorry for barging into you."

"Don't worry about it. You know I'm headed into town. Could I give you a lift?"

"Well…" Bailey brushed her hands down her pants. Something didn't feel right. But as it dawned on her that she seemed to be insulting everyone here, she shook off the feeling.

Why pass this up. I've already caused enough headaches.

"Sure. I'm Bailey, by the way."

"I'm Geoff."

"Nice to meet you, Geoff," she said as she fell into step beside him. "What do you do here?"

"Oh, odd jobs. You know, this and that."

She tried not to be obvious as she took in his three-piece suit and leather dress shoes.

His nostrils flared as he replied to her unanswered question, "I have a date tonight. A date I've been waiting a long time for."

Feeling contrite at his offended tone, she apologized, "I'm sorry. I wasn't trying to imply anything. You look fabulous. Any woman would be thrilled to go out with you. The flecks of gray in your hair are hot right now. Women like that." She was sure that they were what was left from his dye job, so whether it was an accident or on purpose, she did have to admit it made him look very worldly and distinguished.

He beamed at her. "Why, thank you. I can't tell you how good that makes me feel. And you, what do you do?"

Noticing him glancing at her clothes in turn, she couldn't help but laugh. Self-consciously, she brushed her hands down her wrinkled, stained t-shirt. "I usually look much better than this, honestly. It's just been a crazy day." *Week. Month. Take your pick.* "I'm an interior designer in Victoria."

"Hmmmm, Victoria, how did you end up there?" *Odd question.*

"Moved there when I was twenty. Loved it, so I stayed."

"You got tired of living on the prairies."

"I wouldn't say that. It was just time for me to move out on my own. My mom…" Glancing around, she noted they were surrounded by trees. She could no longer see the large mansion—a feat she didn't think was possible. The back of her neck started to tingle. "Uh, where are we going?" She looked back over her shoulder to the winding cobblestone path they'd been following. Ahead there were only more trees.

"I live in a house back here. My car is parked just ahead. It's not far."

Though she was far from at ease, she continued with him. "How long have you lived here?"

His face took on a haunted look so fleeting that Bailey wasn't sure she'd actually seen it. "A very long time."

"It must be something to live here and enjoy this place whenever you want?"

"You have no idea, child. No idea."

Suddenly, the path took a sharp left and they came out of the forest onto a service road. A midnight blue sedan was parked there.

"Get in."

She stiffened. Her senses were ringing like a church bell on Sunday morning. She sensed something… His smile seemed genuine but she noted that he cocked his head such that she couldn't quite see his eyes. He was patiently holding the door.

This is Guy's world. Not mine. Everything is fine.

"Thanks." Stepping forward, she shook off the bad vibes again, putting it down to exhaustion and hurting an elderly lady who'd done nothing but invite her into her home. She wasn't about to hurt another old person.

He nodded and walked around the car as she slid into the passenger seat. As he climbed in, she noticed his ring. It was ugly and gaudy and looked like he'd have to be a weightlifter to wear it. She looked a little closer. *A ruby?*

"What did you say you do here?"

"I didn't." He started the car and shifted into gear, easing them forward.

Bailey's temple started to throb as her stomach clenched like she was in an inverted roller coaster.

How does he know I lived on the prairies?

Not questioning what her body was telling her, she grabbed the door handle to fling herself out. But he was too quick. He slammed on the brakes, throwing her into the dash, his large hand tangled in her hair, forcing her head to connect rather forcefully. He grabbed her arm and slammed her back. The cold whisper of metal caressing her cheek convinced her to stop struggling.

Nausea churned in her stomach, clutching at her throat. Her breath was shallow. Her mouth dry, she whispered, "Who are you?"

He moved in close, his chuckle as grating as nails over a blackboard, shaking her to her core. "Aaaahhhhhhhhh but the question is, my dear, who are you?"

44

She's the spitting image of Mother. I can't believe it. It was like looking at Mother when I was a small child. Of course, she'd have never been caught dead in those horrid clothes. Really, Guy," she arched her brow at him, "couldn't you have bought her some nice, clean clothes?" She patted her perfectly coiffed silver hair. "You could even have put them on your expense account."

Guy smiled lightly at her attempted humor. Her eyelids drooped almost as much as her shoulders did. He'd never seen her this tired.

"Can you help me lay down or do you need to call Penelope?"

He eased her down onto the bed. "Enough with the guilt trip, Grams. Things happened. We arrived. Don't worry, I'll make sure she gets cleaned up before dinner. You'll be dazzled. Okay?"

Tears filled her eyes. It was almost Guy's undoing.

"Don't, Grams."

"All those years lost. I can't wait to tell Gina and Daniel. It will be such a shock. I'm not sure how she'll take it. She's been shut down for so long. I'm not sure how well I'm taking it." Resting against the pillows Guy positioned behind her, she lifted her shoe-clad feet onto the bed. "It's such a miracle." She closed her eyes. In that moment she looked so worn out and helpless. The blueness of her veins stood out like road maps against her paper-thin, pale skin. Age had caught up with her in less than an hour. That shook Guy. He'd never thought of her as old. Even at seventy-eight, she had always been so full of energy.

He leaned over and kissed her cheek, feeling guilty he'd forgotten to do that when they'd arrived.

"You're a good boy, Guy. Thank you. Now let me rest." She patted his face, something she'd never done before. "Thank you for my gift." With that she closed her eyes and drifted off to sleep.

He knew he should get back to Bailey but there was something so fragile about his Grandma that he was reluctant to leave her. Something was off.

From the corner chifforobe he pulled out a throw blanket and gently laid it over her before leaving. He stood in the hallway, taking in several deep breaths before heading down the curved staircase to where he'd left Bailey on the third floor. He stepped onto the balcony, pausing to take in the view. The majestic beauty always caught him, pulled at him. The serenity of the place was so much like a well orchestrated song, able to transport the listener somewhere beautiful.

He stuffed his hands in his pockets as he turned, fully expecting Bailey to have a smart comment about his behavior, only she wasn't there. He looked around and then walked to the edge to scan the area. If he was to guess, he'd bet her independent and curious nature got the better of her. He went back inside. As he wandered through the house, he checked both swimming pools, especially his favorite, the one with the retractable wall, and then the four hot tubs and then six of the twelve vacant rooms.

The nausea grew stronger as he searched. Tamping down his overactive imagination, he knew there was one place he hadn't yet checked. It was where he always went—the kitchen. Heading to the back side of the house, he found the lady that really ran the place.

"Hello, Penelope."

She was arranging a buffet style flower bouquet to adorn the second dining room, the one with a magnificent outdoor view of the gardens. She spun around at the sound of her name. Her face lit up.

"My Guy."

He grinned back. She'd been calling him that ever since he was ten and was the same size as her. She launched herself at him. If his Grandmother had been around, that would never have happened. He caught her and gave her a big bear hug, easily lifting the tiny woman off her feet. "My Penelope."

She giggled as he set her down and looped her arm through his. "What can I get you to eat? I've made cinnamon buns."

Guy groaned. She'd been making and feeding him her world famous buns all his life. They were so irresistible he'd have killed someone to get to them. He was just glad he wasn't around all the time anymore, or he'd look like a baby elephant.

"Actually, Penelope, I'm looking for someone—"

A flustered young woman of about twenty-five flew into the room. "Miss Penelope, Mr. Carter, our meat supplier, says he's not taking blame for the lost order. Said it was our fault."

"Guy, good to see you. I'll have time later?"

"Yeah, sure Penelope. Go give him hell."

She stood tall, all five feet of her, put the same fierce look on her face which had scared Guy a time or two and marched out of the room. Just before exiting she gave him a wink over her shoulder.

The woman had been his savior. Everyone and everything had been so starched and proper when he'd moved there as a child, he'd been afraid to go near anyone or anything. He was a wild young boy unsure of his identity, a pawn in an ugly game of money and revenge. Then there was Geoffrey reinforcing that he was unlovable, something he'd already believed about himself. Geoff had made his life hell. Penelope had befriended him, though. She'd gotten to him through her food. Even now, he'd crawl across burning coals to get to the dishes she served. Not only could she cook but she'd been the one to teach him how to throw an uppercut as well as a few moves not sanctioned by any martial arts. But they'd been very effective. The skills she'd taught him had stopped a bully or two from beating him into a pulp, convincing them to finally leave him alone—all except Geoff.

Sighing, Guy walked to the ten-foot table specially designed to hold fresh-cut flowers. Every five days they were completely replaced. He secretly believed it was Penelope's way to do what she loved. No one else was allowed to touch it. He leaned over to smell their exquisite scents and admire the array—orchids, lilies, carnations and roses. It was beautiful.

He glanced out the window that looked onto the rear of the property. Two of the four massive fish ponds, stocked with foreign exotic fish, were the focal points within the uniquely designed Japanese Garden. It was so lush with plants it had once been his favorite hiding place.

Looking beyond the five acres of gardens, trees obscured some of the scruffy, forbidden area. It had been off limits to him, reinforced by Geoffrey more than once, especially the time he'd explored the boarded-up old shack at the far edge, unseen from the main house. The beating Geoffrey had given him for playing around the old building had cured any curiosity he might ever have had about it. It had just been another excuse for Geoffrey to hurt him. Guy had never told anyone but he'd learned to stay out of his uncle's way. And since he'd failed miserably at piano, cello, the harp, the flute and even the guitar which he'd thought he'd be fabulous at, he'd had plenty of time to find ways to avoid the man.

His grandmother had finally stopped paying for lessons, much to the delight of the poor musicians who'd had to work with his tone deafness.

He went back through the house again, stopping every servant he encountered to ask about Bailey. When no one had seen her, he realized he needed to listen to the forty-pound weight that was churning in his stomach. Pulling out his cell he made a call.

"Graham. We've got a problem. I can't find Bailey."

"What do you mean?"

"I mean…" he proceeded to tell him what had transpired since they'd arrived. "I need you to find Geoffrey."

"On it. I'll be there in fifteen minutes."

Putting away his phone, he realized he'd been asking everyone the wrong question. Heading out the front door, he looked for Emilio, the head gardener.

Rounding the west side, he strode toward the elaborate greenhouse with nearly eight thousand square feet of state of the art equipment. Emilio was working on growing tropical plants and large overhead fans whirred as they worked to keep the place at a constant temperature. Walking through the front door, Guy headed off to his right and stepped through the open door to the head gardener's office—a smaller greenhouse, where he was working on developing flowering hybrids.

"Hello, Emilio."

Carefully setting down the pot in his hand, Emilio turned with a big grin on his face. "Guy. Good to have you back. You stay long?"

Guy smiled and shook his hand. "Not sure. I'm looking for a young woman—"

Emilio grinned. "It's about time."

"Ha ha. No, I brought a young woman with me to meet Grandma. Only she's disappeared. Have you seen her?"

"No. No young woman."

"How about Geoff, has he been around today?"

Emilio shifted his eyes.

"It's okay, Emilio. I promise he won't find out you told me."

He gave one sharp nod.

"Do you know how he got here? I didn't see his car or his driver."

"He drove." Emilio started arranging soil and seeds in a long container.

"Thanks, Emilio." He left knowing he wouldn't get any more from the gardener. All the employees were terrified of Geoffrey. Guy once thought he'd been the only recipient of his wrath but he'd soon learned that anyone Geoffrey, who considered everyone his inferior, was subject to his violence.

So Geoffrey's here. Where the hell is he? And what's he going to do to Bailey?

Guy didn't understand it but he knew Geoff had Bailey. He called the guard house only to be told, "No, Geoffrey hasn't come through the gate." Guy had spent so much of his life running from the ogre that it dawned on him how many times he'd seen Geoffrey at the estate but not his car. So how had he gotten onto the fenced and gated property without coming through the front entrance?

Thumping his fist against his thigh, there was one person who could answer his questions. He headed back into the house and flew up the five flights of stairs, two at a time. He knocked but entered the bedroom without permission. Her eyes were still shut. He gently shook her.

"W-what?"

"Grams, I need to know about Geoffrey."

She closed her eyes, and when she reopened them they were full of anguish.

"What's he done?"

"I think he's got Bailey. I can't find her. He's here but didn't come through the front. Where is he?"

If it was possible for her skin to grow any paler, it did. Her voice wobbled, "Help me up and into my chair."

He assisted her into a seated position. Once she was steady, he got her to her feet and held on tightly as he walked her the ten steps to a rocker situated by the window. After she was seated, he stepped back. She immediately looked out over the massive gardens, some planted just for her, so she'd have the best view from her window.

"He's really not an evil man, just a wounded one. Get me a glass of water, please."

Stepping to the oak cabinet, he pulled open the big doors, retrieved a glass from the shelf and filled it from the water cooler. He handed it to her then stepped back, shoving his hands into his pants pockets as he waited. Patience would hopefully get him some answers. There was one thing he'd learned early on, rushing Dorothea got him nowhere.

"My mother tried to love Geoff but she always let him know he wasn't good enough, which humiliated him to no end. Dad wasn't any better. They should have been thrilled to have a son. I was nine when Geoffrey came along. I loved him from the moment I saw him. I took him everywhere and he idolized me." Smiling sadly, she looked Guy in the eye. "At least until he did this." She pulled up the side of her silk dress to show him a jagged scar that started at mid-thigh and continued below her knee.

Though he tried to maintain a poker face, he could not mask his horror. "How?"

Tears ran unimpeded down her face. "When he was seven or eight, he had a nightmare. I had gone to him to comfort him, but he didn't want me; he wanted Mom. There'd been a huge party here that night. She'd let him come, only to make him a laughingstock. She'd had his pants hemmed different lengths. His shirt was too small. Two different shoes. She'd made him wear it all and then pointed it out to everyone, how simple he was that he couldn't even dress properly. I tried to rescue him but he got mad and pushed me. I fell. Just bruised, nothing more. But that night after his nightmare, when he was running up the stairs to mom and dad's suite, I followed. My parents were yelling."

She stopped, taking in a long, shaky breath. "My mother was calling my father some really ugly things. That's when it came out that Geoff was his son, not hers. Image was everything to my mother. It seems a maid had tempted my father. I don't know whatever happened to the girl, but my parents kept the baby and she simply vanished. That night tainted everything. Geoffrey changed. He was angry all the time. He wouldn't let me near him. It broke my heart. I felt like I had been his mother. And he didn't want me. I always treated him like he was family."

Guy leaned down and hugged her as sobs wracked her body, emphasizing the frail bones that felt like they would snap under his hands.

"When Geoffrey turned eighteen, he was going to leave home which I think my parents were quite happy about. They were tired of paying off and trying to cover up all his illegal stunts and immoral behavior. He went out of his way to humiliate them, not unlike what mother had done to him. I'd left home but came back to celebrate his eighteenth birthday. He got very drunk. He'd taken down one of Dad's many swords that once adorned the walls. Some dated back to the fifteenth or sixteenth centuries. They were massive, beautiful. I don't know whatever became of them. They disappeared after that night."

Guy felt his hands curl into fists. He wanted to punch something but knew Dorothea didn't need to see any more violence. She'd seen and experienced more than her share.

"I was the golden child. I could do no wrong in Mom's eyes. To Geoffrey it must have been another slight against him. Anyway the night he came of age, he had a huge party. There were lots of lowlife scum, the type he surrounded himself with. They filled the pool with booze and broken bottles. Drugs were everywhere. Sex. There were people doing 'it' wherever they pleased. There was this young woman who was on something. She was wild. I told her she'd have to leave. We got into a bit of a tussle. Next thing I know, Geoffrey had a sword. He was swinging it around like he was dueling and he stabbed me in the leg."

Her thin chest heaved with emotion. "He always told me he was sorry and that he'd been trying to get the woman off me. But I knew... I knew in my heart, he'd done it on purpose. That young woman was one of his whores."

"Why didn't you turn him in?"

"I couldn't. He was like my child. I felt I could fix him." She laughed harshly. "I've been trying to do that my whole life. And I'm still making excuses for him. No more. He's evil. If he hurts that beautiful child, I will kill him." Pushing herself to her feet with the energy of a twenty- year-old, she strode to the door. "There's an old house a century old on the back part of the property. Geoffrey wanted it. Said it was his sanctuary. It's all boarded up and unsafe. I'd bet anything that's where he is."

"Where are you going?"

"I'm coming with you."

Guy took her arm and steered her, with difficulty, back to her chair. "No. You'll wait here. Don't worry, I'll bring Bailey back. I promise." He gave her a quick kiss and sailed out of the room. As he was nearing the ground floor, he heard the sound of Graham's vehicle. He raced out to meet him, jumping in the Hummer before it had fully stopped.

"The old house." He'd told Graham about it and the beating Geoffrey had given him, one night they'd been melancholy over their beer.

"How do we get there?"

He pointed to the cobbled path. "Take that."

Graham's eyes widened but he gunned the Hummer and shot down the ornate, colorfully-flowered path.

"You do realize your grandmother will string you up by your nether regions."

Guy grimaced. "Yeah but I think she'll forgive me. If I'm right about Geoff—"

No more words were spoken as tires turned beautiful flowers into scented mulch.

45

"You'll never get away with this." Bailey tested the plastic wrist cuffs. They didn't budge. Every time she moved they sliced into her skin like shark's teeth. He placed his hand firmly against her back and pushed her forward. She tripped and was barely able to remain on her feet. They rounded a dense growth of trees and entered a small clearing. He directed her to walk toward the thick foliage. A vision of a remote cave loomed in her mind, a dark, dank hole he could throw her into where she would never be found. She wasn't going to stick around to find out as she sought an opportunity to run. His knife blade rarely left her skin and her t-shirt was glued to her back in several places by blood oozing from the cuts he'd already had great pleasure in giving her.

He pushed her to walk around the side of the massive overgrown area where the stench of mold, mildew and rotting lumber assaulted her. There was an underlying pungent reek that was so strong, she coughed and tried to bury her nose in her shoulder.

He laughed. "Don't like the gourmet scents I've made? You disappoint me." Shoving her hard, she tripped over the vines and thick undergrowth, twisting as she fell to land on her shoulder. Rolling over, she glared at the man with the sick, demented smile and the most malevolent eyes she'd ever seen. She was beginning to believe she really had seen an evil presence in them earlier.

"Stay there."

He moved aside the cascading vines. Behind them was a solid structure, from which he removed a few boards. She rolled over but a quick stab of his knife into her arm kept her immobile. She could do no more than lay there and watch. He flipped open a small door before jerking her to her feet and shoving her toward the hole.

"Climb in."

The door was three feet off the ground, three feet high and three feet wide, not an easy place to climb into. As she hesitated, he planted his hands on her butt and heaved her through with the force of a missile launcher. Unable to brace herself she landed head first. Black and white spots danced before her.

He scrambled over the top of her before she had time to recover. Then he grabbed her by the shoulder and the crotch and tossed her the rest of the way in, his lower hand digging in much more than was necessary. She shuddered. A look of lust contorted his face. He stood over her, pressing his fingers to his nostrils as he drew in deep breaths.

A violent revulsion shook her body. Fear and panic fought for control, moving over her in waves like a pipeline tide rolling over itself.

Hang on. Hang on. Don't give in. Guy will come. DO NOT GIVE IN! A tiny voice of sanity repeated over and over in her head. Guy would get there in time. She couldn't give up hope.

"Get up."

Not wanting his hands on her again, she scrambled to her feet. Swaying slightly, she stared at the man she'd somehow make sure would pay for this. He gestured for her to go up the stairs. After taking in her surroundings, she noted that although the exterior looked like nothing more than vines and trees, the interior appeared as solid as a vault as if he'd built a house within a house. Then it hit her like a sledgehammer. That's exactly what he'd done. He'd left the shell of an old place and built a new one inside. Sturdy two by fours framed several unfinished support walls. The plywood floor was covered in dust but all of it was new.

"Couldn't find an interior decorator? You know, if you'd asked I'm sure we could agree upon a price."

He growled at her.

No sense of humor.

She moved up the sturdy wood stairs. At the top, he shoved her to the left. The upstairs appeared much the same except here the walls were finished. He opened the only door, hustling her through it.

The room might have looked completely appropriate in the mansion. A king sized bed with a multi-colored silk spread in autumn colors filled one end of the room. Two large mahogany dressers stood against one wall. Two oak closet doors completed the room. It was very masculine but insanely classy in such a setting.

The dread that had been clawing at her veins earlier threatened to do so again.

The last memory I have on this earth will not be this man raping me.

"I see you did a better job of getting a good decorator in here. May I suggest you stick with the one you found. Not good practice to change when in the middle of renovations. No two designers ever see a place quite the same. And since you seem happy with—"

He punched her with the force of a bat cracking against her jaw, and her head whipped back. Unable to catch herself, she stumbled, falling against the wall. He shoved his face into hers.

"Shut your mouth, bitch. I thought I'd dealt with you a long time ago. You will not ruin my life!"

She scanned her memory but she had no doubt she had never met him before. Someone like him she'd never forget.

"I'm sorry about that. I know I sometimes do things without thinking—"

"You have no idea what you've done." Stepping back, he grabbed her upper arm in a vise grip and forced her toward the twin oak doors just off to her right.

"I need—"

He jerked her hard, snapping her body around like a pretzel as pain radiated through her body. The plastic cuffs continued slicing into her skin, a constant reminder that her hands were secured behind her back. He dragged her through a clothes closet that was easily twice the size of her bedroom.

In an instant, all that had happened over the last seven days charged at her. Weakness threatened the stability of her knees. The emotional clutch, sitting at the back of her throat, caused her nostrils to flare and tears threatened to fill the corners of her eyes. Bowing her head slightly, she struggled to pull herself back under control. It wasn't until he unlocked another door, flipped on a dim light and pushed her through that her disturbed state became one of sheer horror. Her mouth went dry. Her breathing became choppy, labored. Any thought of escape or help vanished. This was to be her grave.

The state-of-the-art electronic equipment caught her immediate attention, the shiny metal standing out starkly against the black color of literally everything else in the room—a thin carpet, the walls, the ceiling and even one tiny window. Her eyes widened as it registered what she was seeing. Sticks of dynamite adorned the walls at intervals around the room. She couldn't blink as her gaze followed the path of the connectors, going from one stick to another. Wires, hanging as though hastily strung, dropped behind a small, innocuous square box in the corner that looked as innocent as a clock radio. The number twenty blinked at her. The detonator was set and waiting for its final command.

Time stood still as the import of what she was seeing hit her. "Why?" she gasped.

He straightened to his full six-foot-two height as though it improved his status. "Because you will ruin everything. You never should have been. I did everything to prevent you. Everything. Yet you came. The joy for everyone." His fist came so fast she didn't have time to brace for it. It landed full in her stomach with the driving impact of a boxer's punch. With the wind knocked completely out of her, she doubled over, crumpling to the floor. Bile rose in her throat. Pain radiated, spiraling outward.

He strolled across the room and casually flipped a switch. The wall became a larger than life screen. It wasn't until he'd pressed the third button and she saw Guy's grandma staring out her bedroom window that Bailey understood. He continued to flip through live video feed from the main house.

Her instincts kicked in. "So I'm the basis of all your problems. I don't remember meeting you before. Can you refresh my memory?"

She'd seen a lot in her life. Not much shocked her— not the ugliness of people, the selfishness, or the malice. But she'd never seen anything like him. The muscles in his face contorted, displaying ridges and dips that looked more like a mask than something that was humanly possible. His eyes went black. Lifeless. It was the most vicious, hideous thing she'd ever seen.

"Oh, we met my dear. You were only a few hours old, so I'll forgive you for not remembering. You never should have been. I was giving Gina a concoction that should have prevented a baby. But you. You had to be born. Damn you." He pointed his finger. "I had everything planned. Then you came along and ruined it. Threatened all I had built up."

"I was only a baby."

"BUT A LEGITIMATE ONE!" His face was almost purple with rage. He stormed toward her, driving his fist into the wall over her head and missing only by inches, thanks to her quick slump sideways. He backed away, his eyes glazed.

She couldn't help but cringe as she waited for an impact which thankfully never came. "But what about—uh—Dorothea's daughter? M-my mother?"

"Was not interested in the business, which broke Dorothea's heart. Of course it was really easy to screw up that relationship. Gina hated her mother for a long time." He laughed. "But with you, she was already making plans to groom you, to bring you into the fold. To teach you to be president of this company, my company. Which means she'd have started looking a little more closely at what I was doing. Even back then, the company was paying me well for things that never existed." He chuckled at his own joke. "That was not going to happen. You were not going to mess up everything I worked for. She was talking about you being her little golden princess. Her opportunity to make things right. She was always trying to make things right. To make up for our parents' shortfalls. To make up for how our parents treated me. This company was mine. Should have been mine. I deserved it. Not her. She already had the one thing that meant anything to me and she planned on giving it to you as soon as you were educated. You. So I took away what had meaning for her. I am not the acting CEO. I own this company. She just doesn't know it yet. You were not going to take what was mine."

He straightened his tie. "How did you survive? I'd gotten rid of you. The woman who took you died. Why didn't you? That would have solved everything. Everything."

The time to get away from him was now. She scooted on her butt along the wall. Something tore into her hand, causing her to wince in pain. Her first thought had been to shift away but then it dawned on her that whatever had ripped her skin just might cut through the plastic cuffs. Quietly and slowly she lifted her arms methodically up and down over the sharp object. Things could not end this way. Guy flashed in her mind. She hadn't ever really given him a chance—*them* a chance. She did what she knew, which was how to protect herself. Could they have had anything? Would she get another chance to find out?

The ties hadn't been cut through yet but she felt they were close to snapping. She just had to keep Geoff from figuring out what she was doing. When he glanced her way, she squirmed as if protesting the hard floor.

"Do you know how much I paid to make you disappear?" he bellowed. Then he smiled at her with the smugness of a victor.

"Well obviously not enough because I'm still here."

He growled as fury radiated off him like a furnace. He stormed to the window, grabbed the black covering as though about to pull it back. It was then she heard the loud hum of a vehicle. Praying it was someone looking for her and not one of his accomplices, she kicked out with her foot. The metal stool sitting in front of his electronic equipment clanged loudly as it crashed into the table. He whipped around. Rage contorted his face. He stormed to the detonator and punched in a code. The flashing stopped. The countdown began.

19:59

19:58

19:57

19:56

She stared at the numbers that were steadily dropping one at a time, slowly, methodically.

"You're finished. And all because of me." He laughed. "Oh, the people that will cry over your death. It will be music to my ears."

"You really think you're smart enough to get away with this?"

In two steps, he was above her. He clipped her jaw and her lip immediately bloomed into a fat puff ball as buzzing filled her eardrums like an angry beehive. At that moment, the wrist ties gave way. She leapt to her feet, driving the top of her head into his nose. The bone cracked, the sound reverberating, followed by an animalistic howl as he stumbled backward. Blood gushed between his fingers as he tried vainly to stop the flow. She spun on her heel and rushed for the door but barely made it three steps before his hand lashed out, grabbing her shirt. Fighting for all she was worth, she twisted, raised her arms and ducked at the same time. The top slipped over her head. She was free. She ran for the door.

A loud thwack pivoted her head around to the right. She didn't know if he was a bad aim or if she was just damn lucky but his knife was now embedded in the wall three inches from her chin. Panicking, she raced through the closet, out of the bedroom, grabbing and slamming the doors behind her. Using the railing, she jumped down the stairs three at a time. On the main floor, she raced for the entrance. She was about to shove out the makeshift door and dive through when a bullet whizzed past her ear.

"You're mine."

Raising her hands in surrender, she turned slowly. Her gut clenched as the thundering of her heart drowned out all else.

He shot again. The impact crumpled her leg, dropping her to the floor like a sack of potatoes. She landed heavily on her side. The pain took a moment to register but when it hit, she clenched her jaw, refusing to give in to the searing agony burning through her calf. As she clamped her hand over the wound, blood flowed like a gentle fountain between her fingers. She collapsed in front of the opening.

"You will suffer as I have suffered."

With the last vestiges of strength she had, she lifted her head and faced her captor. "Go ahead and kill me, you bastard. But be prepared because I will haunt you for the rest of your life. I will see you in hell."

46

"Where is this goddamn place?" Graham spun the wheel as they hit another hole, jerking them sideways.

Guy looked around at the unfamiliar area. He hadn't been back since he was a boy, and now it didn't resemble his memories at all. Everything was massive, wild and overgrown. They suddenly burst out of the trees into an open field.

"Stop!"

As he closed his eyes, he went back in time to the day he'd gone exploring. He struggled to shut out the memory of Geoff, the beating and how much of a monster he'd been that day.

He wandered around the gardens for a while but got bored. Besides, the gardener was following him around, making sure he didn't touch any of his prized flowers. Then he found a narrow dirt path that took him into the forest. He followed it, weaving back and forth until he'd finally come upon a clearing. Encouraged by the sunshine in the open space, he stopped to pick flowers for his Grandmother that were unlike any he'd seen in her gardens. When he was about half way, he spotted the top of a house peeking above the trees, urging him to explore.

"That way." He pointed straight across the open stretch in front of them. As he let go of the last vestiges of his memory, he found it ironic that he'd wandered for hours but after Geoffrey had beaten him, he'd found his way home in record time.

"The police are coming, right?"

"Bean said they're on their way." They bounced over the rough terrain but Graham didn't slow down.

Guy stared eagerly ahead but there was no sign of a building. As they approached a large cluster of massive trees, he grabbed Graham's arm. He hit the brakes immediately. They climbed out and moved silently through the grove, pausing periodically to listen and observe. All he saw was a forest. Frowning, his eyes returned to the densest area.

"It's here. I know it. Where the hell do you hide a shack?"

"Let's split up. I'll go about a hundred and fifty feet that way," Graham pointed off to his left. "You walk toward me and then we'll zigzag back and forth as we go forward."

They moved off.

I'll kill you Geoff. I will kill you.

Guy and Graham methodically searched the area. They had been walking for only a couple of minutes, when Graham crowed; had the situation not been so dire, he might have smiled at Graham's bird call—a cross between a choking chicken and a dying crow—but it helped him to realize he needed to stay focused on saving Bailey and not killing Geoff. Guy needed his wits about him. He moved toward Graham and it wasn't until he'd almost reached him that he realized the dense area they'd passed could actually hide a house, overgrown and camouflaged by plants. Though it gave the appearance of a place swallowed by undergrowth, Guy's gut told him it was Geoffrey's concerted landscaping. He was in there.

Not sure what they'd find, they remained together, stealthily making their way around the perimeter. Even after circling the area, they couldn't find any opening and because they hadn't been paying attention to where they stepped, they might have trampled any evidence that might have shown where Geoff had entered the building.

"Shit! I know they're in there. The question is how did they get in? We may have to start pulling boards." Frustrated after the second lap around, Guy kicked the ground. The fern that looked like it had grown over fluttered and moved. He bent down and pulled on one of the fronds. It came away in his hand. Crab walking forward he kept grabbing and moving the fake plants that had covered what looked to be a path. When he reached a wall, he yanked and pulled aside the vines to reveal a trap door. Two boards had been removed and were leaning off to the side, hidden by dense undergrowth.

"You bastard…"

Bailey's voice was muffled but distinct. He ripped at the wall until Graham reached past him and stuck his hand in a hidden hole, grabbed the handle and pulled. Spotting long brown hair and trickles of blood running along a bra strap and over bare skin, Guy reached in. He grabbed the back of the waistband with both hands and hauled her out. Fighting for all she was worth, just as she cleared the door her left arm connected with his jaw. Losing his footing, they fell sideways. Her fists pummeled him as she scrambled to get away.

"Bailey. Bailey! It's me. I'm here to help you."

The sound of a gunshot gave Guy the leverage he needed. He grabbed her wrists and pulled her into the bushes behind him, stopping when he realized she was hobbling. Her eyes were wild and unfocused, peering at him through her mane of tangled hair. He pulled her close, hugging her until he felt some of the tension leave her body. He wanted to say so much to her but now wasn't the time. He did what he hoped would convey what he couldn't say. He kissed her hard. At first there was no response but then she returned his passion in full, holding him tight. She was clinging to him as though she never wanted to let him go. It was the sound of more shots that pulled him back to the present. He gently pushed her away, giving her one more quick kiss before thrusting her at Graham.

"Take her. I have to get Geoff." He moved past them and snuck back to the opening. Geoffrey was standing in the middle of the floor, his head thrown back, his body shaking with laughter. It was deep and guttural and sent a cold arrow right to Guy's core.

What did you do to her, you bastard?

All his life he'd wanted the opportunity to beat the man to a pulp. It had been an obsession. He'd trained. He'd sweated. He'd waited. And now the moment was on him. He had enough reasons, if not for what he'd done to him throughout his life, but also for what he'd done to Bailey.

Geoff raised his arms toward the ceiling and shouted, "Come and get me, you bastard. Come and get me. I've served you well."

The sirens howled in the distance.

Graham stepped out of the thick foliage, supporting Bailey. "Guy, we have to get out of here. He's planted explosives. They're set to go off any minute."

Guy glanced at them before returning to the scene playing out inside the house. Geoff seemed to be in another world, unaware of what was going on around him. "Go. I'll be right there." He climbed through the hole. His uncle had to have heard him but didn't acknowledge him.

"Geoff, we have to leave."

"Who the hell do you think you are?" He swung around, aiming the gun at Guy. His finger stroked the trigger. A smile of revenge lit his face. "Brave Guy, saving the damsel in distress. How sweet. Always the little suck-up. Ha-ha-ha-ha-ha-ha-ha."

"We need to get out of here. This place is going to explode."

"You think I'm stupid, boy. I set the damn dynamite. This isn't the way I planned on going out but getting to take you along will be a bonus. Dorothea will be devastated at losing her little pet."

"Why do you hate her so much? She did everything for you."

"She was the golden one, the one with true blue blood." Spittle flew from his mouth as he yelled, "Mine's just as good dammit. Mine's just as good." The black, dead pupil was all Guy could see over the muzzle of the gun.

There was no doubt Geoff would shoot him and there was no way Guy could save both of them, so he took the only choice he had. He dove through the hole behind him. He jumped to his feet and ran, like he had the time Geoff had beaten him as a kid and threatened his life. Shots pinged around him as he weaved. His arm felt like it was on fire but he didn't stop to see why. He burst out into the open field, thrilled to see the Hummer, jumping in through the open back door. Graham hit the gas pedal and spun the wheel at the same time, whipping them around to bounce and jerk their way over the grassy field. They were about halfway to the tree line when the explosion rocked the ground beneath them. The deafening force shoved the Hummer like a bulldozer on full throttle. They fishtailed sideways but Graham struggled to correct their course while fighting to keep the vehicle moving forward. Once the power of the explosion abated, they slowed, looking back, jaws slack. Flames shot skyward in every direction. Chunks of wood, tree branches and debris flew through the air, some landing within spitting distance of them.

"Get out of here, Graham." The words were barely out of Guy's mouth before they were on the move again, maneuvering around the debris field. They didn't slow down until they'd reached the cobbled sidewalk. They drove past Emilio, who wore a horrified expression, not because a building had blown up and was landing all over the place but because of the damage done to his beautiful gardens.

"Did you call the fire department?"

"Yup, they're on their way as well. I called Bean to let him know what was going down. I think we'll let him sweat a bit about whether or not we got out. I think this lady needs to get to the hospital." Graham indicated Bailey who was strapped into the passenger seat, slumped against the door, a hastily applied tourniquet tied around her calf.

"What happened?"

"He shot her in the leg. Cut her up a bit. Physically, she'll be fine."

As they approached the gate, Guy called ahead. "Open the gate, Jim. We're on the way to the hospital. The fire department and the police are on the way." When they reached it a few seconds later, it was open and Jim gave them a thumbs-up.

"Looks like you could use the hospital too?"

"Huh?" Until that moment Guy hadn't felt the pain. Now there was a burning fire radiating from his shoulder. Moving his arm from where he cradled it against his chest, he pulled his shirt up and over his head, groaning only slightly as everything threatened to go black. He wrapped the shirt tightly around the wound where the blood was running freely. He had no idea if he'd been shot or if it was the result of his dive to ground. He just knew it hurt like a bugger.

"Did you learn anything from that son of a bitch?"

"Yeah. He was and always will be a bastard."

47

I didn't steal you." Dorothea looked at him beseechingly.
"Let her sleep, Gram." Guy gently touched Dorothea's
shoulder. She was slouched in the overstuffed chair beside
Bailey's bed.

"Come on. I'll take you to your room." Since she didn't
argue nor offer resistance, an indication of how tired she
really was, it was easy for Guy to help her to her feet and
escort her to her bedroom.

"It's a day of no more secrets." Looking at him with
pain-filled eyes, she patted the stool in front of her.
"Come. Sit. There are some things you need to hear."

Frowning, he did as she asked.

"In this family there are too many stories; too many
half truths and too many lies." She bowed her head. He
squeezed her hand in a gesture of reassurance. Tears
streamed down her face and dripped off her chin, yet
she made no sound.

He gently brushed away the moisture. "Stop. You can't go back and change anything. Beating yourself up isn't helping anyone."

"I know but I can't stop. He was my brother. I knew he was a bully, but I never thought he was evil enough to hurt others like he did. The stories that are coming out—they can't all be true. Can they?"

Guy pursed his lips but didn't answer. He was sure they hadn't even touched on the horrors that Geoff had inflicted. Guy put his arms around her and let her rest against his shoulder. The newspapers were having a field day with stories about Geoffrey. The gates to Geoff's life had been blown wide open. It was hard to sift through what was fact and what was fiction but Guy didn't doubt that a lot of it was true. He just hadn't wanted his grandma to learn of them that way.

Five prostitutes had been found in a marshy field a few miles further east of the house he'd blown up. Prostitutes that would never have gone to the police were telling the media about the depraved man that had visited them regularly. None of them had been confident they'd still be alive when he'd finished with them. He had beaten all of them, permanently scarring many and performing atrocities that even the newspapers hesitated to print.

Then there were the people he'd bilked out of money. After stealing their life savings, he had brutalized them so they'd been too frightened to go to the police. The only person that found anything nice to say about him had been his receptionist. He'd been distant but fair with her. She never commented on whether she believed what was said about him. The horror the man had inflicted on so many people made Guy sick to his stomach.

"I don't know, Grams."

"You're a good person, Guy. I'm sure he left his scars on you, too."

He shrugged, not wanting to discuss with her what the man had done to him.

"There are things I should have told you."

"It's okay—"

"This is my tale to tell. You just listen. No more half-truths." She pressed her hand to her chest. "Anna was a maid here. She got pregnant. Rather than tell us about it, she left. I tried to find her but couldn't. A few years later, I had a private investigator track her down—and found you. There were rumors she'd been raped and conjecture about the father but Anna never told us. She was a beautiful lady. Her mother, your grandmother, Maria, had worked for our family for forty years but when she retired, she was bitter, hated this family. She blamed this family for her daughter's fall from grace. I think Anna was in love and her mother didn't approve of the relationship. Maria became nasty and made up stories."

His eyes widened and he could tell from her anxious expression that she was waiting for his reaction. He knew most of what she was telling him. Geoffrey had felt it important that he know his lack of heritage. He schooled his features and smiled warmly at her.

"She was urging Anna to sue us; to say Joseph, your grandfather, was the father. He wasn't. Anna made that clear to us. And I know he would never have cheated on me. She fought her mother. But when your mother died in a car accident, your grandmother wanted to use you as a pawn to make money. I couldn't stand what she'd done to Anna and then what she was trying to do to you." She sighed heavily. "I have always loved you like you were my own. Unfortunately, you had become a piece of property to her. I didn't steal you, but I agreed to pay but only if I got to raise you."

"Very lucky for me." Guy knew there was more to the story and that Dorothea had searched for almost a year to pull him out of the foster care system, his real grandmother had thrown him into.

Dorothea curled into herself, her head dropping to her chest. Startled, he leaned forward just as she raised her eyes to him. "It was lucky for me, too. Joseph died two years later and if it hadn't been for you, I'd have been alone. Gina was grown and gone and not wanting to have much to do with me. You were my son. My grandson. I hope you know that hasn't changed."

He hugged her. How long they sat there, he had no idea but at some point he became aware of her sagging against him in exhaustion. She was sleeping. He picked her up and laid her on the bed. He called Penelope to sit with her.

Guy left them alone, relieved that his grandmother was in good hands. Not only did she have a loyal staff but good friends as well. She'd need them. Stopping on the third floor, he walked onto the balcony rather than return to Bailey's room. He took in several deep breaths of the cool morning air.

"Craziest week I've ever had."

He spun around to face his friend and partner. "Yeah, not one I want to repeat any time soon. God, Graham."

"I know. We all have our skeletons but whoa I don't know anyone who can top your uncle's. Geoffrey was one sick puppy... if everything they say is true."

Guy shoved his hand through his unruly, thick hair that badly needed washing. He winced at the movement.

"How's the arm?"

"It's aching but the bullet just grazed me. I didn't even need stitches."

Graham hooted. "That's only because the doctor and Godzilla, the nurse, couldn't strap you down long enough to sew you back together. God, the look on that nurse's face when you grabbed her and kissed her on the mouth and then told her it had been a long time since you'd had a real woman. I thought she was going to be a puddle at your feet. Yeck!"

"Uh, but it got me out of having stitches." He smiled. "Man, I need a shower. You?"

"Yeah. I guess I should. I'm just going to finish my beer. Sure you don't want one?"

Guy shook his head and headed back into the house. He went to Bailey's room to check on her. She was sleeping soundly. The raw indents around her right wrist from the plastic cuffs looked like a neon sign against the white coverlet. His whole body tensed as he thought about what his uncle had put her through—had put all of them through. Not wanting to wake her, he stepped back, gently closing the door and heading to his room beside hers. He stripped and stepped into the shower. He turned it on as hot as he could and soaped himself down four times before he just stood there and let the water cascade over him. He shut his mind to all that could have happened and focused on the fact that Bailey was safe. Everything had been resolved. And he wasn't the outsider Geoff had wanted him to believe he was. Dorothea's trust, the craziness of all that had happened, meeting Bailey, was like a kick in the pants; one he'd probably needed for a while. It didn't matter where he came from. This was his family, his responsibility. He'd never really been sure where home was but he knew now.

He heard a distinct plop.

Guy opened his eyes and cocked his ear.

It was repeated.

He froze. With no idea what the noise was—especially coming from inside his bathroom—he started to reach out when the curtain was suddenly whipped aside. He jerked backward, his feet performing a fancy shuffle that barely kept him from landing on his butt. Bailey, in all her glorious skin and one white bandaged calf, climbed in beside him.

"I..." He tried to keep his eyes on her face; but beautiful though it was it wasn't quite as strong as the lure of the rest of her.

She put her finger to his lips. "I'm not asking. I'm taking. I've had a bitch of a week." She shook her head and smiled. "But you were always there for me. You saved me."

"So this is a pity fu—"

Her hand pressed over his mouth, muffling his response. Her slick body slid against his and that was just about enough to undo him. Groaning he pulled her in tightly, letting his hands roam over her back and down over her tight butt. His lips devoured hers. Her hands slid down over his shoulders and although there was a short jolt of pain reminding him of his injury, he ignored it and continued to explore all that she was offering.

He wasn't sure what brought him to his senses, maybe her brushing his wound, the whimper she let out when she stepped wrong on her injured leg or good old guilt. Breathing hard, he gently pushed her back. His hands slid up to cup her face as he softly kissed her ravaged mouth.

Heaven.

He pulled away, delicately extricating himself from her grasp and smiled sadly at her. "You are one sexy lady—"

"Is this your brush off? Don't worry, I can take a hint." Turning quickly, she stepped out of the tub, staggering when she landed on her injured leg.

He shut off the water and then grabbed two plush, white towels. Handing her one which she immediately used to cover up, he wrapped the other around his waist.

She bent to pick up her clothes—a white, mid-calf nighty, one his grandmother had purchased for her at a store she'd insisted they open at 4:00 a.m. Bailey's jerky, quick movements suggested she was very angry with him. He pressed his hands together and put them over his nose. Breathing deeply, he took a moment to tell himself he was doing the right thing. She looked him in the eye. The hurt in the depth of those blue-green eyes was like seeing waves break upon the beach. All hope was gone.

"To hell with it." Groaning, he threw all caution to the wind and pulled her into his arms. She was rigid.

"Look. I was trying to be a gentleman and not take advantage of you. You've had the week from hell. I don't want this added to your list of regrets."

She smiled and leaned into him. "I'm taking advantage of you. I plan on celebrating the end of several lousy days. I thought you might like to join me. If I'm wrong…" With that she stepped back, dropped her towel, opened the door, walked across the dark green carpet and slid beneath his sheets. Her limp and the cuts crisscrossing her back caused him to hesitate for a second but the sight of her sliding into his bed was more than he could resist. He dropped his towel and followed like a well-trained puppy with one thought reverberating through his mind: there is a God.

48

Bailey snuggled back into the solid warmth surrounding her as she drifted in a threshold consciousness. For the first time she could remember, she felt wholly and completely safe. It was that thought that brought her awake. She opened her eyes to a pencil sketch of an old clown walking with a cane. It was beautiful in its simplicity and yet the expression on the clown's face was of sad awareness.

She wondered what would make a clown, that bastion of happiness, sad.

The feeling of warm, naked skin pressed against her back snapped her out of her reverie and her sleepy state.

Guy. Wow. She couldn't help but smile at the amazing night they'd spent together. He was one special man. She'd had a crazy whim to climb in his shower after awakening alone, scared and tired of running. So for a change rather than leaving, she'd run toward something she wanted. And she'd definitely wanted Guy.

As though he were aware of her thoughts, his hand splayed over her stomach while the other rubbed down her thigh. A shiver of electricity shot through her. Knowing it was now or never, she inched herself away. She made it to the edge of the bed before those two strong arms she'd just untangled herself from wrapped around her and pulled her back.

"Eeekkk."

"Where are you going?" he said groggily. Rolling over, he pulled her on top of him.

"Go back to sleep. I need to get back to my room." The dim light coming in through the window suggested it wasn't quite dawn.

"No."

She looked down at the handsome face inches from her own. The slightly crooked nose was so tempting she ran her forefinger down the center of it.

"Fist fight."

"Oh?"

"Grade nine. Mason wanted my girlfriend, Becky. I took offense, so I punched him. Bit of a mistake. The kid was built like a Mac Truck. Luckily, he only got the one punch in. Not so lucky for me, a broken nose and a badly sprained hand."

Bailey chuckled then leaned forward and kissed first his nose and then his hand.

"Thank you. I don't feel so bad about it anymore." He smiled as he claimed her lips. He tucked her in beside him. "How are you feeling?"

"Okay."

"How about emotionally?" He peered into her eyes.

She met his gaze before looking away. Her hands jerked the blanket back and forth in a tug of war. "Screwed up. I don't know what to say. My life isn't mine. I—"

"Do you want to talk about it? I can maybe shed some light on all that's occurred." He rested his forehead against hers. "I'm really sorry this all happened to you."

She nodded, not sure if she was really ready but glad it was only the two of them.

"It seems Mr. Lund had a heart attack and is in the hospital in Edmonton. He's recuperating and should be fine. Just in time to go to jail, with what we've learned so far on that jump drive you gave us. There's enough to put him away for years and we haven't even cracked half of it."

"He was my mom's lawyer. How did she get tangled up with him?" She snorted in disgust. "Like I should be surprised. My life was full of losers. Only the one I thought was different than the drug dealers and prostitutes really only wore nicer clothes and hid it better."

"It seems he was involved with your—Donna and Doug Zajic. Lund married above his social status and must have thought when Doug Zajic, a member of Parliament, came into his life, he was set. I'm still not clear but it would seem that Mr. Lund lived a life of…" Guy stared at the wall for a few seconds. "I don't even know how to put it. He liked boys. Young ones. There's no proof other than a mention of photos but I think-"

She sat up. "Oh my God. He was badgering me about a picture. At the time I thought it was odd but didn't pay much attention. He seemed very anxious to know its whereabouts and had mom ever shown it to me. I told him she'd burned a picture once. He seemed to relax and be quite energized by that." She looked at Guy. "Don't tell me she had a snapshot of him with a young man."

"I wish I could tell you that but I think it was of a young boy. It seems your mom was using it to blackmail him. He, in turn, blackmailed Doug. Maybe he had evidence of Doug's abusing Donna and convinced him if he didn't pay Lund would leak it to the media. Not something a government official could handle. He also manipulated your mom and made her life a living hell for screwing with him. It seems he had quite a list of people he was blackmailing. One of the accounts that Graham was able to crack looks like a tidy nest egg in an offshore account in the vicinity of twenty million dollars."

"That son of a bitch. We lived like dogs. Sometimes I'd go days without eating. Any food I could scrounge I'd give to Mom so she could keep working." Bailey paused. "Isn't that interesting? I always thought Mom worked but other than the candy store in Calgary, I don't know where or what she did. I know when she got desperate and depressed, I was the one who had to bring in the money."

He rubbed her shoulder, carefully avoiding the nicks covering her skin. "Was that the scams she had you do?"

"Yeah." She hung her head, letting her hair partially hide her face. "In all honesty, I'm the one who started it. I was desperate—hungry, cold, and tired of not having anything. I played up to this sharply dressed man; I got him interested in what a young girl could do for him. When he had his pants down, I took his money and ran. It was easy. Mom was angry at first, but she knew we had few options. From there, the ante went up. And I got better at it."

Guy pulled her into his arms. Settling against the headboard, he stroked her hair. "You were a kid trying to survive in an adult world. I don't think you did anything wrong. Or anything different than any other kid would have done."

"The newspapers. I don't understand the newspapers."

He looked at her quizzically.

"Mom collected just about every major and some minor newspapers she could get her hands on. Why?"

"Hmmm. What if she was trying to keep up with what was happening in the political arena? If her husband was an MP, there were decent odds he'd be in the newspaper. If she was as distrustful as I think, then maybe she wanted to make sure he wasn't coming after her? Going to find her?"

Bailey thought about that. "It makes sense. If I remember correctly, she always read the business and political sections first. Then she'd comb the rest of it for information. The ones that I threw out—" her hand flew to her mouth.

"The house. I haven't cleaned out the house. I only have a week to do so. I don't think I even locked it. Guy—" Horrified that she'd forgotten about her mom's place, she tried to move but Guy stopped her.

"It's okay. I was there after you and I locked it up. Don't worry; we'll get it cleaned up."

Ignoring his reference to 'we', she pondered who she could call to pack it up; get rid of everything but her suitcase and clothes. As soon as she had that thought, she realized she didn't care anymore. She only knew she couldn't go back there. There might be answers in all those papers dating back to the year she ended up with Donna and the years they'd moved but she wasn't sure she wanted any more information. What she knew was that life hadn't turned out the way it should have for her. Resting her cheek against Guy's chest, she couldn't resist the urge to rub against the soft dusting of hair, not because it was so amazing but because she needed to feel something real. "Who's been chasing us?"

"It appears the first guy you met in your mom's house was sent by Lund. He was a petty thief. I don't think Lund meant for him to do more than follow you. The other guy we aren't certain but best guess is he was hired by Uncle Geoff. He couldn't afford to have you come back here."

They'd already talked into the wee hours about Geoffrey and his role in her life. She wasn't looking forward to hearing it all over again with the real members of her family. Feeling sick over all that had transpired just because she'd been born, she let her hand slide up Guy's forearm, shoulder and then down over his chest, moving lower. Her tongue flicked out and lapped at his erect nipple.

"Conversation over." He slid under the covers letting his hands glide down the sides of her body and then back up to caress her full breasts.

She smiled a sad, knowing smile. Her glance flicked to the picture beside the bed. She now understood the clown's look. Letting go was going to be hard but she knew she could now and she wasn't about to let something amazing, like this, pass her by. She gave herself over to the incredible sensations coursing through her body.

⚜

"Bailey. We need to talk."

She glanced over her shoulder, thankful Guy was staring out the window. She'd easily distracted him earlier from what he'd wanted to tell her.

"Oh. I thought we took care of that." She limped over to him and breathed on his neck.

He laughed as he faced her. She leaned in and standing on tiptoes, placed her lips over his. He hesitated only for a moment before he deepened the kiss. Tears instantly filled her eyes. She did everything in her power to stop them from overflowing.

There was a rap on the door.

"Guy? Your grandmother is waiting for you. She wants you there now."

Guy jerked back. "Penelope. Tell her we'll be there right away."

Not knowing what else to do, Bailey buried her head against his shoulder. She took three deep, even breaths and swallowed the lump of guilt lodged in her throat. Her life just wasn't meant to have a happy ending.

She pulled back and spun away. She stumbled as her injured leg wasn't ready for such a rapid movement.

"Hey. What's the hurry?" Guy's arm whipped around her waist to support her. "We need to talk."

"Guy…" She pushed him away and walked to the door. "Let's just go. Let's get this over with. There'll be lots of time later to talk." She smiled what she hoped was a winning one, although she felt anything but.

He held her gaze for a long time. Finally, he moved toward her to cup her face. "Promise me you'll listen to me afterward."

She looked at the scuff mark on his chin. She reached out and gently touched it. "Sure." She opened the door and headed for the stairs. Guy stepped in front of her and redirected her to the elevator. Once inside, he grabbed her and hugged her tightly. Bailey couldn't resist kissing him.

One last time.

49

Guy and a guilty looking, red-faced Bailey entered the second floor salon. Dorothea was sitting on the love seat, something that made Guy pause. He'd never seen her sit there before. He took in the rest of the room. Glancing at Bailey, he knew she was right to be tense. Nothing would be the same after this.

Extending his hand, he walked forward. "Hello Daniel, Gina." Due to their breeding, they both acknowledged him but their eyes were glued to Bailey's as hers were to them. The light of recognition was there in one another's eyes. Only the reasons behind what happened were still to be revealed.

It was Gina who first broke the silence. "My baby." Running forward, she wrapped her arms around Bailey, both women crying as they hugged for the first time in twenty-nine and a half years—and very possibly, for only the second time in their lives. Daniel hung back momentarily but he didn't want to be left out. He wrapped his arms around both women and held on. The three let their tears cleanse away the pain of separation.

Guy was having a hell of a time swallowing the boulder-size lump stuck in his throat. His grandmother, he noted, was in much the same shape. He walked over and sat beside her.

"I don't know how much to tell them." Her hands worried the fabric of her blue silk dress, something she'd never done before. She'd never asked for anyone's guidance in her life.

"No more secrets, Grandma. No more. There have been too many for too long. It's gonna hurt but then the healing can begin. You don't have to do it. Graham and I have pieced together most of it. Thank you for holding off for a few days, so we could all rest." He kissed her cheek and then stood as Graham entered the room. Graham's eyes opened wide, he started to fidget and look anywhere but at the scene in front of him. Guy walked over and slapped him on the back. "Think of it as getting in touch with your softer side."

Graham, the guy females sought out when they needed a strong shoulder, choked out, "Hell." Guy found himself in not much better shape as he turned his back on the scene and stared out the window, blinking several times. Once under control, he made his way to the bar and poured himself and Graham a straight whiskey. They clinked glasses, looked at each other, nodded and downed them. Unsure where they fit into things, they both stood awkwardly in front of the fireplace.

Gina was busy finger-brushing Bailey's hair from her face and staring at every square inch of her. Daniel's arms remained around both women.

"I don't want to break this up but I think it's important we talk about what has brought us here, and to find a way to heal and move forward. Aunt, Uncle and Bailey, please sit down." They never looked at him but they moved as one unit to sit on the couch.

Rubbing his face, Guy let out a long sigh. "I don't even know where to start with this."

"Let me, Guy. I can fill in some of the background." His grandmother sat forward, clasped her hands in her lap and thrust her chin upward. "Geoffrey was only my half-brother. I think that secret is what drove him over the brink. No one was supposed to know. Not even Geoffrey. But my parents weren't the best at keeping their feelings to themselves. They always treated him differently, my mother as though he was lower-class. I guess since his real mother was a maid, she felt she was justified. My father looked at him as a reminder of getting caught with his pants down. Not something he took lightly. Geoffrey used to have to work so hard. The ugliest jobs. The longest hours. And when he didn't do a perfect job, because that was impossible, they beat him. Not just pull down your pants and get the belt across the butt, no." All the color drained out of her face. Pale and shaky, she continued, "No. They tied his hands to the barn rafters. Stripped him naked and whipped him." Her hand flew to her mouth as the horror of what she was saying hit her. "I saw them. I did nothing. I was so scared. Geoffrey hated me so much that he stabbed me with a sword." She waved at the cane and her injured leg. "He was eighteen and drunk. I had come home for a visit. He was already into some pretty bad stuff but I didn't want to know. I knew on some level that he'd hurt me deliberately, but I didn't want to believe it. I made sure no one knew it was him." Deep sobs shook her frail frame.

"Another time, he beat me with a cane. He thought I didn't know it was him. But I did. I forgave him. He wasn't responsible. He wasn't. Mother did this to him." Her body shook as though there wasn't much holding it together.

Guy wrapped his arms around her as did Gina, who had stepped forward to comfort her mother.

"Oh, Mom. It wasn't your fault."

There was a loud indrawn breath. "Oh, Gina. My beautiful daughter. You don't know the worst of it." Taking a deep breath, she whispered, "He stole your baby."

Gina reared back as though slapped. Her jaw moved several times but nothing came out.

"What? Why? How long have you known this?" Angry now, Gina stood and glared at her mother.

"She just found out. I know this is painful, Gina, but please hold on until we tell the whole sordid tale." Although she complied, Guy wasn't so sure that their relationship, strained for years thanks to her mother's interference in Gina's life, would survive this latest family saga. Gina backed up, her eyes wide as she plopped onto the couch. Bailey reached out and clasped her hand.

Graham took over at this point. "It seems that Geoff was living a life of debauchery, money laundering, drugs. Whatever was illegal, he was probably involved. At some point, he met this brother and sister—John and Mary. She worked as a nurse and got hired on at the hospital where you planned on having your baby."

Gina gasped. Daniel sank wearily into the cushions as the import of that sunk in.

"She'd been there six months when you arrived and had Cassidy. She took the baby. It seems it was all planned out." Guy bowed his head for a moment before straightening and looking at each person in turn. "The next part is a little unclear. We think she had to go into hiding due to the reward you offered. After five months, they must have figured they were safe, so she took a plane headed to Vancouver—only the plane went down in Alberta. Back in those days, if a baby was traveling on an adult's lap, there wasn't a record made of an infant being aboard. So when the plane crashed, all those listed on the manifest were identified as dead. No one realized that a baby was on board or missing. Again not sure how—" he looked at Bailey, "she survived it. But she did. Determined, even then."

Graham winked at Bailey. She pursed her lips in acknowledgement. Guy tried to catch her eye but she refused to make eye contact with him. Something had changed. She sat ramrod straight, her fists clenched on her thighs.

"Again pretty sketchy but it seems that Donna Zajic was leaving her abusive husband that same night. She came across the crash, found the baby and took her with her. Cassidy became Bailey Saunders and lived…"

Bailey's face hardened and she shook her head firmly. "I lived okay. As you can see, I came out of it all right. It had to have been the good genes I started out with."

Gina and Daniel both broke down. Bailey took on the parent role and held them close, murmuring it was okay now they were together. She was fine. She'd had a good life.

The pain and agony descended like a thick fog, the weight of which was having a devastating effect on his grandmother, who sat slumped in her chair. Kneeling in front of her, Guy took her cold hands in his.

"I love you, Grandma."

Huge tears rolled down her cheeks but she refused to look at him.

50

It was crazy and she knew that but something was pulling her back there. It had only been two weeks since it had all occurred. Following the cobbled path, she looked at the devastation. The petals from the ruined flowers had already been swept up but the tortured plants still remained. She barely paid them any attention as she limped her way down the winding path toward the field.

Staring at the debris spread across the meadow and the black hole left by the explosion, she realized that was as close as she wanted to get. So much destruction and it looked so much like her life—charred and broken. It had been a long time since she'd felt sorry for herself. But this… this was so much more. This resembled her existence; an existence which had meant nothing.

Numb from all that had happened, not sure what she wanted or where she wanted to go, she stood there. Her parents had agreed to leave her on her own for a few hours. She'd asked them to give her some time to come to grips with it all. It had hurt them but they'd accepted it, at least for a short while, promising to come back for her. Bailey was mixed about that. She wasn't sure she could be what they wanted. She had no social skills. She didn't know one fork from another—you pick one up, stick food on it and shovel it in. No couth, no manners and no class. She may have had the right blood but she didn't feel she fit into their world, only she didn't know how to tell them. The scariest part was that she didn't want to disappoint them.

As she shook off her thoughts she realized she'd stayed for one reason and she was avoiding doing anything about it. Her shoulders drooped as she turned to head back to the house, knowing she had to stop postponing the reality of what she needed to do. She stopped when she saw Guy standing a few feet behind her, watching her.

"How long?"

"Long enough. You look like you're carrying the world."

She shrugged half-heartedly as she moved past him. He fell into step beside her.

"Laying ghosts to rest?"

"Something like that." She still hadn't been sure why she'd needed to see that the building and all Geoffrey's evil were gone but she had. That at least gave her a sliver of reality to hold onto.

"Thank you for giving me some space. Some time to get to know... my parents. For all you've done—"

"Whoa." Guy stopped, touching her arm, waiting for her to stop and face him. "What's this formal crap?"

"I– look– you– we– it's just not– Jesus. Stop looking at me like that."

"Like what? Like I'm falling in love with you?"

"Wh-what?" Her brain threatened to shut down. She couldn't have heard him right. She strode down the path, and he fell in step beside her. When she reached the gardens, she knelt down and tucked one of the sickly, ripped plants back into the soil.

"Don't worry about those; they're all going to be replaced. Grandma's just been a little distracted. Emilio has already ordered new ones. I'm sure they'll be even more impressive."

Still kneeling and focusing on what she was doing, she asked, "What were they going to do with me?"

He offered his hand, urging her to stand. "Let it go. It's not worth thinking about anymore. All of them were sick and evil. They're all getting their just rewards."

"No. Not them. I mean Mary and John. What were they going to do with me as a baby? Why did they take me?"

"Do you really want to know?"

She nodded, the lump in her throat preventing her from talking.

"They'd sold you on the black market. You were headed to a family in the States. I don't think they knew you'd been abducted. I'm sure they were a loving family, one that would have been good to you."

She smiled sadly as she thought about all the people who'd been hurt. "They lost too. I wonder whatever happened to them."

"I don't know."

Guy slipped the backpack off his shoulders. "I have something for you." He unzipped it and pulled out a cassette player.

Bailey gasped. "The cassette. I forgot."

"Here. I think you should listen to it. I'll give you some time alone and I'll come back later."

She stared at the machine but made no move to take it. "I—"

He hit play.

"Bailey, I hope you never have the opportunity to listen to this but I feel it is important to make it. You're such a beautiful child. One any woman would be proud of. You're so bright. So quick. You're my shining star."

There was a long pause. Bailey looked at Guy but he shook his head.

"I only wish I had the right to call you mine. I found you; of all places, in a plane crash near Turner Valley, Alberta. I don't know how you survived but I couldn't leave you. I couldn't go to the police. Doug, my husband, would just get one of his government buddies to get him off. He was a mean, abusive man. I'm sure he had every police officer after me, every border waiting for me. I never meant to keep you. But after a few days of holding you... you filled something within me I didn't even know was missing. You gave me such hope. Such love. You looked at me with those baby blue eyes, so trustful. So happy. No one had ever given me that. Not freely. I couldn't let you go. You were my angel. You saved me."

There was a slow, indrawn breath.

"You're seven now. I've loved every single day we've been together. The cabin that Mr. Lund lets us use has been our sanctuary. Mr. Dresling, who looks after the place for Mr. Lund, has taken a shine to you. He's the grandfather you'll never know. I don't even know whose child you are..."

There was soft sobbing and silence for a time. Bailey reached to hit the stop button but Guy grabbed her hand and gently held it.

"That's not really true. Forgive me Bailey... I guess I should say Cassidy. That's your real name. If you look in the body of Miss Piggy, you'll find some newspaper clippings and a photo, one I'd been hiding from Lund on his own property."

Bailey heard the voice continue on. The voice she'd always believed was her mother. The woman now confirming she really did belong to someone else. Her life had been a lie. None of it made sense. Bailey wanted to slap her hands over her ears and run but she forced herself to focus on all Donna had to say.

"It's a photo of Lund. I hope you never have to use it, but I want you to have some security. Don't trust him. He's a junkyard dog dressed up in silk. Don't be taken in... I had no choice, Bails, I had nowhere else to run..."

She talked more about how he'd helped her to hide from her husband was all those years. He'd kept them safe but at a price.

"I love you, Bails. I hope life has treated you well. If you're listening to this, then you've learned a lot about your life—your real life. I never meant to hurt you, Bails. I was just selfish. I did love you. And I tried to protect you."

Donna shared details about her life with Doug Zajic and how abusive he'd been. She'd kept them moving so he would never find them. Lund had been their look-out, warning when Doug might be getting close. She was sure he'd have killed her and it had frightened her to think what he would have done to Bailey.

Bailey bowed her head, unable to hold it up any longer. She wasn't aware of the tears streaming down her face until Guy's fingers brushed them away. Jerking back, she looked at him. "I don't know how to deal with any of this." She pulled her hand out of his. "I keep thinking, why me? I was a baby. What did I do wrong? All these people conspiring for their own means and I'm the pawn caught in the middle? Dammit, it's not fair." Bailey stopped when she realized Guy wasn't responding. "Nothing to say?"

"Not about that, nope. But I do want to tell you a few things. I want to make sure things are up front, so there are no surprises." He cleared his throat. "There's a possibility that Geoff is still alive."

"WHAT? How?"

"They found a body in the explosion—or I should say human parts. Not enough to ID the person. The interesting thing is his gaudy garnet ring survived; found on a charred, barely recognizable finger. The police are ready to say it's him but it's too suspicious to me. It's my theory, not anyone else's. They'll do DNA but that takes time. I haven't shared it with many people, but I wanted you to know."

Bailey knew that meant he hadn't told his family. She thought about what he'd said. "You know I didn't know the man long but..." She stared into space. "I could see him planting a body, planning out everything, right down to his escape. I bet he fled the country."

Guy nodded. "I think so, too. I just wanted you to know my hunch." He reached for her hand. "Your life may not have started out the way you would have wanted. The way it should have. You have every right to be angry—but is that going to change anything?"

Turning her back to him, she looked at the destroyed gardens; so symbolic of her life. Several men were scurrying around, digging up and removing the damaged plants. All would be replaced. She took in a deep breath, wishing her life could be replaced so easily.

"No. But it won't be easy to let it go, either."

"I know. But I'll help."

"Thank you for not sharing my life with Gina and Daniel. I don't think they could handle it. I'm not sure what I'll tell them. I—" Shaking her head, she looked away. "We spent the last few weeks together. They're wonderful people. I'm just not sure they could handle how my life was, up until now. I can't tell them."

"Gina and Daniel are lucky and very happy to have you back. They never had children after you were taken. I don't know if they tried, but Grandmother said Gina never stopped searching for you."

"Look. You don't really know me. I'm not classy. I don't know the difference between when to serve a red wine or a white. I couldn't tell you the difference between a Renoir and a Picasso. That week was... it's not me. I'm driven. I work twenty-hour days, hundred-hour weeks. Okay, well I don't anymore. I've... it's been... I don't do well at relationships. I've tried. I have nothing to offer you."

"Oh. So you're going to charge me for the sex?"

"What the hell are you talking about? See, I swear. I swear a lot when I'm stressed. I move. A lot. Five years that's the longest I've been anywhere."

"You still have your place in Victoria, right? Can I ask what happened to the TV show?"

She scrunched her face, not sure what to tell him.

"My TV show. Well..." she shrugged. "They were very understanding when I tried to explain about my week and why I couldn't be there by their deadline. They did, however, wish me well in the movies. They didn't believe a word I said; not that I can blame them. So we agreed to part ways. However, yesterday, I got a call offering me the same TV show at double the income. I smelled Grandma in that one. She didn't admit nor deny it."

"So did you take it?

She shook her head. "No. It was wrong timing, wrong circumstances... just wrong."

"You still have your business in Victoria?"

She looked away before answering. "No, I took down that shingle as well."

"And so now you are?"

"Unemployed?" She giggled and danced out of his way, when he growled at her and shook his fist.

"Look, I'm broke. I've been busy paying off bills for my mother. I can't enter into a relationship with someone who comes from money." Waving away his look of get used to it, she continued, "You've got money, I don't. I could clean out your bank account and wipe you out faster than termites could eat through a wood house."

He pulled her into his arms and kissed her deeply. She groaned. "You're not playing fair," she murmured against his lips.

"I don't intend to. If you can play dirty, so can I; enough of the excuses. I get your being scared. I'm frightened beyond belief. I never thought I'd find someone. I never thought I was worthy. I've always been the outsider. The person who never quite fit in, never quite belonged."

She cupped his face in her hands, feeling his pain.

"We both have skeletons. All I'm asking is you give us a chance. Move east. Start over. Let me love you."

Holding herself rigid was all she could do to hold out against the nibbling of his lips across her face and his hands roaming south.

"Damn you. Don't tell me I can move in with you. I need my own space. We need to spend time together and apart."

He kissed her hard and fast. As he pulled back, his smile was so full of happiness. Her mind was telling her to be rational, to think it through but her heart fluttered and then settled into a steady, determined beat. It was slow in coming but it blossomed into a full grin that could not only be seen on her lips but felt throughout her body as well. Looping her arm through his, she leaned against him.

He brushed her hair from her face. "Bailey, it's time to let go of the past. This is a new adventure for you. It doesn't have to be bad like so many past experiences. This is up to you how it plays out. Just give it a chance."

She looked at him and then glanced away. The vision of the charred trees Geoffrey had blown up was still very vivid. Sometimes she awakened and could have sworn it was happening all over again. Geoff had kept hatred in his heart and look where it had landed him. She knew how tough it could be to let go of all that was unfair, to really believe there was something more for her, something good. She only had to look at Guy's big blue, honest eyes, to know she had a chance.

The one thing that did come clear was she didn't want the life she'd had. She didn't want the life her moth– Donna– her mother had. *She loved me. She tried to protect me. If she hadn't come along when she had, where would I be?*

Turning her palm upward, Guy instantly put his hand into hers. Smiling, she looked up at the heavy black clouds that were moving in. She couldn't help but laugh.

"So… care to help me move?"

A Note from the Author

Thank you for reading **Captured Lies**. I hope you enjoyed reading it as much as I enjoyed writing it.

Review It: If you liked reading **Captured Lies, please review it**. Your review is important. It not only helps me create better stories but it helps others to find my books.

Recommend it: Tell your family, friends, coworkers, bookclubs, etc.

Thank you. You truly do make a difference.

www.maggiethom.com

Contact Maggie: maggie@maggiethom.com

About the Author

by Portrait Couture, Regina Akhankina

Award-winning author Maggie Thom has written many types of stories but finally settled on her love of puzzles, mysteries and roller coaster rides and now writes suspense/thrillers that will take you on one heck of an adventure.

She is the author of *The Caspian Wine Suspense/Thriller/Mystery Series* – *Captured Lies* (Award Winning), *Deceitful Truths* and *Split Seconds* – and her other individual novels *Tainted Waters* (2013 Suspense/Thriller Book of the Year through *Turning the Pages Magazine*) and *Deadly Ties*.

Take the roller coaster ride. It's worth it. Get your free ebook of Captured Lies at www.maggiethom.com.

Her motto: Read to escape… Escape to read…

"Maggie Thom... proves her strength as a master of words, plots and finely chiseled characters... she weaves a brilliant cloth of the many colors of deceit." Dii – TomeTender

Want to learn more about writing? www.womenwritesmovement.com

77900285R00189

Made in the USA
Columbia, SC
07 October 2017